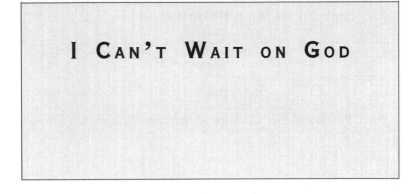

I Can't Wait on God

ALSO BY ALBERT FRENCH

Billy

Holly

Patches of Fire: A Story of War and Redemption

I CAN'T WAIT ON GOD

·

Albert French

Anchor Books · Doubleday
New York   London   Toronto   Sydney   Auckland

An Anchor Book
PUBLISHED BY DOUBLEDAY
a division of Bantam Doubleday Dell Publishing Group, Inc.
1540 Broadway, New York, New York 10036

Anchor Books, Doubleday, and the portrayal of an anchor are
trademarks of Doubleday, a division of Bantam Doubleday Dell
Publishing Group, Inc.

Library of Congress Cataloging-in-Publication Data
French, Albert.
I can't wait on God / Albert French. — 1st Anchor Books ed.
p.   cm.
1. Afro-American criminals—Pennsylvania—Pittsburgh—Fiction.
2. Fugitives from justice—United States—Fiction.   3. Homewood
(Pittsburgh, Pa.)—Fiction.   I. Title.
PS3556.R3948I3   1998
813'.54—dc21   97-42256
CIP

ISBN 0-385-48364-3
Copyright © 1998 by Albert French

TO EVERY HAND THAT'S EVER REACHED.

When shall I find peace and rest within myself again?

—Anne Frank, Tuesday, 14 March 1944

· ONE ·

Pittsburgh, 1950

Summer night air was always sticky kind of air, had that stinkin mill smoke stuck all in it. Them old freight trains comin into Pittsburgh would come around that curve, rumblin, rollin, and shakin them houses down over the hill from the tracks. Them folks livin down over the hill from the tracks was used to hearin them trains comin on by, used to hearin the dogs barkin and howlin at them trains. Sometimes when them trains make too much noise, some folks wake up, grunt, then turn on over and go back to sleep. But that train noise and that hot, sticky air would still be out there. Them summertime nights could be long nights, too, if it was real hot. Them nights could stick around long after that freight train took its noise with it and went on by.

Gus Goins's place was down off the tracks, down in that alley behind Fiance Street. Gettin up into Gus Goins's place didn't take any thought. Folks could find their way through that dark dirty path leadin up in there real easy and kept goin up in there all night long, especially durin them mill payday nights. Gus always had some kind of light hangin off that old shack porch of his. But before folks could get to that light, it be pitch black, stinkin, too, from them chicken coops Gus kept in the yards there. But folks found their way, slip, slide, and stumble til they got to where they were going, kept comin and goin all through the night. Them chickens never did get any sleep, they couldn't even hear them trains goin by for all that loud jukebox music comin out off that back alley shack.

Gus Goins didn't smile too much. He had one of them round, light-skinned faces and some dark shiny hair that he always kept greased down and combed real nice, but when he be sellin you somethin, he could grin then. Gus Goins sell you anything, you know you could always get some chicken any-time and that moonshine he be sellin bring folks back from their grave to get some more.

In that back room at Gus's, them cards and that money be just a-flyin. Bloodshot eyes be eyein too, lookin that cold-face black queen right in her eyes. Pete Turner was as black as any of them spades he was holdin, but had them ugly yellow teeth from all that cigar juice he keeps up in his mouth.

Al Johnson was a quick-talkin man, ask anybody anything at anytime, always up in somebody's face about somethin. Al Johnson is starin across that card table at Pete Turner, been starin at him for a while.

"What ya goin ta do?" Al Johnson done ask Pete Turner again. Pete Turner ain't answerin and ain't takin his eyes away from them cards he's holdin and starin at.

Al Johnson gets to rockin in his chair and sayin at the same time he's rockin, "What ya goin ta do, huh? Shit, damn, make ya play."

Wendell Hill is sittin at that card table, too. He's leanin back in his chair some and givin a little laugh and lookin over at Al Johnson. Then he's sayin, "Pete ain't got shit. Ya dones got the fool's money. Let the nigger have his time."

Out in that front room of Gus Goins's folks are just a-talkin and sippin on whatever they got in them paper cups. Cissy Hall been in there way before it got dark. She's tellin all she knows about anything she can think of. She done told Bertha Wilks all about that Lando Parks sneakin up there around Herman Stokes's place and tryin to mess around with that German white woman Herman brought back from the war. Cissy told Bertha, "He thinks ain't nobody seenin him standin over there in that empty lot tryin to get that woman to come out. Ah done seen dogs wit better sense than ta be standin out in the middle of broad daylight and thinkin they's hidin and can'ts nobody be seein what's they up ta. Any damn fool knows what's goin on."

Bobby Rose has that Indian-colored skin and that thick black curly hair. He used to try and tell folks his mama was full-blooded somethin. Folks be tellin him, "Man, git out of here wit that shit. Ya ain't nothin but some full-blooded Mississippi nigger. Ya need ta go back where ya come up here from."

He's tellin Olinda Harris, "Ya know ya's ain't meanin that." Then he's askin her, "Why ya doin me likes this fore, huh? Come on now, why don't ya be sweet likes ya can be, huh?"

Bobby Rose and Gus Goins's moonshine is about the same thing now. Them words comin from his mouth is just a-covered with that moonshine smell. Sometimes Bobby Rose ain't sayin nothin, just standin there and lookin down Olinda Harris's dress, tryin to see as far as he can see down there. But that moonshine still makin noises, make him moan and grunt a little.

Olinda Harris has them dark starin eyes and that brown skin that shines just like them buckeye nuts that be fallin off that tree up at the end of the alley. Sometimes folks be comin down the alley, be thinkin about things they be needin and things they ain't never goin to get. Sometimes they slow down a little, take a look at that pretty brown buckeye bustin out of that ugly green skin of its. Folks look down at it, give it a thought, let that thought take a few steps with them fore that need they carryin in their head smack at the inside of their skull.

Bobby Rose is still lookin at Olinda Harris. She's lookin back at him, cuttin her eyes at him, givin him some looks that make that moonshine splash up in his head. She's twenty and knows how she looks and what them looks can do for her.

Dicky Bird is sittin in the corner. Got him some chicken in his mouth and chewin as fast as he's talkin. He's talkin to Bill Lovit, but he don't know, and might not care if he did know, that Bill Lovit ain't listenin to a word he's sayin. Bill Lovit ain't been right since the fire. Sometimes he still gets to cryin. Folks say that's all right, say they'd cry too if they come home and find they house all burnt down and all them seven children burnt past knowin which one was which.

Dicky Bird is tellin Bill Lovit all about Miss Macune. Miss Macune lives up there at the far end of the alley. Folks don't see her much. She keeps herself in that big house all by herself since that man of hers died, and that's been some twenty years or more. Dicky Bird is sayin, "Ah wents on in there. Ah tells ya, that woman was talkin ta somebody the whole time Ah was in there. And it sure wasn't me, Ah tells ya that. And there weren't nobodies in there cept me. She wants me ta come back up there and gits them leaks she's got. Them pipes ain't nothin but rust. Ah tries and tell her that. Ya know, tells her she needin some new plummin in there. She gits ta talkin ta me and at the same time she talkin ta whoever ain't there. That's when Ah come on out of there."

4

Gus Goins's jukebox got to seemin like it was bouncin. Somebody want to hear somethin that would make them move, wanted to hear some drums beatin, hear that music that gets sweat to rollin. Olinda Harris gets to swayin with that drum beat. Bobby Rose tries to get closer to her, move with her sways, but she don't let him. That blue dress she's got on becomes a blur of color in his eyes.

The black, sticky, hot air of midnight is still, hoverin above Gus Goins's place in the alley. The beat of some drum and now the squeal of a horn get stuck in the air, squiggle there. Alley cats stray in the night, eyes glowin and tails curled. Gus Goins's chickens squat in them coops, quiver when them alley cats come by. That music is still jumpin. Olinda Harris's hips sway and roll. Dicky Bird is watchin and still chewin on that chicken, just about got them bones clean. Folks sittin back in the corner just watchin the night go by. They might take a little sip out their paper cup, give somebody close to them a little talk, then they get to starin at Olinda Harris or just starin at the nighttime goin by. Jeremiah Henderson is sittin way back in a dark corner, he's sippin from his cup, but he ain't watchin Olinda Harris or talkin to nobody. Folks know he keeps to himself, got that kind of stillness about him. He ain't got to say nothin for them to know he's there.

Back in that back room, Al Johnson has some sweat comin down in his eyes and is up in somebody's face. "What ya talkin about, huh? What ya talkin about, motherfucker? Ah want my motherfuckin money, man. What the fuck wrong wit ya? Ah wants my money."

Richard Norris is shoutin back at Al Johnson, "Man, ya goin ta git yer money. Ah done told ya, now gits out my face wit it."

Pete Turner done lost all the money he had and tries to borrow some more. Asks folks, "Lets me hold somin? Ah gits it back for ya fore the night's over."

Folks tell Pete Turner, "Ya gots ta be crazzy."

Mosquitoes were buzzin and bitin at anything in the light hangin out on that back porch when Pete Turner went on out the door. He went on past where the glow from the light failed to go any farther, then stumbled and slithered up the dark path that goes to the alley. Some cat curled its back up in the dark, hissed and vanished in the night, only leavin the brief death of its sound skirtin in the air.

Pete Turner reaches the alley, takes a few stumblin steps until he gets to one of them back alley fences. He stops, sways while the splashin sound of his urine hits the fence. He jerks away from the fence and starts up the alley, leavin some short grunts behind.

Olinda Harris has left, took her sweet ways on home. Bobby Rose still talkin about her, sayin, "Ya all just wait. Um goin ta get that, yeal."

Gus Goins's moonshine takes Bill Lovit on home, too. Takes him up the alley, then he cuts across Dunferline Street until he's on Susquehanna Street. The moonshine he's carryin in his gut begins to carry him as he passes through the lot still filled with ash and jagged burnt timber that been his house, reaches the shack he's built in what been his backyard. The moonshine whispers, too, tells the dark dead faces of his children to leave him be.

Jeremiah Henderson looks up and keeps starin into Dicky Bird's face while Dicky Bird's sayin somethin about the late hour and, "Yeal, Ah think um goin on out of here. Gots ta git me some sleep . . ." Dicky Bird's words drift as soon as his eyes fall from Jeremiah Henderson's face, then he gets up and staggers away. Jeremiah Henderson says nothin, stares into the dark space where Dicky Bird's been.

Gus Goins's chickens were stirrin, some distant alley dog was barkin. Dark eyes on a dark face looked into the night, searched where the dark lay low along the alley fences, glanced away to where the alley began or ended. To where it became Homewood Avenue, where streetlights hung far in the night. Jeremiah Henderson lowered his eyes from them lights. Closer by, the browns, grays, and greens of the row houses were only black in the night that Jeremiah Henderson walked through.

· · ·

When the sun came up, it came up over them hills up in Wilkensburg. Then it wasn't too long fore them sun rays started lightin up the alley. Officially, the alley was named Annon Way—somebody that was important named it that. But folks livin back in the alley didn't know who and never asked either. Annon Way hadn't changed much since they put it back there to make some room for them wagons to get down in between them front street houses. Then somebody built some back alley houses and them folks that didn't have that front street—livin money could live in them back alley houses. Back alley folks seemed to be a little different from front street folks, seemed to do a little bit more sittin on them steps and porches they had back there. When nighttime came, a lot of them front street folks from all around would get to comin back in the alley. Everybody knew how to get back up in Gus Goins's place. Before that Second World War got started, white folks used to live back in the alley and out on them front streets, too. After the war, Coloreds started tricklin in them alley houses, right before the white folks started gushin out.

Mister Allen got one of them alley row houses first, got that second one from the end. He told folks that house was just what he was lookin for. Lester Jones got that row house on the end. Mister Allen said he could have had that one on the end if he would have wanted it, but he wasn't givin that white man all that extra money to be on the end of anything. Mister Strayhorne moved right next door to Mister Allen. He'd been knowin Mister Allen from way back down in North Carolina. Mister Strayhorne's wife, Lilly, say Mister Allen's a fine man. She say, Mister Allen got plenty of respect for himself. She say she wish some of them damn fool–actin niggers that be comin around there get some of that respect Mister Allen gots.

Mister Allen is out on his sittin porch tryin to get as much of that mornin quiet as he can get fore them alley children get to runnin around and yellin all day. Some of them alley dogs have got to barkin and Mister Allen looks up, squints his eyes some, and looks down the alley and sees that old cart comin up through them early mornin shadows. Mister Allen can't see Dicky Bird, just that big old rotten wood cart with them old horse-wagon wheels comin. Mister Allen puts his head back down, he don't have to see Dicky Bird to know it's him comin, that cart and Dicky Bird is the same thing anyway. Next thing Mister Allen knows, Dicky Bird is lookin up in his face sayin, "Mornin, Mister Allen."

Mister Allen looks down at Dicky Bird, gives Dicky Bird a little mornin grin, then says, "Mornin, Dicky Bird."

"How ya be ta-day, Mister Allen?"

"Um just fine here, Dicky Bird. Looks like we gots us a nice day comin. Ah hope it ain't too hot."

"Yes, sir, Mister Allen, this here heat can gits ya."

Some alley woman gets to callin her cat. Dicky Bird wipes some of that cart-pushin sweat off the back of his neck, looks up at Mister Allen, and says, "Ah hears Mat Hicks is dead."

Mister Allen gives a little gasp, then asks Dicky Bird, "Where ya hear that?"

"Ah seen Eddy Pope this mornin and that's the first thing he tells me."

"Lord have mercy. Ah just saw Mat Hicks up on Homewood Avenue, couldn't have been but a day or so ago. We stood up there and talked a good bit. What they say happened to him?"

"He just fell on over. Eddy Pope say they all up Mott's place just sittin around. And the next thing they knew, Mat just sittin there and not movin or sayin nothin. They say his eyes were wide open, but he wasn't movin or sayin nothin. Eddy say he yelled over to Mat, ask him what was wrong wit him. Eddy say Mat ain't said nothin back at all. Then Eddy say it was just like watchin some tree fall. Ya know, ya cut it and it don't seem ta fall, it just seem to stand still. Then all of a sudden it comes down. Eddy say Mat topple on over like that. They'd know he was dead then, know he wasn't havin any liquor in him."

Dicky Bird goes on up the alley, pushin that cart of his. Dicky Bird has some pickin to do, pickin at what folks didn't want anymore. Mister Allen goes on with his early mornin thinkin. Mister Allen still sittin quietly, sometimes starin down the alley and sometimes just lookin down at them shadows layin on the porch steps. There's a quick rattlin sound, then some real fast-soundin footsteps fillin that quiet mornin air. Mister Allen looks up, knows he'll see Jimmy Maben comin out his house. Jimmy Maben gives Mister Allen a quick, "Good mornin, Mister Allen. How ya ta-day?"

"I'm fine there, Jimmy. How you?"

Jimmy Maben's hurryin down his steps and tellin Mister Allen, "Got ta make this day, ya know."

Mister Allen yells out, "Dicky Bird was by here a little while ago. He say he heard Mat Hicks is dead. Say Mat just fell on over."

Jimmy Maben slows his gettin-to-the-mill walk with a quick turn of his head. "What?"

Mister Allen goes on and tells Jimmy Maben what Dicky Bird done told him. Word sounds seemed to hang in that mornin air for a while as Jimmy Maben walked on down the alley still shakin his head. But that mill was waitin on him, told him to hurry that step. Mister Allen used to work them mills, worked out on that Curry Furnace in Rankin, used to walk them five miles every day to get there. Watchin Jimmy Maben goin on down the alley, Mister Allen wished he was going, too. But he had to come out that mill with what back he had left. He told folks, "Now I like to work, but thirty years out there can get you. I miss that payday comin."

That Miss Duncan come out on her porch. She has that row house down next to Jimmy Maben's. She call herself Miss Duncan, but folks know she ain't never married that LeRoy Duncan. She just pretends to be that man's wife while she spendin all his money. Everybody knows that. She gives Mister Allen an early mornin what-ya-lookin-at look. Mister Allen gives Miss Duncan a nod of his head, then he looks away, anyplace. Mister Allen don't like that woman's evil ways, at all. Mister Allen can get mighty upset with that kind of actin that Miss Duncan be carryin on with. Miss Duncan goes on back in the house.

Mister Allen had him a good woman. Adline. She was a real respectful kind of woman, always called Mister Allen "Mister Allen," but she got that cancer all up in her breast. Next thing Mister Allen knew, she was dead. Mister Allen didn't marry Miss Allen til he was fifty-five and Miss Allen was thirty. Mister Allen had him a woman before, but he don't say nothin to nobody about her.

Some of them alley children started comin out and puttin some noise in that early mornin air. Mister Allen was still sittin on the porch when he heard that distant rattle of a door comin open. He looked up, knew what he would see, then put his head back down. That noise them children were makin seemed to still in the air, stay there. Mister Allen kept his head down for a while, then slowly looked up and watched that woman of Jeremiah Henderson's go down the alley.

Them new alley bricks were red, but down where Gus Goins's chickens were runnin around, them alley bricks were those old kind, them ones they first put in and ain't thinkin about takin up. They didn't have any color to them that folks even thought about unless it was the green they saw from them weeds growin up between them. Dark eyes kept starin down at the cracks between the bricks.

Gus Goins's chickens flapped their wings and scooted from the sound of quick-clickin heels comin. Willet Mercer kept her head down, wasn't thinkin about Gus Goins's damn chickens. There was a flow to her black hair that seemed to keep with the rhythm of her walk. It was always a quick walk, but like the dark hair, the walk would flow through the stillness of the early mornin, seem not to touch or be touched by the alley.

That early mornin sun would seem to linger, stay up over them hills in Wilkensburg, then all that heat it was bringin would seem to come all at the same time. Everything would get hot; red alley bricks would get to glarin. Mister Allen been gone in the house. Them alley cats and dogs done climbed up under somethin lookin for what shade they could find. Little beads of sweat that was stickin on them dark bare backs of them alley children playin out in that sun got to poppin and makin them backs shine back at the sun. All that yellin and carryin on them children got to doin chased anything that was quiet away.

. . .

Noontime came and passed, and the noise stayed. Willet Mercer kept her head down and her eyes away from all the children that got to lookin at her as she came back up the alley. A little girl stared, saw the flow of the long dark hair. The sun made Willet Mercer's light brown skin shine, then glow red. The little girl saw the color of the skin, saw it as pretty, and kept starin. Alley folks knew little of Willet Mercer. They sorta figured she was in her early twenties. They knew she was Jeremiah Henderson's woman, but sorta figured she wasn't married to him. Sometimes she'd speak, say a quick hello, leave a quick smile, but never had she stopped and talked. Soon as they moved in, alley folks got to whisperin about her and Jeremiah Henderson. Mister Allen told folks, "Ya'll leave them folks be, they ain't botherin nobody."

Them rooms inside them row houses weren't too big and real hot in the summertime. The kitchens were in the back, and folks always had the back doors open to let that cookin heat out, but they kept them screen doors closed tight to keep the garbage can flies out. Jeremiah Henderson was sittin at the kitchen table. He heard Willet come into the house, heard the sound of her footsteps nearin, but did not turn. He sat starin down at the floor. The dark gray linoleum had them little fuzzy blue spots on it. Jeremiah had stared at the blue spots until they went away and came back just gray.

Willet whispers into his silence, "You goin to do it?"

The shadows in the kitchen stayed silent. Some fly had come in through some hole in the screen and was buzzin to get back out, but Jeremiah sat quietly. Willet stood lookin at him for a moment, then spun on her heels and went on up the steps. Upstairs in them row houses there were two rooms and that little bathroom. That front room didn't have anything in it except for some old soft-cushioned chair and some boxes. The back room was where the bed and dresser were. The one dresser had the mirror that Willet is starin into now. Some of that sunlight was comin through the window, even gettin through them blinds that were hangin low, but it was still lightin up that mirror a little. Where the light didn't hit the mirror, the mirror reflected the shade in the room, and the eyes that had stared into it quickly turned away. The other room was always cooler, darker. The windows were covered with long hangin drapes that were slightly parted, like they were waitin on some cool breeze to come through. The big stuffed chair was always comfortable. Willet is leanin back in it, she's kicked them high heels off and that short summer dress has ridden up to her thighs. Slowly she has unbuttoned her blouse, then lit

13

that cigarette. The gray smoke floated into the shade of the room then seemed to still, stay there before it went away.

Alley time didn't always come in minutes that had all them seconds stuck in there. Sometimes it just went on by, then the same time would come back. Same fly still be buzzin on the screen to get out, same dark eyes starin down at them fuzzy blue spots. Another cigarette is burnin, but the smoke is floatin the same way before it goes away.

Willet is starin into the shadows of the room. When she hears the sound of footsteps comin up the steps, she keeps starin into the shadows. Jeremiah is standin in the doorway now, but Willet ain't lookin at him. She brings the cigarette to her lips, sucks the smoke from it, turns her head toward the windows, and blows the smoke from her mouth. She is silent til she whispers, "When are you going to do it?"

Jeremiah says, "I don't know."

Willet keeps lookin at the window, but whispers back over her shoulder, "I'm not stickin around here forever. I told you that."

Jeremiah steps softly til he reaches Willet, then stands silently before her. Quickly she brings the cigarette to her lips and sucks on it until its end turns red and glows. She sucks the smoke deep into her lungs, turns to Jeremiah, and just stares up at him. She blows the smoke away and sits silently.

Jeremiah whispers, "I told you I'd get you to New York. But we got to get the money first."

Jeremiah still sees her eyes lookin up into his face, still lingerin in his mind with the flow of her hair as she spun her face around. "I told you I'm not stayin," she whispers. The room is silent now. Willet's eyes glow as red as the cigarette she is holdin.

．．．

Alley children kept that screamin up all day long, wasn't payin that hot sun any mind. When that sun went on over the alley and way beyond Homewood Avenue, where it started to turn red instead of that hot old yellow glare, them red alley bricks got to coolin. Mister Allen came on back on his porch, figured he sit for a while. Wasn't too long before he seen Jeremiah Henderson come out. Mister Allen sorta kept his eyes on Jeremiah and tried to figure out why he was hurryin so much. Then he tried not to be doin that kind of thinkin that be gettin into other folks' business. Mister Allen put his head back down and let Jeremiah Henderson go on down the alley. Then Mister Allen got his pipe out, put that tobacco in it, lit it, and leaned back in his sittin chair a bit. Then he got to wonderin again without knowin he was wonderin at all. He got to tryin to figure out how Jeremiah Henderson and that woman of his be livin when it seemed like ain't neither of them workin since they moved in there. Mister Allen set for a while and tried to figure out just when they moved in. He knew it wasn't too long ago. Figured it was just fore spring come, then he caught himself thinkin in their business again and went on and thought of somethin else.

Them early summer nights in the alley was still filled up with all that noise. Folks sittin out on them sittin porches hollerin back and forth at one another, tryin to holler over all that noise them children makin. Farther down the alley, folks done already started seepin into Gus Goins's place. In that front room of his, that jukebox was blarin already. In that back room, them eyes were just a-starin at them cards. Al Johnson

15

had his mouth poked out, but it was shut. Gene Holland was sittin across the table from Al Johnson and he had most of Al Johnson's money sittin on the table right in front of him. Al Johnson spent more time lookin at his money than at them cards he was holdin.

Jeremiah Henderson had come in and was standin in the corner of that back room, sippin out that paper cup he's holdin. He takes a quick sip, but keeps his eyes lookin at that door. The later in the night it got, the louder that jukebox in the front room be playin and the more folks got to crowdin in that room, but Jeremiah stayed in the back room. Dicky Bird came back there carryin that plate of chicken Gus Goins fixed up for him. He found him a place to sit and watched Al Johnson lose what money he was tryin to keep. Dicky Bird was still watchin them cards slidin back and forth when he felt Jeremiah nearin him. He stopped chewin that chicken and watchin them cards, then quickly looked up at Jeremiah. Slowly Jeremiah is leanin over and whisperin in Dicky Bird's ear. "Huh?" Dicky Bird whispers back, then says, "Naw, Ah ain't seen him."

"What ya got? Huh? What ya got, motherfucker?" Al Johnson's hollerin across the table.

"Play ya own damn cards," Gene Holland hollers back across the table.

Jukebox music and all that card-shoutin noise was fillin that back room up. But Dicky Bird wasn't listenin to all that noise. That whisper of Jeremiah's was comin in his ear again. Dicky Bird whispered a little loud whisper back, tried to get his words up over all that noise. He's tellin Jeremiah, "He mights be up the Shamrock. Yeal, that's where ya mights see him. Ya know how he be around them white folks up there."

Jeremiah left the back room, slithered through that front room crowd that was wigglin to the music, then he was movin through the glare of that old hangin porch light. Then the path was dark in his eyes, the white chickens in them coops couldn't be seen. Dark alley cats stayed in the dark, hissed and scooted away into the night. At the end of the path, Jeremiah turned up the dark alley, lifted his eyes, and stared at the far lights of Homewood Avenue. His steps quickened, then the sound of his footsteps taunted the silence in the alley. Backyard dogs barked as he neared their fences, passed, and was far beyond their sight. But they kept that barkin up until silence would say, "Silence."

Homewood Avenue lights were bright in the night. All kind of them little black summer bugs, them kind that could fly, were just a-buzzin up in the glow of the lights. But Jeremiah wasn't lookin up at them, or lookin in them lit-up store windows. He kept his head down as he walked, kept his eyes away from anyone comin his way, until he neared that big old bank's clock hangin way up over the sidewalk. A quick look up saw the time in the night; the dark face of the clock frowned as it showed its midnight hour. Jeremiah lowered his eyes, looked back down at the dark gray of the sidewalk, and hurried past the darkness cuddled in some of the doorways.

To alley folks, Homewood Avenue was always "up the alley." Even when it was down the alley, it was always up in their minds. Way up there where money was, way up there where the Belmar and the Highland theaters were. Where the A & P grocery store and all them other shoppin stores always had that good stuff. If alley folks had the money, they could buy whatever they wanted. They could watch them picture shows as long as they sat up in that balcony and kept quiet.

They could even take their bright, smilin, Colored faces into that Isaly's ice cream store, get some of that good-tastin ice cream. They could do that anytime they had that little extra ice cream money, long as they took that ice cream on out the store. Colored faces couldn't sit at them nice tables in that ice cream store, couldn't be sittin in there with them white folks. But it is night now, shoppin store doors are closed, been closed.

Jeremiah looks up again, sees other walkers in the night. He tries to see their colors and puts his head down when he sees the whiteness of their skin. They are passin, two or three men and some women. Jeremiah has walked closer to the curb of the street, but lowered his eyes from the other walkers. The sound of their talk and laughter slowly follows them down the street, and it is quiet again til the faint sound of music comes into the silence. Jeremiah knows he is nearin what they call The Corner, where Homewood crosses Frankstown Avenue. Some folks say that corner up there ain't no good for nobody. Most folks cross that Frankstown Avenue real fast and try not to look up or down the way it comes and goes. They don't want to see some of them Frankstown Avenue men and women that be hangin out in front of some of them bars like trash.

Jeremiah has reached the corner and turns down Frankstown. It is always a dark street, its lights in the windows giving off just a dull glow. That Shamrock Bar isn't far from the corner and the bar doors are propped open in the heat, that beer smell spillin all out in the street. Some of them Frankstown Avenue white men are standin out in front of it, and Jeremiah eases his way through them and on through the door. Inside, jukebox music is floatin in all that thick cigarette smoke. Some woman with long red hair is leanin at the bar and lettin her hips sway with that slow rhythm comin from that music. Other faces are fallin deep into the darkness of the room, where the high, hangin, dim lights can't reach them. The red-haired woman turns around when the bartender yells over her head, "What you want in here?"

Jeremiah looks over her shoulder, stares at the bartender for a moment, then says, "I'm looking for Tommy Moses."

The bartender stares, seems to let his eyes look at things twice he already seen once. "He's in the back."

Tommy Moses was in that back room of the Shamrock where they had the pool table set up. Tommy Moses was sittin on a chair over in the corner. He had bright yellow skin and was real fat; had a lot of loose, flabby skin hangin off him. But his face wasn't fat, it was bony-lookin, and them little eyes he got look like the same kind that them chickens of Gus Goins's have. Tommy Moses got a lot of hair on his head and uses a lot of grease to keep it flat, but some of it still gets to stickin up. He sees Jeremiah come in the back room and watches him stand and look around a little until he sees Jeremiah look at him. He gives Jeremiah a quick nod that tells Jeremiah to come on over to him.

"What ya got for me?" Tommy Moses whispers up to Jeremiah, but keeps his little chicken eyes on them pool-playin men.

Jeremiah leans over and whispers in Tommy Moses's ear, "I got to talk to you about somin."

"What?"

"I need somin."

"What?" Tommy Moses whispers, then quickly jerks away from Jeremiah and shouts to one of the pool players, "I got ten says you ain't goin to make that shot."

The pool player flicks his head back and gets the hair out

of his eyes, got a little smile on his face. He stands starin at the pool table, then softly tells Tommy Moses, "You on."

Jeremiah slowly raises himself back up, but keeps starin at Tommy Moses's face. He hears the crack of pool balls, sees Tommy Moses's face twist all up, then turn into a smile before he hears him shout, "Give me my money, man."

Those chicken eyes keep starin at the pool player, then at the ten dollars in the player's hand. Jeremiah's eyes look to the side a little at the pool player, then look down at Tommy Moses's hand reachin for the money. He watches the fat fingers grab the ten dollars, sees the flash of gold and silver rings on many fingers. Then he watches the fat fingers reach and struggle to get a big roll of money out of Tommy Moses's pocket and add the ten dollars to the big round roll of dollar bills. It takes a little time for Tommy Moses to wiggle himself comfortable in his chair, then he sits quietly and looks at the pool game.

Jeremiah leans over and whispers again, "I got somin I want to talk to you about, Tommy."

"Oh yeal," Tommy Moses mumbles, but keeps his eyes on the game. Crackin sounds of pool balls smackin each other fill the moments. Chicken eyes keeps watchin the pool table.

"Can we talk, man?" Jeremiah whispers again, but his whisper has a crack to it. The words smack at Tommy Moses's ear.

"Yeal, all right," Tommy Moses says, sighs, and begins to wiggle himself up and out of the chair. "Come on, let's go out back with this. This here better be somin good for me. You come up here and get to cuttin me out of makiŋ some of that money."

Out back of the Shamrock was some little old dark yard with a bunch of stinkin, smellin garbage cans and piles of boxes. Tommy Moses wiggled on over by the cans, unzipped his pants and in a moment was splatterin piss all over the cans and askin over his shoulder, "Now, what you got to talk about?"

"I need to hold some money for a day or two. I got somin goin down, but I need a little stake on it."

Tommy Moses wiggles himself til he's got his pants zipped up, then turns around and gets to reachin in his shirt pocket for a cigarette. A light from a match lights his face up, makes that bright yellow skin of his look pink in the night. He takes a few puffs on that cigarette. "What's in it for me? What you got goin down?"

Jeremiah lowers his eyes in the dark. "I want to keep it to me for now."

"Shit, man, you crazzy. Come askin for money and ain't goin to tell me where my money is goin. What kind of money you talkin about anyway, huh?"

Jeremiah looks up, stares at the fat man's skinny face. "I need hold about three."

"You talkin about three hundred dollars? Shit, I know you out your mind now. What you need that kind of money for?"

Jeremiah just stares into the skinny face, but says nothing. Tommy Moses puffs on his cigarette, looks out into the night, then turns back to Jeremiah, sayin, "Man, you got to come up with somin if you askin for that kind of money. What you got for me to hold? How I know you ain't about to skip town or somin? Shit, you got to come up with a whole lot more of what you talkin about if you wants me to be thinkin about this shit at all. You can make that money you talkin about in no time. Shit, you can make that money in one damn night. I can set you up real easy, set you up good."

Jeremiah whispers out from his silence, "What are you talkin about, man?"

Chicken eyes stare at Jeremiah's eyes, and a little smile gets to comin on that skinny face. Jeremiah waits for Tommy Moses to say something, but the fat man just keeps smilin.

Jeremiah whispers, "Look, I need the money soon."

"Man, I told you, you can make the money yourself. Shit, I'd even give you some for what you got."

There is silence in the dark. Then Tommy Moses laughs a little and says, "Damn, man, just turn that woman you got stayin with you out. That's where the money is. Turn her out. Shit, as good as she's lookin, that can be some big money for you. I'd take some of that myself, and you know them white boys in there will pay you top dollar just to eat her pussy. Shit, you can get more money than that bank got down there. Man, I can set you up real good. I thought you would have turned her out by now. That last gal you had was nice, but this one here you got can make the money."

Jeremiah keeps starin at the fat man's skinny face. Tommy Moses is still smilin up at Jeremiah. A whisper eases into the silence. "Let me think about it, man. I'll let you know in the mornin."

"Yeal, man, let me know. Shit, like I said, *I'd* even give you somin for that."

"How much can you come up with?" Jeremiah chokes out, then speaks up a little, lets his words go free in the dark. "I at least need three up front. Can you come up with that?"

"Shit, I got that now."

"I need it up front."

"I'll tell you what, let me have some of that first, and I'll front you what you need. Then I'll set you up real good here.

Shit, you can make that money back in no time. Shit, just like I said, them white boys in there pay top dollar just to eat that fine-lookin thing's pussy."

The corner of Jeremiah's mouth is curlin up a little. The white of his teeth glimmer. He whispers again, tells the fat man, "I'll let you know in the mornin."

Far above the alley, the summer moon was only showin half its face. Its yellow glow was dulled by all that mill smoke floatin around beneath it. But the alley always had its deep shadows along them fences, always kept its shadows. Jeremiah is walkin close to them fences. He has his head down and stares down at the dark red bricks. Even as he moves along the fences, his eyes are still. Alley cats scootin around in the dark can't make him look their way.

Willet's layin across her bed, but she's not sleepin. She can hear Jeremiah comin into the house, hear him comin up the steps. Slowly, she turns to the doorway when he comes into the bedroom. Jeremiah cannot see her face in the dark, but he can feel her eyes lookin at him and hear her sayin, "Well?"

Jeremiah stops in the doorway, stands there silently for a moment, then says, "I found him. He'll let me know about the money in the mornin. I told him I'd have to think about it. You know, bringin you up there."

Willet's silent.

"He says he got the money."

"What's there to think about then?" Willet asks.

· TWO ·

When mornin came, it came without the sun and was all gray. Mister Allen was out on that porch of his. In a bit, Mister Strayhorne came out his house, gave that quick "Good mornin" to Mister Allen and headed on out to the mill. Mister Allen went on with his sittin and got to readin that mornin paper while it was still quiet enough to read. Every once in a while he'd look up, stare up at the sky, and wonder when that rain he could smell in the air was goin to fall. That quick door-openin sound Mister Allen heard made him look down from the sky and see Jeremiah Henderson leavin his house. Mister Allen sorta squinched his face up a little while he got to tryin to figure out where that boy was goin this time of the mornin. Mister Allen watched Jeremiah hurry on up the alley, then shrugged his shoulders a little fore he got to readin his paper again.

The rain didn't come, but them alley children did, brought all that noise with them, too. Mister Allen got up and went on back in the house and tried to keep all that loud carryin-on out his mind. Cool breezes could come down the alley and blow up into some of them windows. Sometimes that cool air would flap them drapes and curtains back, cool them upstairs rooms off. Willet Mercer was lyin on the bed in the back room. That noise them alley children were makin stayed out of the silence in the back room. It was one of those waitin silences that wouldn't go nowhere. Willet wouldn't let it go away. She needed it to wait in, close and open her eyes in, with that dreary light comin through the window.

.   .   .

When the winds blew hard, rain came, but it didn't stay long. Mister Allen looked out his window and was surprised to see that sun tryin to light up the alley some. Them children got out them houses and off them porches as soon as the last drop of water splattered on one of them alley bricks. Mister Allen stood in his doorway and just shook his head as he watched some of them children splashin in them puddles like they ain't had no better sense. In a while he went on and sat down on that porch of his, but every once in a while he'd look up at the sky again and wonder when that rain was comin back.

That dark sky stayed all day, made that day seem like it was goin to last forever. Alley mamas had called the children in, made them eat, then kept them close to the porches. Some of them alley mamas kept their children in the house, told them they ain't needin to be out there with that kind of night comin. Them folks that were still sittin out on their porches got to softenin their talk when the sky started flashin all that lightnin. Then they got to whisperin back and forth when they saw Jeremiah Henderson and that woman of his comin out and start hurryin up the alley. Them folks that weren't whisperin about them was starin just the same and wonderin where they were goin with that storm comin like it was.

．　．　．

Gus Goins was hopin the rain would hold off, go some place else. He knew folks didn't like to come out with all that rain comin down on them. And that money they might have in their pockets wouldn't be gettin to him, he'd have to wait some for it. He was sittin out on that back porch of his tryin to figure out if he should just go on and get some of them chickens' heads off, anyway. Maybe if the rain come hard and quick, it would go on about its business and leave his be. He heard them heels clickin on them alley bricks and looked up just in time to see Jeremiah and that woman of his going on by. He watched as much of that woman as he could see through all them high weeds in his yard he had to look through. He didn't have to see all of her to know who it was. That dark red she had on was still movin and wigglin in his mind like it was movin and wigglin on her when he looked up and saw Al Johnson comin up the path. Gus Goins yells out, "Nigger, you's the last one on earth that needs to be walkin around with that lightin up there. If that lightin strikes anybody, it's goin to be you."

Al Johnson gives Gus Goins a little laugh, then yells back, "Man, Ah just *seen* me some lightin goin by. And it sure wasn't up in the sky. Um comin down the alley and Ah look up and Ah sees me some lightin comin. Ah seen Jeremiah and that woman of his comin up the alley. Ah tell ya, the closer she got, the harder my dick got. Now *that's* some lightin. Ah bet that pussy be so hot it burn your dick off before ya can get it up in there."

Gus Goins laughs some. "I watched that go by here. I wonder where they's goin with that rain comin again." Al Johnson shakes his head and says at the same time, "Man, that rain ain't goin to fall on that woman, wherever she goes."

Wasn't many folks out on Homewood Avenue. What that first rain didn't chase away, the one that was comin was keepin away. Nighttime was still far off in the comin skies. But wasn't nothin left of the last little bit of sunlight that was fallin over Homewood Avenue. Wasn't nothin but dark gray light lurkin over the street. Jeremiah stood in the doorway of Kay's Drugstore. He kept starin up and down the street, tryin to see through all that thick gray. He knew Tommy Moses was on his way, had to be comin. Willet was standin way back in the doorway. She wasn't watchin nothin cept that gray smoke comin from her cigarette.

Miss Macune ain't got a light on in that big house of hers. She turned all them lights off when that thunder and lightnin got to comin. She's sittin in that big front room of hers. She's alone, but she don't think she's alone. She's lookin toward the window and is tellin that husband of hers, Eddy Macune, that the devil got to be bringin this kind of rain that's comin. Now she's lookin over at Eddy Macune and tellin him what she just got done tellin him before she looked out.

Dicky Bird ain't had no house, just had him a shack he built up in them real high weeds next to the railroad tracks. Folks that didn't know it was there couldn't see it. And them folks that knew it was there didn't give it a minute's worth of thought unless they were wantin Dicky Bird to do somethin for them. Dicky Bird's up in that shack now. He got them pieces of plywood up against them windows to stop that rain from comin in when it comes again. And he's hopin that leaky spot on that roof of his ain't goin to get to leakin real bad when the rain come again. He's sittin on the side of that cot of his and starin down through them planks he got for a floor. He can see through them cracks in them. He can see that dark muddy water layin beneath them planks. He's seein the water, but that ain't what he's seein in his mind. He's seein his mama, who he ain't seen in fifty-six years. He knows how long, keeps track of each passin year as soon as spring is over. He told his mama he was leavin, was goin to go on and get on one of them slow-rollin freights going north. He told her he was going to send her some money and come back and see her, too. Dicky Bird knows his mama got to be gone on by now. And he knows he ain't never sent her no money and ain't never gone back to see her either.

Bill Lovit ain't hurryin, cause he figures he ain't got no place to go anyway. He knows his house ain't goin to be there when he gets there. All his babies ain't goin to be there either. Ain't nothin goin to be there cept that dark charred wood layin where his house should be. He knows he's gonna hear his babies' ghosts there cryin for him. He's in that weedy lot that's between Casino Way and Tioga Street. He's tryin to stay on that little path that winds through all them weeds. But that wine in him keeps takin him into them bushes. He's in the bushes now and got that wine bottle turned up high toward the sky. That wine is just a-gushin down into his throat. Some of that wine that can't get into his mouth is runnin down his chin. That wine is still runnin down his chin when lightnin flashes and makes everything look real bright. Makes him look like some black scarecrow somebody put out in the lot. And tilted its head back and stuck a bottle of wine halfway down its throat. That thunder that's comin after the lightnin is shakin the ground everywhere. And the rain that's been wantin to come is comin like it's mad it had to wait so long. Its big cold drops are splatterin all over the place. It just ain't fallin down, it's blowin sideways, too, splashin up against folks' windows. It's splashin up against Bill Lovit's face. But he still got that wine bottle up and don't even feel that water smackin his face, soakin all into his clothes.

Tommy Moses hears all that rain comin down, hears it batterin down on his roof and tappin hard on his windows. But he ain't thinkin about the rain. He knows he's goin to have his dick sucked. And Jeremiah Henderson better have that bitch of his there waitin for him. Tommy Moses is in the apartment he has up on Frankstown Avenue. He's in the bathroom and lookin at himself in the mirror. He sees his face all shiny-lookin after he done shaved and patted it down with that Old Spice cologne he likes. Now he's in his bedroom and lookin at himself in that big mirror in there. He has his dark brown pants on and his bright yellow shirt that goes with his bright yellow skin. He's goin to wear his yellow-and-black plaid sports jacket cause he needs somethin with big pockets in it. He's goin to have some big money on him. And he ain't goin to have that big money on him without havin his pistol with him, too. He knows Jeremiah Henderson carries him a quick knife, one of them long switchblades. He knows Jeremiah had that blade up against Skippy Robinson's throat before the man could see Jeremiah comin at him. David Higgens told him, said he seen it. Jeremiah was shootin crap, made his point, and Skippy didn't want to pay up. Couldn't have been over nothin past a dollar.

·   ·   ·

Homewood Avenue ain't nothin but cold and gray-lookin, with the rain splatterin down on it. The only colors Jeremiah can see is them reds and greens flashin on traffic lights. Them cars that go by every once in a while don't seem to have no color on them, just seem to be all gray-lookin, just like the rain. Jeremiah has his shoulders hunched up and turns his back toward that rain when it gets to blowin up in the doorway he's standin in. Then he turns back, tries to see the big clock out in front of the bank so he can see what time it is. He knows it has to be gettin close to seven o'clock. Tommy Moses better be comin, better not be pullin no no-show shit on him.

Willet's starin at the raindrops she sees splashin out on the sidewalk. Sometimes she can feel the wind from the rain blowin back on her. Slow thoughts come into her mind, bring things she wants to feel again, see again. But she knows Tommy Moses is going to be drivin up soon, better be bringin somethin she wants right now. She knows she got to play him like he wants to be played. Play him good so he ain't got nothin but angels and candy in his mind.

Tommy Moses got him one of those brand-new long Buicks. It's dark blue and got a lot of chrome on it. He keeps it shiny, pays some boy two dollars a week to keep it clean for him. The rain is splashin up against its windshield now. Them windshield wipers can't seem to keep that Buick's window clear enough for Tommy Moses to see where he's going. But he don't have to see where he's going. He knows them Homewood streets, just wants to make sure ain't nothin gettin in his way, don't want to be runnin into nothin that's goin to be dentin up his grille. He's drivin down Homewood Avenue now and got his face up toward the windshield so he can see the front of Kay's Drugstore.

Jeremiah is watchin the slow-movin dark car comin. He can't see who's drivin it, but he knows, can feel, it's Tommy

Moses. A quick honk of a car horn is bein muffled by the sound of the rain. But Jeremiah can still hear it, been listenin for it. Quickly he's lookin back over his shoulder. "That's him, come on."

Willet's been lookin down, hasn't seen the dark car pull up, hasn't heard the car horn. She has a cigarette in her hand and slowly brings it up to her lips and takes a long, slow drag on it.

Jeremiah's tellin her, "Come on," again.

The cigarette's fallin from her hand. It hits the ground and it's still rollin when she steps on it, grinding it a second fore she walks toward Jeremiah. He's lookin at her, tryin to see her eyes, but she's keepin her head down.

Tommy Moses is leanin over in his seat. He's tryin to see out that car's passenger side window. He knows he seen Jeremiah standin in the doorway, but that ain't who he wanted to see. He can see Jeremiah hurryin through the rain, and now he can see what he wanted to see. He can see the blur of red through the gray water hittin and rollin down the window.

Willet's takin quick, long steps. She's keepin her head down and tryin to keep the rain from gettin in her face. But she's reachin down and pullin her skirt up a little so she can take those long steps.

Jeremiah got that big car's door open, he's holdin it open for Willet. She's hurryin past him and steppin up into the car. Tommy Moses is watchin her get in. He's seein her red skirt ridin up her leg, a little of the soft white of her slip. She's in the car now, slidin across the seat, gettin close to him. He can feel the softness of her hip against him, smell the scent of her perfume seepin up his nose. He's tryin to see her face. But he can't see all of it, just the side of it. He can only see the black of her hair hangin down over caramel-colored cheek. The beads of rain rollin down her cheeks. He's wonderin if she's goin to turn to look at him, say somethin to him. But she doesn't, she's lookin down at the dashboard and keeps lookin down.

Jeremiah's in the car and pullin the door closed. The sounds of the rain batterin down on the street seem distant to Willet. She hears Jeremiah sayin somethin to Tommy Moses about the damn rain. Tommy Moses is sayin, "Yeal, man." Now he's askin, "How come you don't have an umbralla here for this fine woman?"

Jeremiah's pushin aside Tommy Moses's question and askin him, "What we goin to do, man?"

Tommy Moses says, "Just like Ah said, we got to talk about things. Talk goes right, everything be just fine."

Willet keeps her head down, keeps lookin at the shiny knobs on the dashboard. Now she's lookin up as the car starts movin slowly. She can see the quick, dark blurs of the wind-shield wipers goin back and forth over the window.

Tommy Moses is sayin to Jeremiah, "What do ya say we ride on up by the ball field. We can talk things out there. Ain't nobody goin to be playin no ball there. We can talk up there, have a nice talk up there."

Jeremiah's askin, "Did you bring some of that help with you?"

"Like Ah say, talk goes right, things can get right, too."

Homewood Field ain't far from Homewood Avenue. It's up there behind the school. The railroad tracks go by the back of the field. Some of them trains stop at the little station up there, let some folks off, let some folks on, then go on about their business. Them old freight trains don't stop, just slow down some. Dicky Bird tells folks that's where he got off the train. Says he didn't know where he was at. But he was hungry and had to get off that train and find him somethin to eat. He said he didn't care where he was at either.

Slowly the rain is passin. It's still comin down, but it ain't doin all that pourin down and blowin around. Tommy Moses is still drivin his car real slow. He's drivin it up that hill that goes up to the ball field. Except for that back and forth wipin sound of the windshield wipers, it's quiet in the car. Jeremiah's lookin out the front window of the car, he's tryin to see where Tommy Moses is going. Jeremiah can see that ball yard fence. But Tommy Moses ain't stoppin and pullin over to the side. Slowly, Jeremiah's askin, "Hey man, where you goin?"

Tommy Moses is slidin some slow words over to Jeremiah. He's talkin real smooth and sayin, "Just up the hill some, man. Just goin up here some. Ah figure we can pull down in that lot by the tracks up there. Ya know, that little lot down under the bridge. That's a nice place to talk. We can talk, watch them trains go by, too."

Tommy Moses is smilin now, he's askin Willet, "Ya like to watch them choochoos go by?"

Tommy Moses still got that little smile on his face. He's waitin on Willet to say something back to him, maybe give him some little tease words he can keep and play with up in his mind. But she ain't sayin nothin back. She's lookin out the window some and hearin them windshield wipers goin back and forth.

Tommy Moses is turnin the car onto that bumpy little street that leads down to the lot by the tracks. He's goin real slow and tryin to ease his car over them bumps nice and easy. He got it down the little hill now and is drivin the car up toward the railroad tracks. There's a fence at the end of the lot and he don't want to get it too close to the fence. He knows there's a gully before you get to that fence and he don't want his wheels to get down in that gully.

The rain has almost slowed to a stop. Except for the light patter of raindrops fallin on the car, there's a sudden silence in it. Tommy Moses has turned the engine off and sounds of the windshield wipers settled somewhere beyond the silence. The dark skies that brought the rain have gone, but the dark gray that came with the storm has stayed. Willet is starin across the tracks. There's a park over there. She can see the mist the rain has left behind hoverin over the grass and seepin through the trees.

Tommy Moses is wigglin around in his seat, tryin to get a little comfortable. Same time he's shiftin around in his seat, he's sayin, "Looks like that rain's out of here just in time for us to get a little talk in."

Jeremiah's leanin back in his seat and askin, "You going to be able to give some of that help I told you I needed?"

Quickly Tommy Moses is sayin, "Damn, man, what Ah tell ya? Ah say we can talk about some things. Ya know, talk. That's what we here for, ain't it, huh?"

"Look, man," Jeremiah's sayin, "I just want to know if you got some of that . . . help . . . with you. Ain't no sense in talkin if you don't have somin with you."

"Hey, Ah always got me somin. Ah carries more in my change pocket than half the niggers ya see got in the bank." Tommy Moses is tellin Jeremiah and tightenin up his skinny face.

Willet wants to cross her legs, get a little comfortable, and light up a cigarette. She has little room to get comfortable between Jeremiah and fat Tommy Moses. She's shiftin her hips and her shoulders a little. She's gettin the space she needs to cross her legs and gettin out a cigarette. That tightness on Tommy Moses's face is loosenin up now. That red skirt slidin up Willet's leg caught his eye and kept it there. She got her cigarette out now and Tommy Moses is quickly gettin out his lighter and sayin, "Here, baby, let me get that for ya."

Willet's stickin the tip of her cigarette into the bright little flame comin from Tommy Moses's lighter. She's takin some puffs on her cigarette to get it lit and seein the glow from the little fire lightin up all them shiny rings on Tommy Moses's fingers. Now she's tastin the smoke, takin the cigarette away from the flame. She's tiltin her head back, blowin some smoke out of her mouth, and givin Tommy Moses a quick nod to tell him thanks. It's real quiet for a moment before Tommy Moses is sayin to Jeremiah, "Look, man, what ya say ya and me go talk? Let's get this talk out the way. It ain't doin nothin but doin some drizzlin out there. Yeal, let's go on over underneath the bridge, get this talk out the way. We don't needs to be botherin this fine young lady here wit our talk."

Willet's alone in the car now, she can lean back and get real comfortable. The car seems so much bigger to her since fat Tommy Moses got out. She likes the car, likes how big it is, likes all the shiny knobs on the dashboard. She sees the dials for the radio, stares at them fore she leans over and turns one. There's a little bloop sound fore a soft hum comes out of the radio's speakers. She's leanin back, waitin on the radio. She can hear the mellow sounds of a horn playin, with some slow drum beats layin down a deep base while that horn gets them high notes. Slowly, she turns around some in her seat to see if she can see Jeremiah and Tommy Moses under the bridge, but she can't. Them car windows are steamed up from the rain. She turns back around, gets comfortable, and lets that horn player soothe her mind, keep them thoughts she don't want to be bothered with out of her head.

Tommy Moses got to watch where he stands, keeps lookin down at the ground underneath the bridge. He don't want to be steppin in all that broken glass from them bottles. Jeremiah's lookin down at the ground, but he ain't thinkin about the glass. He done told Tommy Moses somethin and he's gettin ready to tell him again. Tommy Moses is sayin, "Man, Ah tell ya—"

Jeremiah keeps lookin down at the ground, but he's bustin in to what Tommy Moses is sayin and tellin him, "I can't do what I want to do for that. I told you what I need up front."

"Ah told ya, Ah gives ya somethin up front. But man, ya gots to give me somethin for givin it to ya. Ah gots ta get mine, ya knows how things work. Ya smart, everybody knows ya knows what's up. Gives me somin for my money."

"You got the hundred? You got it with you?"

"Damn, man. Ah told ya Ah gots it."

"What about the three? You got that too?" Jeremiah's lookin up from the ground and lookin at Tommy Moses, waitin for his answer.

"Hey, man." Tommy Moses is gettin his hands extended from his side and lookin like some preacher gettin ready to ask folks to pray. But he's sayin, "Ya askin me a lot abouts my money. Ah done told ya, ya can makes that three. Shit, five, ten times that three. Ah knows that girl can gets that kind of money. Ain't goin ta be nothin to it."

Tommy Moses is holdin up his words, he's waitin to see if he can tell what Jeremiah's thinkin about. He's lookin at Jeremiah's face, tryin to see what kind of play he'll take. He sees the look he wants to see and quickly gets to sayin, "Ain't nothin to it, man. The money's just goin ta be waitin. Ah gits the room in that boardin house up there. Ya know, the one across from the Shamrock. Then, Ah walks her into the Shamrock. Walk her around some. Ya know, lets her be seen. Then, she goes on over the room. And Ah knows a good ten, maybe fifteen of them white boys goin ta want that. Ah knows they come up with a good fifty apiece for somethin that looks that good. Ya know me, Um goin ta gets the money from them before they go over. And Ah gets them to give me twenty dollars more. Ya know, just in case they go over their time. They don't go over their time, they get that twenty back. Shit, man, ya see ya can get way more than that three tonight. And that's after Ah gets my little cut."

"What's your cut?" Jeremiah wants to know.

"Twenty percent and what Ah gots to pay for the room. But that ain't goin ta be a flat ten dollars. Ya can see, man, lots of money waitin, just waitin. And that's just tonight, a couple nights a week and ya can have all the money ya be needin. Shit, plus a whole lot more."

Jeremiah's lookin back down at the ground, starin at it and sayin, "Let me think about it. I got to talk to her about it."

Slowly, Tommy Moses is sayin, "Yeal, go on and talk to the little lady. But like Ah say, Ah gives you a hundred up front on the deal. Tell her that, tell her Ah gots that now. But ya tell her Ah wants ta try some of that out, ya know, see what Um goin ta get for my money. Tell her when ya get done talkin ta her and she likes the deal, tell her Ah want to spend some little time wit her. Ya know, get ta know her. Ah gots a big backseat."

Jeremiah's walkin back to the car, that quick step of his

hurryin through the dark. The night that was comin came quick and easy. That passin storm had already taken the light away. Tommy Moses is pissin up against the wall beneath the bridge. But he's still got his eye on Jeremiah, watchin him quickly slide through the dark. Willet turns to the door when she hears it bein opened. She looks up at Jeremiah, stares into his face. She can't keep her eyes on it. He's turnin it from her as he gets into the car and closes the door. Quickly, he's lightin a cigarette, takin a couple puffs on it. Willet's silent, waitin on Jeremiah to say something. She can hear the sounds of his breathin. He cannot see her lookin at him, but he can feel her eyes on him. She wants to know what Tommy Moses said under the bridge, she's tired of waitin for Jeremiah to tell her. "Well, what did he say?"

Tommy Moses is waitin, keeps his eyes on the car in the dark. He can see the car, see things he wants to see in his mind. He can see that red skirt ridin up her leg, that soft white of her slip ticklin his eyes again. He can still feel her hip up against him, smell her perfume that seeped up his nose. He hears the car door bein opened.

Jeremiah's gettin ready to slide out of his seat and get out of the car. Willet's whisperin to him, "That fat pig better have the money."

"He got it." Jeremiah's still lookin at Willet, seein the weak light of some faraway streetlight fallin on her face enough for him to see her eyes starin at the dashboard. He whispers to her, "You got what you need if he gets to actin a fool. I'll be over by the bridge."

Tommy Moses sees Jeremiah gettin out of the car and comin back toward the bridge. He's watchin Jeremiah comin until he sees Willet slowly gettin out of the car, too. He can see the red in the night, see it movin, see it lookin alive and whisperin to him. A smile is comin to his face, he's seein what he wants to see. Willet's openin the back door of the car and gettin in. She's doin it slowly, too.

Jeremiah walks toward Tommy Moses with his head lowered. As he nears, he's lookin and tryin to see Tommy Moses's eyes in the night. "She'll do it for you."

The smile on the fat man's skinny face has become soft, almost gentle. He's lookin past Jeremiah to the car, but he's tellin him, "Yeal, man, Ah thinks we can work together here. Like Ah told ya, Ah knows ya smart. Yeal, man, we goin ta make a lot of that money, too."

Slowly and as soft as the fat man's smile, Jeremiah's sayin, "Yeal, I think we can. Listen, I want to hold that hundred now."

"Oh yeal, man, yeal, ya can hold a hundred. We doin business now. And ya knows Um a businessman, good businessman. That's why ya come lookin for me, cause ya knows Ah do good business."

Jeremiah's tryin to watch Tommy Moses's hands in the dark. But the fat man has quick hands, has them bills counted real fast. And the rest of his money back in his pocket before Jeremiah can see how much there is. "Here's a hundred," Tommy Moses is sayin as he holds out the money for Jeremiah to take.

Willet doesn't look over to the sound of the car door bein opened. She's lit another cigarette and leaned her head back against the seat. She will not let the noise the door is makin come into her silence. The car is saggin a little to one side as Tommy Moses gets in. He's slidin over the seat, gettin closer to Willet. He's tryin to make himself comfortable, get his arm stretched over the back of the seat. Willet can feel his hand movin across the top part of the seat behind her head. Now she can feel his fingers touchin her hair. She takes a real slow drag on her cigarette and blows the smoke out of her mouth just as slow as she sucked it in.

Tommy Moses is whisperin, "Ya one fine woman."

Willet is silent.

Tommy Moses is slowly lettin his eyes dance in the dark. He can hear the soft music comin from the radio and his eyes move with the rhythm of music over Willet's lips, breasts, and legs. He's touchin her hair, lettin one of his fingers go through her hair and rub the back of her neck. He's whisperin to her again, sayin, "Yeal, ya one fine woman here."

Willet is silent.

Tommy Moses whispers, "Why don't ya come on over here? Get a little closer ta me. Come on, get a little closer. Ya knows Ah can take good care of somin like you. Sees that ya gits everythin ya wants."

Willet keeps starin over the top of the front seat and out the front window of the car. She can see the dark outline of the trees in the park across the tracks. She keeps starin at the trees in the night, but whispers very slowly, "What can you do for me?"

There's a smile in the dark that Willet does not see. Tommy Moses is smilin. She knows he is movin closer to her, she can feel his fat stomach bulgin out against her. His fingers are rubbin her neck, tryin to pull her closer to him. He's whisperin, "Ah can do a lot for a fine woman likes you. Come on now, show me what ya can do with that fine self ya gots."

Willet can smell Tommy Moses's breath, feel the heat of it and the wetness of his tongue lickin at her neck. She takes a quick drag on her cigarette, leans forward, and puts it out in the ashtray.

Tommy Moses pulls her back.

Willet lets herself be pulled to him.

Tommy Moses is buryin his face into her breast, usin his quick hands to unbutton her blouse.

She's puttin her hands behind his head.

He likes the feel of her hands.

She's pullin his face closer to her breast.

He's lickin at her breast.

She's pullin his face closer.

He's lickin on her stomach.

She's lookin out into the night.

He's pullin her skirt up, rubbin her legs.

Far off, a train whistle's blowin.

She's closin her eyes, listenin to the whistle blow.

Her panties are bein pulled off. He's jerkin them down her legs. And gettin to his knees on the seat. Quickly, he's takin off his jacket, unbuttonin his shirt, pullin down his pants. She's lookin up at him, seein the fat layers of his flesh wigglin from his every move. She can smell the thick, sour odor of his sweat. He's comin to her again, reachin for her arm, and pullin her toward him.

The train's nearin, shakin the night.

He's pullin the back of her head.

The rumblin sound of the train is nearing.

Her face is bein rubbed in sweaty, fat flesh.

"Come on, baby, do me," he's tellin her.

Train lights come into the dark.

"Come on, do me, do me."

The train's passin, shakin the ground.

She's kissin his stomach.

He's moanin, "Do me . . . Do me . . ."

The loud rumblin of the train is poundin the car.

"Do me, come on."

Slowly, she's reachin into her purse.

Window lights from the train flash in the car.

She has the knife in her hand.

He's pushin her head down farther.

Train wheels squeak loud in the night.

A quick clickin sound stings the air.

"Hey, what ya—"

She's sneakin the knife through the dark. Now she's stickin it into his fat stomach, pushin it deeper, pullin it out, and stickin it in again. He's makin loud, quick gaspin sounds, jerkin around, tryin to grab at her in the dark.

The train's passed, lights goin away in the night.

Jeremiah's been standing beneath the bridge, sometimes lookin up at the passin train. Couple times he's tried to see in them brightly lit windows of the train, see if he could see the people on board before lookin back into the night, over to the car. He's seein the car door openin now. He's seein Willet slowly gettin out. He's watchin, waitin to see Tommy Moses get out, too. He hears Willet whisperin his name through the dark. Quickly he starts walkin over to the car. He's slowin as he's gettin closer to her, able to see that her skirt is stuck high up on her legs. Her blouse is all open and hangin out over the waistline of her skirt. Her hair has come undone, loose and hangin down over her face. But her head is up high, rigid. A silence is surroundin her, and Jeremiah nears it quietly. When he's near enough to see her face, he turns and looks toward the car, then back to her, whisperin, "Hey, what's goin on? What happened?"

She is silent.

Jeremiah looks over to the car, tries to see Tommy Moses. He turns back to Willet whisperin, "Hey, what's happening? You all right?"

He's close enough to try and see her face, but he can't. He looks down at her open blouse. It's soaked with somethin. He sees her hand hangin down at her side and the knife in it. He looks back up at her face quickly and stares at it, tries to see through the hair coverin her cheeks and one eye. The other eye is lookin beyond him and toward the open car door. He sighs, whispers, "What the hell did you do?"

Now Jeremiah can see both of her eyes starin into his. "I cut him."

"What?"

"I said, I cut him."

"Goddamn, Willet . . . Shit . . . Is he dead?"

"He stopped moving."

Jeremiah turns and goes over to the open car door. He slows when he gets to it, then tries to see into the dark backseat. Tommy Moses is slumped down on it. Jeremiah can see some of him in the dark. He can see his fat bare yellow legs all twisted up. But he can't see Tommy's face. He's hangin facedown over the seat. He keeps starin at those bare legs, tryin to see if they're movin. Slowly, he's climbin into the car, whisperin, "Tommy . . . Tommy . . . Hey, Tommy." He's feelin down into the dark, touches, shakes Tommy Moses's shoulder, jerks his hand away when it slips and slides through all the blood he can't see.

Willet has brushed the hair from her eyes. She's watchin Jeremiah comin back to her. When he is close enough for her to see his face, she stares at it. That far-off light from the streetlight shows her his eyes. "I think he's dead. What ya kill him for?"

"Cause I felt like it."

"What?"

A long moment won't go nowhere: it just stays in the silence between them. He turns from her and whispers back over his shoulder, "We got to get out of here."

Tommy Moses is bein dragged out of the car. Jeremiah got hold of his arm and is pullin him across the seat. The fat man is heavy. Jeremiah got to jerk hard on his arm just to get him to move. Slowly, Jeremiah's gettin Tommy Moses's head out of the car. It's makin a thumpin sound when it hits the ground. Jeremiah keeps pullin until he gets all of Tommy Moses out of the car.

Willet has stood in her silence, her blouse still open and hand hangin down at her side with the knife in it. She has watched Jeremiah pull Tommy Moses out of the car, heard his fat body slump to the ground. She walks slowly out of her stillness, stops and stands, lookin down at Tommy Moses. Jeremiah is quickly going through the fat man's pockets. But Willet is starin down at the side of Tommy Moses's face that she can see. Without takin her eyes away from it, she's askin, "Is he dead?"

"Yeal," Jeremiah whispers, and keeps going through Tommy Moses's pockets. He's pullin out that thick roll of bills, tryin to see how much money is there. But it's too dark to count, so he's puttin the roll in his own pocket.

"How much is there?"

"I can't tell, but it's a lot."

"Get his rings."

"Huh?"

"Get them rings, too. I want them rings he got."

Jeremiah's hurryin, goin through all of Tommy Moses's pockets. Now he's takin a deep sigh, lookin up at Willet and whisperin, "I can't find the keys, the car keys. Where's that jacket he had on?"

"He took it off, it's in the car. You goin to get the rings?"

"Yeal, I'll get them. We got to get out of here. We need them keys to get out of here."

Jeremiah's climbin into the backseat of the car, feelin and reachin for Tommy Moses's jacket. He has it and is draggin it out of the car, holdin it up with one hand and goin through the pockets with the other. He got the keys, but he's feelin somethin else, somethin heavy. He knows what it is now, and he's pullin it out of the pocket and sayin, "Look what I found."

Willet can't see. She's askin, "What's that?"

"A pistol. He had a pistol."

Jeremiah's stickin the pistol down through his belt. He's takin another deep sigh and lookin around at the night. He whispers, "We got to get out of here. Fast."

"What about him laying out here? Somebody might see him."

"Um going to put him in the weeds. Won't nobody see him down there tonight. It might not be days til they find him."

Jeremiah starts pullin on Tommy Moses's arm. Willet whispers sharply, "Get the rings. I want them rings."

Tommy Moses's hands are wet with his blood, his fingers are all curled up. But Jeremiah's gettin the rings off of them. He's tellin Willet to take the rings and get in the car.

The night is quiet now. Tommy Moses is layin in the weeds by that big black fence right next to the tracks. His jacket and a couple of broken-off bushes are layin over him, tryin to hide him in the dark. Some night bug done already got underneath that jacket coverin his head and is crawlin in his ear.

· THREE ·

Gus Goins was sure glad he got them chickens ready. He had him a full house. Folks he ain't seen since he didn't *know* when had come on down. Must have been tired of stayin in the house with that rain beatin down on their roofs and splashin up against their windows.

When they saw Mack Jack done come through the door, folks sorta stopped what they were doin, let that piece of chicken in their mouth just stay there, let that gin in their glass sit still. Ain't nobody seen Mack Jack since he put his horn down and said he wasn't goin to play no more.

Mack Jack could play some horn, write that music he was playin, too. He could go far away, all the way to Saint Louie and Chicago and play with them big-time bands. Folks say Mack Jack could make that horn sweat and cry at the same time. He'd do that practicin and everybody that could hear that music comin out his window would stop what they were doin and listen. Charlie Gray said he even saw one of them trains stop dead on the tracks to listen to that horn. Some folks didn't believe that, but some did. Anyway, after he came back from one of them long road trips, Mack Jack said he wasn't goin to play no more. Didn't say why.

Mister Hopewell had even come down to get him a sand-

wich, got him a couple drinks, too. Folks would give Mister
Hopewell a nod, ask him how he was doin, then try to slide on
away from him. They didn't want to be shakin his hand and
hear him tellin them he'd be seein them later. Didn't nobody
be wantin to see Mister Hopewell too soon, bein he was the
undertaker. Mister Hopewell knew folks were that way about
him, but he knew he'd be seein them later anyway.

That jukebox music in that back room of Gus Goins's is
bustin through the walls, gettin outside, and bouncin out into
the night. But Olinda Harris don't care where that music is
goin as long as she's goin with it. Horn and piano music is just
a-comin from that jukebox. But Olinda Harris ain't hearin
nothin but that low drum beat. When it gets real low and slow,
she got her hips movin slow and low with it. She got that full,
bright yellow skirt on, she got her legs spread wide and her
hands holdin up that skirt above her knees so she can move the
way she wants to. That yellow is just a-swayin all up in Sam
Barnett's eyes and gettin into his head, too. It's gettin way up
into his head, makin him think he ain't as old as he is. He's
been tellin folks he's seventy-two, but he's been tellin them
that for years. He's sittin back in that chair, sippin on his wine,
and knowin he shouldn't be watchin that young girl dancin like
that. He knows he don't need all that ass-shakin up in his
mind—can't do anything but think about it and that's what he's
doin already.

Lucille Briggs is peekin over her shoulder, takin them
quick looks at that Olinda Harris doin what she's doin. She
knows Olinda Harris got everybody in the room watchin her
dance. Peter Lloyd was talkin to Lucille Briggs and tellin her
how good she was lookin. Now he's lookin right past her shoulder and watchin that other woman dance. Lucille Briggs is

thinkin she don't need that shit. She walks on out that room, thinkin it was too hot in there anyway.

Al Johnson's standin out on that back porch of Gus Goins's. He got his cup of gin with him and is leanin up against the porch post. He can hear all that music, but he ain't thinkin about it. He knows there's a good card game goin on inside, too. But he ain't thinkin about no cards either. He's sippin on his gin and lookin up at that big dark sky. Sometimes he can see some little star tryin to shine through all them storm clouds passin. Sometimes when he can't see it, he keeps lookin til that cloud that's hidin it goes on by. He's tryin to figure out if there's anything better up there in that heaven. He ain't told nobody, but he got a letter up from his sister in Savannah, Georgia, tellin him his mama ain't doin too well at all. His sister told him his mama keeps callin his name out. He hears that screen door bein pushed open behind him and he's turnin around to see who's comin out.

Lucille Briggs is comin out on the back porch to get away from all that mess she don't want to be bothered with inside. She's a big woman, she knows that. But she carries herself good and she knows that, too. She's steppin out on that dark porch. Now she can go on and poke her mouth out, get them little hot pockets of air in her blown out. She don't see Al Johnson til she hears him sayin to her, "Hey baby, what ya doin out here?"

Lucille Briggs looks over and sees Al Johnson leanin up against the porch post. But she don't go over by him. She just moves away from the door a little bit and leans up against the wall and starts to get a cigarette out of her purse. She don't want to be bothered with no Al Johnson. She gets that cigarette lit, blows that smoke out of her mouth, and lets that match fizzle out as it falls to the porch floor. Al Johnson's givin her another little holler. He's askin her, "What ya doin comin out here all by ya self? Less ya knows Ah was out here and comes to see me."

Lucille Briggs takes another drag on her cigarette, blows the smoke out her mouth, and tells Al Johnson, "I just come out here to get me some air. Do you mind?"

"No baby, Ah don't mind," Al Johnson says, turns back around, and sips on his gin.

"How come you ain't in there playin in the card game?" Lucille Briggs is askin a little quiet-like.

Al Johnson doesn't turn back around. He just says quiet-like, too, "Well, ya know, ya can't win everything ya needs in a card game."

"Huh?"

"Uh, it's too hot in there tonight."

"Oh."

It ain't nowhere near midnight yet, but Mister Allen don't like stayin up late at all. He says he needs all the good rest he can get. He's in bed tryin to get some of that good rest. He can hear some of that music comin from down Gus Goins's. But that don't bother him none. He knows if it did, he never would get any sleep. But them dogs out in the backyards are barkin, been barkin. Mister Allen knows there ain't no cat out there. Cat don't stay around no barkin dogs that long.

．　　．　　．

Jeremiah Henderson parked that big car of Tommy Moses's over on Fiance Street. He didn't want any of them back alley folks to be seein him drivin up in that big car. He's comin from

Fiance Street now. He's tryin to come in between them front street houses, tryin to walk real quiet up them pathways between the houses so he can get to his back door. Willet's right behind him. She's buttoned up her blouse and fixed her hair some. She knows she got blood all over her skirt and blouse, even got some on her hands and breast. But she knows ain't nobody goin to see that blood on her in the dark unless they get real close. And she ain't goin to let them get close anyway. Jeremiah's tryin to walk real quiet up through them backyards. Willet ain't, and she don't care if them damn dogs are barkin or not. She's followin Jeremiah with her head high in the night.

Black Eye is Mister Strayhorne's dog. Black Eye don't like nobody comin near his yard when it's dark and he can't see who it is. He's barkin and jumpin up to the top of that fence he's behind. He can get up high enough to stick his head over. Pepper is Mister Maben's dog and he's right in the yard next to Black Eye. Pepper's barkin just as loud as Black Eye, but he's just a little black dog. He can't be jumpin up at the fence. He got to try and get his mouth through them cracks in it.

Jeremiah whispers, "Shis . . . Shis . . ." But them dogs ain't shuttin up for nothin.

Mister Allen is up and out of his bed. He's tryin to see out the window, but he can't see nothin in all that dark. Them dogs are still barkin and Mister Allen wants to know why they actin like that. He's takin the screen out that window, pushin it up a little higher and stickin his head out. He can't see nothin at first. Then he sees somebody comin down through them backyards. He keeps lookin real hard to see who's out there. When he can see it's Jeremiah Henderson and that woman, he keeps lookin. He's tryin to figure out why they're comin the back way from Fiance Street, instead of comin up the alley and goin in

51

their front door like everybody does. He's thinkin they know them dogs were goin to do all that barkin.

Jeremiah got his gate open, he's hurryin through his little yard and up his back steps. He slows, then stops. He doesn't feel and hear Willet behind him. He turns around, sees her slowin almost to a stop and starin up in the night. Mister Allen sees her lookin up at him like he ain't got no business lookin down at her. Mister Allen pulls his head back on in his window, puts the screen back in, and pulls the window back down. He's gettin back in bed but still wonderin what that Jeremiah Henderson and that woman was doin comin in through them yards and all that dark. Now he's sorry he even got up and looked out. He don't want that woman thinkin he's tryin to get in other folks' business. He don't want nobody sayin and thinkin that way about him.

It's quiet now. Mister Allen, Black Eye, and Pepper done went to sleep. Willet is lookin in the mirror. She's taken all her clothes off and took a quick bath. She's lookin in the mirror to make sure she got all of Tommy Moses's blood off her. She can see Jeremiah in the mirror, too. He's sittin on the bed behind her and has Tommy Moses's money all spread out in neat little piles across the sheet. But he ain't lookin at the money. She can see him starin at her. She looks toward him in the mirror and asks, "How much did he have on him?"

"He still had two fifty-five in twenties, tens, and a lot of fives. And about thirty more dollars just in ones. We can sell them rings and get more than what we have," Jeremiah's sayin and tryin to see Willet's eyes in the mirror. He can see her brown skin, darker in the low light of the room. He can see the nipples of her breasts, darker against the brown of her skin. She's combed her hair out, and he can see it hangin gently down over the top of her breasts. She has washed the lipstick off of her lips, and he can see how her lips are still moist and glistenin in the low light. But he can't see her eyes til she turns to him sayin, "Them rings are mine. If I don't want to sell them, they won't be sold."

Jeremiah sighs and says, "We gots to get out of here fore mornin. I know someone's goin to find him."

Willet's lookin away from Jeremiah and reachin for her robe. He sighs when she looks away. Quickly, he gets up and goes to the window, looks out into the dark. But the only things he's seein are what's comin in his mind. He can see a dead man's face. He can see it when it was still alive, when it was lookin at him under the bridge. He can see it dead lyin on the ground. He couldn't see it good, but he can see it in his mind the way he saw it. Mouth open like it was still tryin to get some air into it. Eyes wide open and starin, just starin. He can see it when he covered it up with that jacket.

Quickly Jeremiah turns from the window, looks at Willet, and says, "We got to get out of here. We got to hurry and get goin. We can't let anyone around here see us gettin in the car."

"Can't you see I have to get dressed?" Willet's sayin as she stands lookin into her closet.

Jeremiah hurries, gets his suitcases from under the bed. He's grabbin his clothes out of the closet, stickin everything he can in the suitcases that he doesn't want to leave behind. He knows he ain't never comin back, can't ever come back, didn't want to stay anyway.

Willet ain't hurryin at all. She's takin her time and foldin her clothes neatly. She still has her robe on, hangin open in the front. Jeremiah's sittin on the bed, lookin at the clock and knowin she has to hurry up. He wants to be way out of Pittsburgh when the sun comes up. It's only one-thirty or so. He thinks it should be later. It feels later.

"What time is it?" Willet's askin as she's reachin in her closet.

"It's about one-thirty."

"I'm almost ready. I ain't takin all this old stuff in here," Willet's sayin as she turns from the closet. Now she goes over to the dresser, gets and lights a cigarette. She leans back against the dresser, looks at Jeremiah sittin on the bed with his head lowered, smiles, and says, "You goin to buy me somethin nice?"

Jeremiah looks up, sees her smilin, tells her, "Yeal, I'm goin to get you somin. You know you can get what you want. But we got to get on the road."

Willet keeps smilin, lookin at Jeremiah as she slowly goes over and turns off the light. She's nearin him in the dark, reachin and puttin her one hand behind his neck and begins to slowly rub it as she straddles his leg and moves up against him. She can feel his breath on her stomach, his face nestlin against her breast, his hands goin around her waist. She's leanin over, puttin the cigarette in the ashtray, then puttin her other hand behind his neck.

Jeremiah has closed his eyes, the touch of Willet's hands rubbin gently over the back of his neck is soothin to him. The light scent of her perfume beneath the fresh smell of soap on her skin gets up in his mind, eases all his thoughts. Slowly, smoothly, Willet begins to sway her hips, makin her stomach slide back and forth across his face. Gently, she's pushin him back and he lies across the bed with her breast snugglin against his face. From far off in the night, some of that Gus Goins's jukebox music is comin through the open window. She is slidin herself down Jeremiah's chest so she can see his face, his eyes, and talk softly to him, whisperin, "You're goin to get somethin nice for me, aren't you?"

Jeremiah tries to whisper somethin back, but he can't. Willet's lips cover his. She darts her tongue into his mouth, then pulls her face away from his and tries to see his eyes in the dark.

A quick sigh comes from Jeremiah. He turns and looks away from Willet, whispers, "We got to get goin."

She's kissin him on his neck and slowly slidin her kisses up across his chin til she can find his mouth in the dark again.

•   •   •

Mister Allen doesn't know what time it is. But he knows it's too late or too damn early for them dogs to be barkin like that again. He's hopin they're goin to go on and shut up soon. He was sleepin, knows he was sleepin good when them dogs started that barkin again. Now he's hearin some train comin, blowin its whistle and soundin like rollin thunder in the night. That train's gone now and takin all that loud noise with it, but them dogs are still barkin.

Jeremiah's made about two trips to the car, got his and Willet's suitcases in the trunk of the car. He didn't want to put anything in that backseat til he gets that blood back there cleaned out. Willet's takin one last look at herself in the mirror before she starts puttin all her makeup and brushes in her purse. She can hear Jeremiah callin her from the bottom of the steps and tellin her to come on.

Willet's followin Jeremiah down them dark back porch steps. When she gets to the bottom of the steps, she looks up toward Mister Allen's window to see if he got his head stuck out of it again. Black Eye and that little dog Pepper are barkin at her as she's lookin up for Mister Allen. Jeremiah's out the gate and waitin on her to come on. He knows it is near three in the mornin. The sun will come soon after six.

Except for the far-off sound of jukebox music in the air and the sounds of night bugs up in them weeds by the railroad track, Fiance Street is quiet. It's dark, too. Most of them folks that live out on Fiance Street go on and turn them lights off, get to bed at a decent hour. They wish Gus Goins would turn that jukebox off at a decent hour, too.

Jeremiah's gettin ready to get in Tommy Moses's car. He's lookin up and down the street to see if anyone is nearin in the night. Willet's going around to the passenger door. She's not lookin around, she ain't lookin for nobody. She's not lookin because she doesn't want to see Fiance Street again and that alley behind it, too. And she don't care if somebody's seein her leavin.

Jeremiah starts up the car, lets the engine run for a moment, then puts the car in gear and slowly drives up the street. Willet has leaned back in her seat, looks down at the shiny radio knobs and thinks of Tommy Moses. She sees his big fat stomach up in her face. She can smell him again, hears his voice in her mind. It's there again and she can feel the knife in her hand again. She turns the shiny radio knob.

•　　•　　•

Bill Lovit's still down at Gus Goins's, been there all night and ain't thinkin about leavin. That loud jukebox music, dancin, and hollerin, ain't botherin him none at all. He's sittin on that chair way in the corner of that back room. He ain't got up or moved at all in hours. Folks know he ain't dead or nothin. They know he's just sleepin some of that day off. Pete Turner don't even know Bill Lovit's in that back room, don't even care if he is. Pete Turner's in that card game and got him some winnin goin on. Them cards been smilin up in his face all night. Pete Turner's lookin over at Carl Hughes and tellin him, "Ah sees that, ten bucks. Yeal, Ah sees that, ten. And Ah raise ya ten more." Now he's leanin back in his chair, waitin on Carl Hughes to make up his mind. Pete Turner's havin him some fun waitin, he's takin a sip of his drink, smackin his lips nice and loud, lookin down at all that money he done won.

Carl Hughes's still tryin to make up his mind about puttin some more of his money up. He keeps lookin at the cards in his hands and that money already down on the table. He's thinkin and thinkin hard about what he wants to do. Carl Hughes can think clear, he don't be doin no drinkin and keeps himself out of trouble, too. He got him a good respectable job up on Homewood Avenue. He's been workin up there in Wilson's Hardware Store, works behind the counter. He's the only Colored to have a counter job on Homewood Avenue. Sometimes folks say that Carl Hughes carries his ass too high. Pete Turner's lookin over at Carl Hughes, smilin and sayin, "Take your time. Ah be here. Ah ain't got no place to go. Yeal, Ah can stay here all night as long as this kind of money's comin. Yeal, ya just go on and take that time."

Gary Morgan's sittin at the table and playin them cards, too. He ain't winnin, but he ain't losin either. He's laughin at Pete Turner talkin shit. He knows Pete Turner don't know how to go home with money in his pocket. Carl Hughes ain't smilin or laughin. Them cards he's lookin at and tryin to change in his mind are lookin back at him and tellin him they ain't changin for nothin. They're tellin him he's done lost some more of his money. Folks don't know that out-front counter job he got don't pay him that kind of money he tells them it does.

Leroy Lawson is in that back room tryin to look up to folks when he's talkin to them. But he can't get his head up at all. He always got to keep it down since he got that broken back of his when he was a young workin man. He's old now, way past sixty. He's tryin to look up to Mack Jack, wants to show him that respect he got for him. He's tellin Mack Jack that he sure misses that playin of his. But Mack Jack ain't sayin nothin back down to him. Mack Jack ain't sayin nothin at all, ain't said too much to anybody all night. Elizabeth Green said that the only time Mack Jack talked was through that horn. She said sometimes she could swear she heard words in that music. She said it was like it was tellin you something, make you feel what you were hearing.

Some slow song is playin on the jukebox. It's that kind of music that floats through the room slowly. It's gently rubbin up against folks, feels smooth on their minds. Loud talkin is gettin quiet and sometimes it ain't talkin at all. Bobby Rose got Olinda Harris to dance with him. Ain't no space between them. The sweat from Bobby Rose's face is drippin down on her neck. Her eyes are closed and some bass guitar made them close. Its deep, slow, long sound told her to let her feelins sway in the dark.

Mack Jack's standin in the corner of the room where the dim light fails to go. His dark skin is darker than the dark he's standin in. Folks know Mack Jack doesn't like to be bothered much. Most folks seem to let him be, but they all know he's there. They can't see his face, ain't even lookin at it. But they know he's there, know he's in there that night. If they want to, they can close their eyes, see his face in the dark. A dark face, sometimes dark brown in the day, dark gray, almost black, in the night. Mack Jack don't smile, he just looks at you, never too long before he looks off to some place else. But you can still see his eyes lookin at you. Eyes he ain't supposed to have, ain't nobody that dark supposed to have. Dark blue eyes, shinin like some pretty blue marble some kid wants to keep.

Bobby Rose's whisperin in Olinda Harris's ear. He's tellin her how fine she is. He's pullin her closer to him, makin her breasts mushy against his chest. Her eyes are still closed, she doesn't want to open them. That long, slow song is comin to its end. Someone's puttin another nickel into the jukebox, quickly pushin down on them buttons they want. That jukebox arm that keeps on pickin out them records is movin slow, like it's tired and wants to just put that arm down and tell folks to go on home, leave it alone. But it can't, so it's givin them that next record they want. It's another one of them slow songs for the late night. The bass of the song seems to make the floor slowly rise and fall. Some slow drum beat is makin it do it, leavin them soft spaces between its beat. The drum seems to be callin, a sax hears its call, comes to it, stoops down and wiggles a nice low horn sound in between its beats, then it slowly rises and fills the night with a sizzlin, slow, long wigglin sound.

Mack Jack's starin out of that dark corner he's standin in. He's seein that music he's hearin, sees it dancin and curlin around like Olinda Harris's hips. But he ain't lookin at Olinda Harris's hips, he's just lookin at the music, seein it and givin it a look back. It's a dark look; his blue eyes peer into it.

Bobby Rose is whisperin in Olinda Harris's ear, askin, "Why don't ya let me walk ya on home? Baby, come on now, let me walk ya on home? Ah just want to talk to ya. Let me walk ya on home?"

Olinda Harris ain't sayin nothin, ain't openin up her eyes either. Bobby Rose is kissin and givin her neck soft little licks. But she's keepin her eyes closed and ain't sayin nothin.

The only sound left in the night is that jukebox music comin from Gus Goins's place. But it floats through the air only so far and then softens into silence. Mack Jack is beyond the sound of the music, he's goin through the alley that goes over to Tioga Street. He's walkin slowly beside the back wall of that shoutin church that sets on the corner of Tioga and the alley. But he ain't lookin at the wall of the church, doesn't look at them big side windows of the church. He doesn't see the picture of the face in the dark stained-glass window. In the daytime, it's that face some folks stop and look at, some mamas stop and show their children. Some folks don't stop, might start walkin a little faster, don't want them eyes in that face seein them doin what they're doin. That face can seem to come out that glass, say, I'm Jesus the Son of God. I'm your savior. Come to me.

Ain't nothin in Mack Jack's room cept a bed and a little table with a lamp on it. Even when that lamp is lit, it's still dark in that room. Ain't no kind of light goin to brighten up them dark dingy blue walls in there. The light ain't on. Mack Jack's sittin on his bed lookin out that one window he got. Way far off in the night, the sky is beginnin to brighten. Mack Jack lowers his eyes from the light and stares at the dark floor.

. . .

That light that comes before the sun is beginnin to lighten up the highway. Jeremiah's eyes are tired, they keep blinkin, tryin to see things they're tired of lookin at. Willet has slept some, but she's awake now and lookin out the side window of the car. The air comin from the slightly opened vent window keeps blowin her hair into her eyes. She's lettin the air and her hair do what they want. She has seen signs along the highway and tried to read them when the car lights lit them up. But sometimes the signs meant nothin, just some small town somewhere up ahead. Sometimes she'd see bright lights, look and see some brightly colored sign for some roadside diner. She's still lookin out the window but askin Jeremiah, "Where we at now?"

Jeremiah's sighin, sayin, "We almost to Breezewood. We goin to be out the state soon."

Willet turns from the window, looks down at the shiny knobs on the dashboard, thinks of the radio. She stares at the knob for a moment til Tommy Moses's fat stomach comes into her mind. She can smell it again, then she can see his face when he was still alive. She looks up and out the windshield, sees the far bright light in the sky. Tommy Moses's face is dead again, he's lyin on the ground. Jeremiah is sayin something to her. She keeps lookin out the window, but whispers, "Huh?"

Jeremiah speaks a little louder, says, "Soon as we get out of the state, we can stop, get something to eat. I'm tired, I got to get a little sleep."

Willet keeps lookin out the window.

· FOUR ·

Mister Allen was up early for his quiet time, had his cup of coffee, and was goin out to sit on his porch. That early light was out in the alley waitin for him. The only thing makin noise was them birds, but Mister Allen never did mind birds singin. Thought it was pretty nice of them. He's sittin on the porch now, sippin on his coffee and lookin up the alley. Ain't nothin for him to see he ain't seen before, but he's lookin anyway. He knows he's old and gettin older. And one day comin soon, there ain't goin to be no mornin to look at. Mister Allen don't like to think about dyin. Sometimes he tells folks he's ready to go when the good Lord calls. Then when folks go away, he sorta puts his head down, thinks about that death nearin, and jerks his head back up.

It ain't never too long after the birds get to singin and flyin around before Dicky Bird gets that big pushcart of his out and gettin that early mornin pickins. He's got him a weekly schedule he likes to follow. He seems to know when folks are gettin ready to throw something good out before they know it themselves. He's pushin that cart up the alley, goin on up to Wilkensburg. He knows them white folks up there be throwin away some good stuff today. He's hurryin that pushcart up the alley, them big old wagon wheels he got on it makin all kind of noise goin over them alley bricks. Somebody seein that wagon comin might not be able to see anybody behind it doin the pushin. But Dicky Bird always knows what's up in front of him. He can always find some cracks in that old rotten wagon wood to peek through. He's hopin he don't see Mister Allen out on that porch already and have to stop to do some talkin. Sometimes he doesn't want to stop and talk to that old man. Dicky Bird's squinchin his face up behind that wagon and lettin his big sigh fall down in all that wagon noise when he sees Mister Allen sittin up on his porch.

Mister Allen got his mind and eyes someplace else. And his mind ain't payin no mind to what his eyes are seein. But that noise Dicky Bird's wagon is makin gets to rattlin right into Mister Allen's mind and his eyes get to tellin him, here comes Dicky Bird. All that early mornin quiet and that peace that was in Mister Allen's mind ain't there no more. He's wonderin if Dicky Bird done seen him yet, if he got time to get up and go into the house fore Dicky Bird sees him. He's gruntin a little bit when he knows he can't go in the house. That wouldn't be right.

Dicky Bird's peekin through them cracks in the wood, he can see Mister Allen watchin him comin. He can see Mister Allen gettin to smilin and givin him a little wave.

Them wagon-wheel sounds are still floatin around in that quiet mornin air even after Dicky Bird done stopped pushin it. He's wipin that little bit of forehead sweat off his head and lookin up at Mister Allen, sayin, "Good mornin, Mister Allen. How are ya doin this mornin?"

Mister Allen's smilin, lookin down at Dicky Bird and sayin, "Good mornin, looks like it's goin to be a nice day."

Dicky Bird's smilin back up at Mister Allen and sayin, "Yes, sir. It sure do look like a nice day comin. But that was some rain come down here yesterday. The Lord's tryin ta tell ya somethin when he makes it rain like that."

"He's tryin to tell somebody somethin," Mister Allen's sayin and takin a quick look up to the sky.

"Yes, sir," Dicky Bird's sayin and takin a look up at the sky, too. That sun ain't all the way up yet, but its early yellow glow is brightenin up the sky.

Mister Allen's sayin somethin again about how nice the day is goin to be. Dicky Bird ain't heard all the words Mister Allen said, but he's lookin up at him and sayin, "Yes, sir . . . Yes, sir, gots ta be a good day ta-day, gots that pretty sky up there already."

That noise from Dicky Bird's wagon wheels ain't left Mister Allen's ears yet and he can't wait til Dicky Bird gets that wagon on up the alley. He's sittin there and lookin back up into that sky again. That silence he was waitin for came back til some faraway dog got to barkin and some other faraway dog got to barkin back. Them dogs ain't barkin now and Mister Allen ain't thinkin about them anymore. He's still lookin out at the sky, but wonderin what that Jeremiah Henderson and that woman of his was doin out in the back last night.

Some of that early sunlight is tryin to light up them weeds Tommy Moses is lyin in. But most of it is only gettin caught in all them dewdrops hangin off the leaves of them weeds. It's makin them dewdrops glisten, seem nice and bright in all the gray mornin air. Slow-crawlin mornin bugs are takin their time crawlin over and gnawin at Tommy Moses's cold skin. But them quick-crawlin bugs are hurryin in them holes that knife made in Tommy Moses's fat stomach.

. . .

Jeremiah is tired, tryin to keep his eyes open and on that early mornin gray-covered road. Sometimes that road just becomes a lot of blurry gray mist up in his mind, gets his mind to want to seep into it, stay there. But when it does, Jeremiah shakes his head real quick, tries to make all that gray up in his head become that road again.

Willet's tryin to sleep, curled up on that big front car seat. But she keeps wigglin around, tryin to get more comfortable. Sometimes she opens her eyes, brushes her hair away from them, looks up and out the window. She sees the emptiness of the early mornin gray road, closes her eyes, then tries to get comfortable again. The rhythm of the car, its easy rockin motions, is soothin to her mind, lets it gently seep into different feelins. Sometimes the feelins become colors, different colors. Dark pretty reds, purples, deep blues, and sometimes golden yellows color her mind. She did not like the gray of the mornin road.

Milton Speer was tired, too, wanted to go on home, get in that bed of his and get some sleep. But he knew that old clock up on the wall ain't moved much since the last time he looked up at it. And it would still tell him he had that same damn hour to go before he could finish his all-night shift. He could sit, knew how to sit through that slow-passin time. He could sit and just stare out that dirty, dusty window, see past them fast-passin cars out on the highway. He didn't have to look to know when one of them cars was about to pull off the highway and into the fillin station for some gas, he'd know without lookin. He could hear its gears doin that down-shiftin, its engine groanin into that lower speed, its wheels brakin and kickin up that loose gravel out in front of the station. He's turnin in his seat, knowin he has to get on up, knowin he has to put that good-mornin smile on his face and pump that gas.

That early mornin sunlight is pawin at Milton Speer's eyes some as he steps out into it, sees that big, shiny new car rollin up to the gas pumps. He gets to hurryin his step a little and puttin a quick grin on his face.

Jeremiah's easin the car up to the gas pump, lettin it slow to a stop, set, and quiver before he turns its ignition key off. Slowly, the hummin sound of the engine stills and a quick silence comes and settles in the car. He wants to seep into it, take deep long breaths. But he can't, he's got to keep his eyes on that old skinny-lookin white man comin and smilin at the car.

Willet feels the silence in the car. It's touchin her, gently rubbin her mind. She shudders, opens her eyes, and brushes the strands of hair coverin them away. The early mornin sun is brighter and tryin to lighten up the lingerin dark shadows the passin night has left in the car. Quickly, Willet turns from the light comin through the window and looks over to Jeremiah. "Where we at, why are we stopping?" she's askin.

"Get some gas," Jeremiah mumbles as he keeps his eyes on the smilin man comin to the car.

Milton Speer's grinnin, takin some quick looks at all the shiny chrome on that big new car. He's seein it still shiny through all that road dirt stuck on it.

Jeremiah got his window all the way down and his eyes still on that quick-comin, smilin white man.

"Good . . . Good mornin," Milton Speer says with a little

stutter. He's tryin to keep that smile on his face when he sees some nigger sittin up in that big, shiny new car.

Jeremiah nods his head toward the smile, says, "I need some gas. Can you fill it up?"

"Sure can," Milton Speer's sayin and takin quick looks past Jeremiah and into the shadows in the car. He can see long dark hair, see it curve down over the side of a beautiful face. For a quick moment, too quick, he can see a pair of eyes glowin like a dark sun. He can see them starin at him before they turn away. Milton Speer's turnin his eyes, too, lookin away quickly. But he's still seein that blur of sight in his mind, still feelin what he felt when he saw that skirt up high, showin them dark legs all curled up.

Milton Speer's grin is gone, he's got his head down as he's pumpin that gas. Jeremiah's head is lowered, too. He's takin them deep long breaths and tryin not to think of anything.

Willet's gettin herself up in her seat. She's gettin all the hair out of her eyes and lookin out the windows. That sunlight that is gettin in her eyes is makin her turn away from the light and seein stuff she don't give a damn about. "Where we at?" she's askin.

"Breezewood," Jeremiah says in between them deep breaths he's takin.

"Breezewood? Where's Breezewood at? How far have we come?" Willet's askin.

"I don't know, we ain't out the state yet."

Willet sighs and takes a quick look out the side window of the car. She stares at the dirty storefront-lookin gas station, sees signs in the window she ain't readin. Some Coca-Cola sign the early sunlight ain't got to yet is dull red. She turns away from all she doesn't want to see, lowers her eyes into the shade left in the car, and says, "I have to go to the bathroom. Tell that man I have to use the bathroom."

Milton Speer put all the gas in the car it was going to take. He knows he ain't cleanin this nigger's windows. But he's puttin that grin back on his face and tellin Jeremiah, "That will be four dollars and thirty cents."

Jeremiah is squeezin his hand down into his pocket, tryin to get his fingers around that big wad of Tommy Moses's money. Milton Speer's waitin for his money and tryin not to look past Jeremiah, take them quick looks he's takin at that dark, beautiful face he can't see all of and them legs that skirt ain't coverin.

Jeremiah has that big wad of money out of his pocket, but he's holdin it down low, tryin to peel off just enough of them dollars that man's askin for and not show him all the money he's got.

"Tell him," Willet whispers.

Jeremiah gets a five-dollar bill peeled off the wad of money, quickly hands it up to Milton Speer, then says, "The lady has to use the bathroom."

Cept for the highway sounds of passin cars, it's quiet. Jeremiah's lookin up at Milton Speer and waitin on him to say something about a bathroom, but ain't no words comin out that grinnin mouth.

"Do you have a bathroom here?" Jeremiah's askin.

"Well . . . Well, yeah . . . But . . ." Milton Speer's sayin and stutterin while he's reachin down in his pocket for some change.

"I have to use the bathroom," Willet's sayin as she leans

over in her seat and looks past Jeremiah. She can see Milton Speer, see that grin on his face get smaller, go away.

"Miss . . . Miss . . ." Milton Speer's sayin and bendin down so he can look into the car. "Miss, I ain't supposed to let you all . . . I just work here. Mister Weaver, he owns this here station . . . He's a little particular about who uses his restroom facilities," Milton Speer's sayin, gettin a good look at all that face he's been wantin to see.

Willet's silent, starin at that face lookin at her.

Jeremiah's lookin up at Milton Speer.

"I'm real sorry, miss," Milton Speer's sayin.

Jeremiah's waitin til Milton Speer looks back at him, then catches his eyes lookin at him.

"I'm . . . I'm sorry," Milton Speer's tellin Jeremiah.

Jeremiah's silent, but keeps starin up in Milton Speer's face.

The highway sounds of them passin cars can't fill up the silence.

Softly and very slowly, Jeremiah's sayin, "The lady here has to use the bathroom. You understand that, don't you?"

"Yeah, but . . ."

Quickly, Willet shifts in her seat, leans and pushes up against her car door. It flings open.

Milton Speer's up on his toes, lookin over the top of the car, seein Willet's glarin eyes. "Where's the bathroom?" She's shoutin over the car.

Jeremiah's reachin down under his seat feelin for the handle of Tommy Moses's gun. He feels it, gets it in his hand.

"Miss . . . Miss . . ." Milton Speer's callin out over the car to Willet.

Jeremiah's got the gun hidden next to his leg.

Willet's glarin at Milton Speer.

"Miss . . . I'm sorry . . . you can't use it here."

Willet won't stop glarin.

Milton Speer sighs, shakes his head a little, and says, "Go on . . . you can use it. Just be a little quick if you can and tidy up when you done in there."

Jeremiah eases up his grip on the gun. But he keeps his eyes on Milton Speer, watches the man walk away from the car and go sit down on a little bench in front of his gas station window. Willet's pushin the bathroom door open and flickin the light switch on. She closes the door and hurries past her blurry reflection in a mirror. The toilet seat is still chilled from the coolness of the passin night. The echoin sound of urine splashin into the toilet bowl fills up the silence in the small, damp-smellin bathroom. Some fly woken by the light wants to get warm and is buzzin around the hot bulb. That buzzin sound is scratchin at Willet's mind, won't let her thoughts still. She's lookin up from the toilet seat, watchin the quick dark blur of the fly buzz around the light. That fly is on the mirror now, crawlin around. Sometimes it crawls real slow, stops, then quickly starts crawlin again. Willet's lookin in the mirror now, she's washed her hands, tried to rinse her face. She's leanin closer to the mirror, puttin on her lipstick. The fly scoots across her face in the mirror, Tommy Moses's fat stomach is in her face. She stops puttin on her lipstick, stares at the fly. It's slowly crawlin across the mirror. Quickly she flings her hand at it. It flies away, buzzes up around the light bulb. She looks back in the mirror, stares at herself. Her half-red lips do not brighten the thoughts in her mind, only a small spot on the mirror. Deep in her mind where feelins can't even make words yet, they just buzz like that damn fly back on the mirror again. A quick flick of the hand and the fly is gone again. Smoothly but hurriedly Willet's glidin the tip of the lipstick over her lips again. A sting of silence frightens her a moment, makes her hand stop, stand still while she stares into the mirror. Dark eyes look into themselves, then quickly turn away.

Milton Speer's sittin and leanin back against the window ledge. He's been lookin out over the highway, sometimes just starin at them far hills the sun's brightenin up. He doesn't want to look over at that big new car, see that nigger sittin behind the wheel, and think of that nigger's woman usin the restroom. But her usin the restroom ain't that big thought he doesn't want to think about. He's still starin at them hills, but he ain't seein them. He's seein them dark eyes, feelin that heat he felt when he saw them legs curled up the way they were. He's feelin that space between him and that nigger's woman that he can't reach through, can't even think through. He's hearin that restroom door openin, the quick sound of fast-walkin, light footsteps comin. He's turnin, lookin over his shoulder and seein Willet hurryin past him. He's watchin her legs make that skirt she's wearin look alive, look like it's dancin all by itself. He's hearin himself sayin, "You have a good day now, miss."

Willet looks over her shoulder, glares back at Milton Speer, lets her glare linger as she says, "Kiss my ass."

"You better watch your mouth, hear? I was nice enough to let you use the restroom. I think you should show me some courtesy here," Milton Speer's sayin and sittin up on his bench.

"Go to hell," Willet's sayin as she hurries and gets in the car.

"You goddamn nigger bitch you," Milton Speer shouts, gettin to his feet.

Jeremiah's startin the car. "Let's get out of here."

But Willet's not listenin, she's rollin down her window. "Don't you call me a nigger . . . I'll kill you."

Jeremiah's putting the car in gear quickly, pushin down on the gas pedal. The car jerks forward, its wheels squeak. The mornin air is rushin through the car, blowin Willet's hair into her face and eyes. Slowly, she's rollin the window back up and takin deep breaths and starin into the space in front of her. Now softly she is sayin, "I want to go see him."

"What?" Jeremiah's askin.

"I said, I want to go see him," Willet's sayin and starin down into the car where the sunlight cannot reach.

Jeremiah's silent, he can hear all the sounds of the road. The air makin that gushin sound outside the window, the car's engine is makin them groanin sounds, but Jeremiah's silent. Willet lights a cigarette, slowly blows the smoke from her mouth, leans back in her seat, and stares out at the road.

That sunlight gettin into Jeremiah's face is keepin his eyes open. But that sleep wantin to get into his head keeps clawin at his eyes, makin them blood-red. He's reachin up and rubbin at his eyes and tryin not to think about that thought that's stuck in his mind. He knows he got that money he's been wantin, can get to where he's been wantin to go. He knows he got to keep goin, too, get away from that dead man still in the dark of his mind. He's takin deep, slow breaths now and grindin his teeth some. He knows he has to say somethin, can feel them words burnin in his throat. Softly he's askin, "What you want to go back down there for?"

Willet is silent, just keeps starin out at the road.

"It ain't the right time to be goin down there," Jeremiah's sayin.

Willet does not take her eyes from the road. She lets her silence speak for her. It stills the moment.

The long road miles come slow, then quickly fall behind. Willet's cigarette has burned out, but she's still starin silently out at the road. Some of them brightly colored road signs and billboards wasn't nothin but colorless blurs streakin through her mind. Jeremiah ain't thought about them signs either. He knows he can't say nothin, but he's got to say somethin again. He's quickly takin his eyes off the road and lookin at Willet. She doesn't look back, but he's sayin, "We can't go down there now. It ain't the right time. It will take us a whole day just to get down there."

"I said I want to see him." Willet keeps starin out at the road.

"I'm tellin you it's not the right time."

Willet turns her head, stares at Jeremiah. She keeps starin til he looks away, back at the road. Now she's sayin, "I told you I want to see him. I don't care how long it takes to get there."

. . .

Mack Jack's not up yet, but he's not asleep. He's just lyin on his bed and starin up at the ceiling. Some of that mornin got through his window, tryin to brighten up that dark room of his. It can't, falls weakly to the floor. The ceiling is still dark, always is. But Mack Jack ain't lookin at the ceiling, just the dark. Sometimes that dark can become somethin it ain't, it can become a face. A young firelit woman's face glowin in the night. She can have eyes that can stare down at him. He can look back at them, see them lookin like a black cat's eyes painted with firelight. He can see her face, high cheekbones of a goddess, a nose that profiles beauty. He can stare at her lips, see them become red, wait for them to smile, keep waitin. He can see her long, dark, shiny hair, see it swiftly blow across her face. He can see her turn, her movements sway into a dance. He can watch her hips slowly play in the dark. She can turn back to him, slowly run her hands through her hair, then quickly come to him. She can look down at him, dance over his face, let him think he can smell the scent of her lust. He can want to make his music, make her stay and dance. But she ain't there, maybe never was. But that outside day is, another day, sunlight and everything he don't want. Them day sounds are comin through the window. Some loud-talkin woman's tellin all her business. Some faraway kids are yellin about nothin. The ceiling is just the ceiling now, empty and endless nothin. It's tellin him he's nothin, go on and stay in the bed, be dead, get away from all this nothin shit.

Slowly, Mack Jack's sittin up in the bed, but he's keepin his head down and away from that light comin through the window. That sun ain't got to him yet but his face is drippin sweat down onto his chest. He's wipin his face off with his hands, keepin his eyes closed so he don't have to look at nothin. He's tryin to keep his mind closed, too, so he don't have to think about nothin. But all that outside day noise is breakin in anyway, makin him yell at it. Can't nobody hear him, but he's screamin at all that outside nothin, he's tellin it to leave him alone.

Some alley folks knew what day was comin and what it was time to do. Maybe it might be time to get that rent money together for that landlord on the way. It might be time to get ready to go up Homewood Avenue, get that food while it was still fresh. Darnell and Calvin Clark wasn't thinkin about what day or time it might be. Neither was Pucky White. They knew their mamas wouldn't be callin after them for a good while. They done already had their breakfast and it wasn't even near lunchtime yet. Darnell and his brother, Calvin, looked so much alike, with that coal-colored dark skin they had and that short black lambs' wool—like hair, some folks quit tryin to tell them apart. Darnell was the oldest. He was twelve. Calvin said he was twelve, too, but he was eleven. Everybody knew Pucky, knew he was one of them Whites, could tell him comin from a mile away. All them Whites had that high yellow skin and that nappy, thick red hair. Pucky had that red hair and that bright yellow skin, too. But Pucky was fat. Wasn't twelve years old yet and already had him a double chin and a belly hangin down over his belt. He had them short fat legs with them big thick thighs that rubbed together every step he took.

Darnell, Calvin, and Pucky had their own way of goin somewhere, even if they didn't know where they were goin. They'd start one way and end up someplace else. But they always had their secret pathways of gettin someplace. They could go down the alley some, sneak through some backyard that nobody wanted them in. Climb some fence and crawl through the hole in another one til they knew their mamas couldn't see them no more. Sometimes they could sneak around them Homewood Avenue back alleys, get in that junk and see what they could find. Sometimes they'd sneak up by the tracks, stay in them high weeds. Sometimes it can be nice and shady up in there, but they can stay there too long, can sit that still. Their mamas done told them a thousand times, don't ya all be on them railroad tracks, but they're on them now.

Darnell and Calvin are up on their tiptoes, tryin to balance themselves on that rail. Pucky's tryin to balance himself, too, but he keeps lookin back over his shoulder, lookin for one of them comin trains and stumblin off the rail. Calvin's keepin his balance, lookin back at Pucky and yellin, "Come on Pucky . . . Ain't no train comin."

"Um comin," Pucky's yellin back at Calvin and tryin to get back his balance on the rail. But in his mind he can see one of them new, big, fast diesel trains comin. Sometimes he thinks he hears one comin and stumbles off the rail again.

"Ya scaredy cat, Pucky. Ain't no train comin," Calvin's yellin again.

"Ah ain't scared of nothin. Shut up. Um comin," Pucky yells.

Darnell's way up ahead on that rail, got his arms held out like he's some trapeze artist in some circus. It ain't long before he can look down the tracks and see that bridge that goes over them. He's yellin back over his shoulder, "Come on . . . Let's go down by the bridge."

Pucky looks up from that rail he's tryin to walk on, sees the bridge way down the tracks, and yells back up to Darnell. "We can'ts be goin way down there."

"That ain't far, Pucky. Go on home if ya don't want to go . . . It ain't far," Darnell's yellin back over his shoulder.

It doesn't take a lot of sun to get Pucky hot, make that sweat start rollin down his face, get him to thinkin about some water. He ain't tryin to walk on that rail no more. He's walkin along the side of the tracks, but sometimes he still looks back to see if one of them fast trains is comin. Even when he doesn't see one comin, he can still see it in his mind. He can remember his mama tellin him about stayin away from them tracks.

He can remember her sayin, her voice tellin how that little white boy was run over by a train and it cut him in half.

Darnell's close enough to the bridge to see, feel the silence of the dark shade beneath it. It seems to be waitin on him, darin him to come runnin through it. He's stoppin, turnin around, and yellin, "Come on, ya all."

Pucky's caught up with Darnell and his brother. Now he's tryin to run as fast as they are. Darnell's yellin as he runs beneath the bridge, tryin to hear his echo. Pucky's slowin down, sees all that broken bottle glass lyin on the ground. Calvin's tryin to catch up with his brother, beat him to the other side of the bridge. Darnell's callin out, "Last one over the fence eats doggy doo."

Calvin sees his brother jump up on the high black fence and try to scoot over the top of it. He hurries.

Pucky's yellin out, "That ain't fair . . . Ain't fair . . . Ya all starts first."

"Is, too . . . Is, too . . ." Darnell's yellin back over his shoulder.

Pucky's tryin to get his fat self over the fence. But he ain't hurryin, knows he's last. He's gruntin and still tryin to get his leg over the fence. He's gettin tired of hearin, *"Pucky eats doggy doo . . . Pucky eats doggy doo . . ."*

"Ain't fair . . . Ain't fair," Pucky's yellin back between them grunts.

"Come on, Pucky . . . Hurry up . . . Let's go up on the bridge, thens we can go over to the park . . . Last one over the bridge looks like a big monkey's butt hole," Darnell yells, and starts runnin through the weeds.

Calvin starts runnin, too, tryin to keep up with his brother. But Pucky ain't hurryin no more. He ain't thinkin about runnin through them weeds. That sweat rollin down his forehead is gettin in his eyes, makin them burn. He can hear Darnell and Calvin yellin back at him to come on. But he done made up his mind, he ain't runnin no more. He's takin his time gettin through them high weeds, makin sure he stays away from them sticky kind of bushes. He stops, but his heart don't, it's poundin faster. But he can't move, run like he wants to, go be with his mama. Tell her the bogey man got him. That sweat rollin down his forehead ain't hot no more: it's cold. It's makin him shiver, freeze. He can't move his eyes, keeps starin down at that big fat man he sees lyin in the weeds. He can see all that sticky blood lyin around him. He can't see the fat man's face, it got something over it. But that blood ain't covered and it's got bugs crawlin in it, too. "DARNELL . . . DARNELL . . . CALVIN . . ." Pucky can hear himself callin out, feel himself movin, see them green blurs of weeds passin him.

Darnell and Calvin ain't never heard Pucky yell so loud. They've stopped runnin and start starin at Pucky runnin up through the weeds. Pucky ain't stoppin, ain't slowin down for nothin. Them high weeds and bushes that won't bend, get out of his way, he's runnin over, makin them make them quick crackin sounds.

"Ya see a snake? . . . Ya see one?" Calvin's yellin out.

"SOME MAN'S IN THE WEEDS . . . SOME MAN'S THERE. HE'S GOT BLOOD COMIN OUTS HIM."

· FIVE ·

Sometimes Gus Goins didn't like to be bothered with folks at all. He'd get one of them porch-sittin chairs of his and take it around the side of his place, sit it in that cool shade, and hope nobody would see him back there. He's been sittin back there most of the last passin hour, just sippin on some grape Kool-Aid. He could tell when somebody was comin up that yard path of his, could hear them chickens flappin their wings and fussin. He could tell when somebody was comin, just wantin somethin. And he could tell when somebody was comin and needin some-thin, just by the way they'd get to callin his name. He already would know who it was as soon as they'd open their mouth. He's gettin up now, comin out of his shade. Al Johnson's callin his name. Gus Goins knows by the way Al Johnson's callin his name that Al don't need or want nothin from him. But he got somethin for him and whatever it is, it's enough for him to get up for.

Al Johnson's face got sweat just a-drippin off it. He sees Gus Goins comin from around the side of the house and hurries on over to him. Before Gus Goins can get a word out of his mouth, Al Johnson's sayin, "They done found Tommy Moses dead. Found him up there by the tracks, up near that bridge that goes over to the park. They sayin somebody done stabbed him."

Gus Goins gets to shakin his head some, twistin his face up.

Al Johnson's sayin, "They sayin he was dead when they found him. That little White kid found him. You know, that little Pucky. He was up in them weeds and found him. The police be up there now. They say whoever did it done tried to cut his guts out."

Gus Goins is still shakin his head, but sayin, "Shit, I guess that fast shit he was into turned around and came back at him."

Al Johnson's wipin some of that sweat off his face and sayin, "Yeal, somebody wanted that nigger dead. Ain't no lyin about that."

Alley mamas were up from their porch-sittin chairs and leanin over them porch rails whisperin back and forth about that bad talk that was goin around. When they ain't whisperin back and forth, they're callin at them children, makin sure they stayin in sight. Pucky's mama got him in the house, holdin him and wishing he'd stop shakin. She's still pattin him on his back, tellin him, "It's all right, baby, it's goin to be all right."

Mister Allen's been sittin in that big livin room chair of his, didn't even know he was asleep until he woke up. He's sittin there now, wonderin what time it is. He knows he has to go up to Homewood Avenue today, should have gone up already, before that sun got too hot to be walkin in. He's yawnin, lookin at his watch, and tightenin up his face when he sees it's near twelve.

Ellen Maben's out on her porch, she's whisperin about that bad talk to Norma Gaines. Mister Allen's comin out his house and gettin ready to go down his steps. He's made up his mind, figures he'll go on and get done what he has to do. He's already seen Ellen Maben leanin over her porch rail and runnin her mouth with that Norma Gaines. He's figured he can just give them a little nod when he walks by, go on doin his business, and keep them out of it. He's thinkin he's got past them when he hears that Norma Gaines whisperin, "Mister Allen . . . Mister Allen."

That sun already got Mister Allen hot, he's got his straw hat on to cover his head from it, but that hat ain't helpin his neck at all. He's stoppin, turnin around to that Norma Gaines, and that sun that was burnin his neck is smackin him in the face. He's tryin to get a good smile on his face as he says, "Yes, Miss Gaines."

Norma Gaines is a big, fast-talkin woman. She always keeps her hair pulled back and kept in a ball, makin her eyes look bigger than they are. She can't keep her eyes out of her talkin, got to be battin them, rollin them, and everything else. Mister Allen don't like that kind of talkin.

"Mister Allen . . . Mister Allen." Norma Gaines keeps whisperin until Mister Allen knows he has to take a few steps closer before this woman's goin to say what she got to say. He's tryin to keep that smile on his face, give that woman whatever respect he has for her.

"Did ya hear abouts what happened to Tommy Moses?" Norma Gaines is quickly askin Mister Allen. But she ain't givin him no time to answer before she's tellin him. "He's been killed, somebody killed him with a butcher's knife and left him dead rights up there by that bridge. That one that takes ya over to the park. Pucky and them was the ones that finds him up there. Sees him all cut up and everything . . ."

Tommy Moses didn't know Mister Allen. But Mister Allen knew about that Tommy Moses, knew he didn't carry himself too well, wasn't respectable at all. Norma Gaines is still talkin, got her eyes tellin some of the story, too. Mister Allen's heard enough of what he didn't want to be listenin to in the first place. He knows he got to say somethin before he can get away from this woman. He's shakin his head and sayin, "That's a poor shame, somebody do somethin like that, have them children comin up on it. I don't know where's this here world headed to."

Alley children that were playin, hittin balls, jumpin rope, and just chasin each other around knew to let old folks pass. Mister Allen hurried his step a little as he passed through the children, gave a smile to them kids he seen lookin at him. He's past them children now and tryin to get past them thoughts he has in his mind of that Tommy Moses. Mister Allen's lowerin his head, lookin down at them red alley bricks. He's mumblin, and before he knows it he's sayin, "Damn fools."

· · ·

Colored folks and white folks the same didn't mind gettin out of the way for Lenny Boughner. Even those folks that didn't know who he was. Folks that knew him knew he was a cop, maybe a captain or somethin bigger. They knew he didn't say much, but when he did, you could hear him a mile away. Folks had to look up at him, him bein way over six feet. Gus Goins knew him well, seen him bust many a nigger's head wide open.

Lenny Boughner's makin a few gruntin sounds, and that crowd standin around Tommy Moses's body is gettin out of his way.

Everybody in Homewood knew Jason Dyer, called him Blinky because he had that bad habit of always blinkin his eyes, couldn't stop it if he wanted to. He's been Homewood Avenue's beat cop for years. Blinky's hot and thirsty, been standin out in that sun for more than an hour watchin over dead Tommy Moses. He's had to yell a few times at that crowd gatherin around to get a peek at somethin dead. Some of them folks in the crowd wanted to get too close, get in them weeds to see if they could see whose face was dead.

Blinky's lookin up at Lenny Boughner and watchin him come through the crowd. Folks in the crowd are lookin up at Lenny Boughner, wonderin what he's goin to do. Those folks that were talkin got real quiet. Blinky hurries and lights a cigarette, quickly blows the smoke out of his mouth, then watches Lenny Boughner go into them weeds where Tommy Moses is lyin.

Some of them flies crawlin in that blood in the weeds are quickly flying up in the air when they hear Lenny Boughner comin near them. Some ain't paying Lenny Boughner no mind, keep eatin. Tommy Moses's face ain't as yellow as it used to be. That bright yellow of it is pale, dull gray-lookin. Them chicken-lookin eyes of his are still open, but ain't seein nothin. His mouth is stuck open, too; a little bit of his blood is still seepin out of it.

Lenny Boughner's stoopin down in them weeds, lookin at fat Tommy Moses. He's got to keep battin at them flies that are gettin off Tommy Moses and gettin on him. He's lookin at them knife holes, seein if he can see how many there are. He's seein

Tommy Moses's shirt all open, his pants unzipped. He's pushin, rollin Tommy Moses over and reachin down in his pants pockets. The crowd's watchin, tryin to see what they can see. Blinky's lightin up another cigarette while the one he lit before is still smolderin on the ground where he just threw it.

Lenny Boughner's got his handkerchief out and is tryin to wipe his hands off as he comes out of the weeds. He's lookin over at Blinky and sayin, "Where's the goddamn coroner? That fat son of a bitch is gonna be stinkin up the place soon."

Blinky's glancin down at his watch and sayin, "They ought to be here by now." Now he's lookin up at Lenny Boughner and askin, "Well, what do you think?"

"Somebody did us a favor. The fuckin question is who," Lenny Boughner's sayin, then starts lookin down at the ground at that dried blood trail leadin his eyes back over to the weeds. He's lookin back up at Blinky, sayin, "Yeah, looks like they stabbed his ass up here, then dragged him down in them weeds. Whoever did it took every dime that nigger had."

Blinky's sayin, "That fuckin car of his ain't nowhere around either."

"That won't be hard to find around here," Lenny Boughner's sayin, then starts lookin over at the crowd. For a slow moment he stares at them, then shouts, "GET THE HELL OUT OF HERE. GO AHEAD, GET THE HELL OUT OF HERE RIGHT NOW, ALL OF YOU."

• • •

There was still some shade that high noon sun hadn't brightened up yet. But that news about findin Tommy Moses dead was gettin everywhere. Folks that never heard of a Tommy

Moses was findin out that somebody got murdered up by the bridge, and they found the body down in the weeds. Mister Allen was up on Homewood Avenue now, tryin to get his shoppin done. But everybody he seen wanted to stop him and talk about Tommy Moses.

Dicky Bird was in Bruston, pushin his cart behind them big homes they got up there. He was havin him a good day, found him a real pretty lamp somebody threw away, got him an old sewin machine he knew he could get a couple dollars for. Dicky Bird was havin a good day until he ran into Orval Nixon and Orval got to tellin him about Tommy Moses. Dicky Bird didn't want to stand and talk too long, didn't want that good luck he was havin to die, too. He said him some real quick good-byes to Orval Nixon and was back pushin that cart. That heat comin down on him wasn't botherin him at all until that chill stopped him right in the middle of all that heat. Dicky Bird had to stop pushin that cart, get his sweat-wipin handkerchief out, and wipe that cold sweat comin down his face. Dicky Bird's rememberin that the last time he heard Tommy Moses's name was when Jeremiah Henderson whispered it in his ear. Dicky Bird's thinkin real hard, and the more he thinks the colder he's gettin.

Al Johnson's still down Gus Goins's. Gus went into the house and brought out some of that good bottled liquor he keeps for himself. He knows Al Johnson likes it and he's in the mood for a taste himself. He and Al are chasin that good liquor down with that grape Kool-Aid. They're talkin about stuff to make that time they're sittin with go away, but it ain't movin.

Alley dogs get to barkin like they all went crazy at the same time. Al Johnson's sayin something, but Gus ain't listening. He's got his eyes squintin up and is tryin to see out into that alley. He can't see anything but he keeps lookin cause he knows them dogs ain't barkin like that for nothin. Al Johnson's still talkin, tellin him somethin when he hears that car comin down the alley. It's comin fast, like it don't care what gets in its way. Gus keeps lookin out at the alley and wonderin who's drivin like that when he sees that car comin. It stops real quick and his yard chickens start runnin and flyin up for the sky. Al Johnson stops talkin when he sees that car stop, but his mouth stays wide open. Gus Goins is sighin, mumblin, "What the hell is he doin down here? . . . Damn it."

Lenny Boughner is gettin out of his dirty old black police car. He's walkin slower than he was drivin, takin his good old time comin up Gus's path. When Lenny Boughner is close enough, Gus Goins yells out, "Well, Captain, what brings you down this way? I know you ain't comin all the way down here to say hello, now. The only thing I can think of that would get you down here would be to arrest Al here for bein so ugly."

"Ugly . . . Ugly," Al Johnson's sayin with a laugh. "I'd be the last one arrested for bein ugly."

Lenny Boughner gets an ounce of a smile on his face. But it don't stay there too long. He gets up to the porch, stops, and puts his foot up on the step. He gives Al Johnson a quick little nod, then looks at Gus Goins. It's quiet for a moment. Them alley dogs stopped that barkin and them yard chickens went on back to peckin at whatever they could find. Slowly, Lenny Boughner's takin a cigarette out, lightin it. When that smoke comes out his mouth, so does "Gus, we have a little problem here."

Gus Goins gives Al Johnson a quick look out the corner of his eye, then looks back at Lenny Boughner and says, "Problem? What kind of problem?"

"Just a little problem," Lenny Boughner says.

"Oh . . . Well, Captain, I'll be glad to help you if I can."

"I think you can, Gus."

"Oh?"

"I guess you know about that piece of fat shit they found?"

"You talkin about Tommy Moses?"

"Yeah, you know damn fuckin well who I'm talking about. Come on now, Gus, don't play that dumb shit with me. You probably knew he was dead before they found his fat ass."

"Captain, I ain't heard a damn thing about that til Al come and tell me. That ain't been bout a couple hours ago. The only thing I know is them kids found him up there. I don't know when the last time Tommy was down in here. He liked that Frankstown Avenue fast money. The money that come up in here ain't that much and don't come that fast. Folks down here got that slow money and don't likes to let it go."

"You don't know nothin about this, huh?"

"I tell you if I did. But I don't know, ain't heard nothin here. But I'll tell you what it sounds like to me. It sounds like some of them Frankstown Avenue boys come after Tommy, that's what it sounds like to me."

"It don't sound that way to me, Gus."

"Huh?"

"I said it don't sound that fuckin way to me. It sounds like we have a little problem. You see, I was just on Frankstown. And it sounds like the other night somebody come in the Shamrock lookin for Tommy. Somebody no one knew, some young Colored, tall, dark-skinned. Now, somebody told me that Tommy was braggin about this new bitch he was going to get up there sellin ass for him. Now, they said this young Colored fella was supposed to be settin up this girl for Tommy. And Tommy

87

was goin to meet this guy and girl last night. Tommy didn't mention any names, but he did say this Colored fella and this girl lived down here by the tracks. I figured you just might know some names for me."

"Shit," Gus Goins is mumblin, lookin down at them porch boards. Al Johnson's takin himself a real quick sigh. He's got some quick thoughts comin in his head tellin him he don't need to be anywhere near what he's hearin.

"I ain't heard nothin down here," Gus Goins is lookin back at Lenny Boughner and sayin.

Al Johnson ain't sayin nothin. He's hurryin, gettin his pack of cigarettes out his pocket. But he's takin his time gettin a cigarette lit. He's keepin his head down, starin into the cuff of his hands where that match is burnin.

"So, you haven't heard anything, huh?" Lenny Boughner's sayin softly, almost whisperin.

"I can't say I have . . . No, I ain't heard of nobody runnin some girl up Frankstown," Gus Goins is sayin.

"So, I came all the way down in this chicken shit to waste my time, huh?"

"Sorry, Captain, but I ain't heard nothin."

"So we have a little fuckin problem here, huh? I don't like wastin my fuckin time, Gus. I don't come down here fuckin with you. I let you sell that fuckin piss juice you make. I let you run your fuckin card games. I don't give a fuck about your crap games. But I got a fuckin problem. I don't like it when my desk sergeant tells me somebody's dumpin dead bodies in my area. I don't give a fuck if it is that fat ass layin up there. It's still my fuckin area. I want some fuckin names, Gus. And I don't want to wait too fuckin long, either. Don't piss me off."

"Goddamn, shit," Al Johnson mutters as Lenny Boughner walks out, takin his time back down the path. Gus Goins waits until he sees the dirty old police car leave before he sighs and says, "Ain't but one nigger down here that would go pull that shit. Him and that woman of his ain't nothin but some goddamn fools. I don't need this kind of trouble comin up in here."

. .. .

Tommy Moses had known of Mack Jack, knew he could make a horn come alive. He knew Mack Jack when he saw him, knew enough to just give him a little nod and let him be. Mack Jack didn't know Tommy Moses's name, just knew his face when he saw it. And right now, Mack Jack doesn't know Tommy Moses is dead. He ain't come out that room of his yet. It's way past the noon hour and that sun ain't goin to get no brighter. It ain't goin to lighten up that dark shady corner of the room where Mack Jack's sittin in his own silence. That outside noise, that loud talkin and them kids yellin, is still comin through the open window. But it ain't makin no noise in Mack Jack's mind. Them voices he's hearin ain't comin from the outside and they ain't yellin. They're whisperin little words, sometimes the same word over and over. Sometimes Mack Jack can't hear the words, ain't no words, just colors in his mind. Different colors that make him feel their color. That dark gray with that bright red is there, then that red's gone and ain't nothin but that gray. And them faceless voices come back, whisperin them words. Fingers he can't see, just feel, get to pokin at him. Long, dark red fingernails he can see now, feel now, scratchin across his chest. Dark yellow is gettin in that dark gray in his mind. That yellow's gettin bright, burnin like fire in the gray. That woman's dancin, but she ain't lookin at him. Firelight is glowin from her long shiny earrings. She's gone and he smells dirt, that damp dirt. He hears whispers, soft whispers.

·   ·   ·

Edmund Yates didn't have the slightest idea of how old he was. Didn't anybody else know either. But everybody knew he had to be near a hundred. His skin had more time on it than any clock they ever seen. It was dark skin that hung loosely from his face. Had them wrinkles that didn't have no end. The only hair he had left was gray, dirty gray. Folks say when he used to talk, he could talk about them old, old days. He could talk about that Lincoln time. He said his brother, Randolph, seen Mister Lincoln, seen him down at that Gettysburg, seen him when he gets off the train there.

Edmund Yates don't talk no more. He just sits out on that porch of Miss Alberta's roomin house when the weather ain't too bad. She gave him one of them first-floor rooms, sorta takes care of him. She said he ain't got nobody else. He's sittin on the porch now, with that shawl up around his shoulders. That heat can't bother him no more and he can't hear that good to be hearin all that street-talkin noise. His eyes are closed, but he ain't sleepin. He's openin his eyes, lookin up to see if he can see who's come out the house and onto the porch. Mack Jack's lookin at him, too. Slowly, Mack is walkin over to Edmund Yates, touchin his hand, and leanin over and whisperin somethin in his ear. The old man nods his head, then slowly, quietly, Mack Jack walks away and on down the porch steps.

• • •

That air rushin into the window and them cigarettes Jeremiah was smokin was the only things keepin him awake. Hours ago, some highway sign read WELCOME TO VIRGINIA. Jeremiah had seen the sign, kept on drivin. Willet had seen the sign, lowered her eyes, leaned back on her seat, and let the air comin through her window rush through her hair.

Centerville, Virginia, didn't sit too far off the highway. Folks comin up on it couldn't help but see it. It had one of them big courthouse-lookin buildings and one of them churches with its steeple stickin way up in the air. Jeremiah had seen them highway signs tellin him WELCOME TO CENTERVILLE. He's tellin Willet, "We got to get some gas and find someplace to eat."

Jenny Jo Curbin had just turned fifteen, had long red hair and a face covered with freckles. She'd been helpin out her daddy at his fillin station since she was eleven. Her daddy'd tell folks if he couldn't fix somethin, Jenny Jo probably could.

Jeremiah sees the young redheaded girl rushin up to the car. He can see the big smile on her face and hear her hollerin ahead, "Good afternoon, how you all today?" She's lookin in the window at Jeremiah now, still got that smile on her face and askin, "You want me to fill it up for you?"

Jeremiah's smilin back a little and noddin his head yes. Jenny Jo turns quickly, yells over her shoulder, "Sure is a nice car you got here," then hurries on to put in the gas.

Willet sits quietly, glancin out of her window at the gas station. She sees its little brightly colored signs hangin about, some man in a car bay bent over and fixin some car. Jeremiah's sayin somethin to her and waitin for her to answer, but she doesn't.

"That will be four dollars and seventy-six cents," Jenny Jo's back at the window tellin Jeremiah. He's reachin in his pocket gettin the money she's askin for. He's givin her one of them five-dollar bills he has and askin her, "Is there anyplace to get somethin to eat around here?"

"Oh yeah," Jenny Jo's sayin and reachin in her pocket for change. "You all can go down Arlene's, you can eat down there. She's real nice and can fix you anythin you all want. My daddy even goes in there to get her pies." Jenny Jo's still talkin, tellin Jeremiah how to get to Arlene's. He's pullin out slowly as Jenny Jo's tellin him, "You tell Arlene that Jenny Jo sent ya. You tell her I said hi, ya hear?"

Centerville wasn't that big, but had its back side of town. Them paved streets didn't go that far, stopped, and then dirt streets started. Some of them Colored folks livin back down on them back streets got to lookin at that big dark new car goin by. Some of them young men standin out in front of that pool hall–lookin place kept their eyes on that big car passin and tried to see as much as they could of that woman in it. Dudley Wright and Elmer Charles were out sittin on that bench in front of Arlene's. Both of them were way past rememberin the day when their last tooth fell out their mouths. Neither one of them could see too far. But when that big new car pulled up close to them, they got to lookin and at the same time whisperin to each other, "Who this here?"

Willet's sittin quietly in the car as Jeremiah turns its engine off. She's takin a couple of quick looks around, seein the old tobacco-colored front of Arlene's, seein some black and white sign in the store front—lookin window. She's seein them two old men lookin at her and she lowers her eyes from them.

"Come on, let's get somethin to eat," Jeremiah's sayin.

Willet's gettin out the car slowly and pullin down at her skirt. That sunlight comin down in her face is makin her eyes squinch up when she tries to see into the shade of Arlene's window. Jeremiah's hurryin, gettin that gun of Tommy Moses's shoved under the car seat and makin sure them car windows are rolled up.

Arlene Darby was a big, brown-skinned, fast-talkin woman. She had big brown eyes that didn't miss a thing while she was talkin. She was talkin to Clifford Miles while he was havin one of her roast beef sandwiches and watchin that big car pullin up in front of her place. She was keepin her eye on that big car, thinkin some big money was comin, too. Clifford Miles saw her lookin and started lookin, too, and sayin, "Oooh, looky here. Where's this good-lookin woman comin from . . . and gettin out that fine car."

"Shut ya mouth up and go on and eat," Arlene says, wipes her hands on her apron, and starts up to the front of the counter.

Jeremiah's lookin around the small restaurant, sees a few empty tables, a bright-faced red jukebox in the corner, sees that dark-faced man at the counter lookin back at him. He sees that big-eyed woman behind the counter smilin at him.

Willet ain't lookin at nothin, she got her head lowered and keeps it down when she hears, "How ya all doin?"

Jeremiah gives the big woman behind the counter a quick nod. He takes a seat at the counter, tries to take a deep breath quietly. Willet takes a seat, too, a quick look at the woman behind the counter, then she lowers her eyes.

"Can I get sometin for y'all?" Arlene Darby's askin.

Jeremiah's tryin to think about what he wants. Willet's gettin out a cigarette and gettin it lit.

"Y'all got people here?" Arlene Darby's askin and widenin the smile on her face.

Jeremiah shakes his head no.

"Oh," Arlene Darby's sayin, then turns quickly and gets a pitcher of ice water off the shelf behind her. She sits that pitcher of water on the counter, hurries and gets two glasses up on that counter, too.

"Here, Ah knows y'all have to be thirsty with that heat out there today the way it is. This will help cool ya off some," the big woman's sayin as she pours that ice water into the glasses.

Willet watches the water fill her glass, hears that little sound of ice clangin around in the pitcher.

"Where y'all comin from?" Arlene Darby's askin as she's pourin the water.

"Pittsburgh," Jeremiah says quickly.

"Oh, Pittsburgh, ya way up there. What brings y'all way down here?"

Willet's takin a slow sip of her ice water, and keepin her eyes away from that woman and her questions.

Jeremiah looks up at the woman behind the counter, puts a little smile on his face and says, "We're just takin a little trip down to see my wife's family."

"Oh, wheres ya from, honey?" Arlene Darby's askin Willet.

Willet keeps her eyes lowered, stares at the glass of water, and says, "North Carolina."

"Ya from North Carolina, honey? Well, Ah be. What part of North Carolina ya from? Ah comes up here from down there. Ah still got people down there. Honey, Ah was born in North

Carolina, right there near Kingston. Ah come up here in nineteen twelve, marries me a man brings me up here. Lord, he brings me here, gives me five children, and drinks himself to death. What part of North Carolina ya from, honey?"

Willet looks up, then quickly lowers her eyes and says, "I'm from Wilmington."

"Honey, y'all gots a long ways to go. But Lord, ain't nothin like that goin-home feelin. Ah sure like to gets back down there to Kingston fore Ah goes. It be a good fourteen, fifteen years since Ah been back down there. My mama died and they sends for me."

Willet's keepin her eyes lowered and stares into the water glass.

· SIX ·

Night bugs were buzzin around them alley streetlights, but nobody was lookin up and payin them any mind. Folks out sittin on them porches was talkin back and forth, but it was that quiet talkin. Some mamas had already made their children go on in the house, didn't want them hearin what they were talkin about. Sometimes that quiet talk would still to a silence. Ellen Maben ain't sayin nothin, she was whisperin over her porch rail to that Miss Duncan. But she's silent now, keeps lookin up and down the alley. She's lookin past that glow of the streetlight and tryin to stare into the darkness. She can't see nothin, but she keeps lookin until she is sure she can't see anybody comin.

Mister Allen went on in the house, didn't like that talk he was hearin and didn't want to hear any more of it. He's sittin in that kitchen of his, listening to the radio. But every time he hears them backyard dogs barkin, he turns that radio down, turns that kitchen light off, and peeks out that back window. When he can't see nothin, he still looks, stares out into the night. The dark out in them backyards was always that slow, creepy kind of dark. It liked to wrap itself around things, seep down in between stuff where it could get darker, lurk quietly until some night cat screams.

Pucky didn't want to go up them dark steps in his house, didn't want to turn that light off and get in his bed. His mama told him he had to go upstairs and go to bed, nothin was goin to bother him. Then she had to go up them steps with him, sit with him with that light on until he went to sleep. Everytime he tried to close his eyes, that dead man would be lyin in the dark of his mind. That blood would still be comin out and them bugs still be crawlin in it. Pucky's sleepin now, but sometimes he shakes, twists, and turns in his bed.

Ellen Maben's still sittin out on her porch when she sees somebody come down the alley. Quickly she gets to shiftin in her chair and stretchin her neck to see who's comin. She takes a deep sigh and leans back in her chair when that walk comin in the dark is tellin her whose face it will be when she can see it. She waits until she can look down off her porch and whisper out, "Al . . . where's you goin at tonight?"

Al Johnson slows his walk, stops, and whispers up to the porch, "Oh, didn't even see you sittin up there. Um just goin on down Gus's for a while. Been sittin there up the house, figured I'd go on down Gus's and sit there. You heard anything?"

"No, I ain't heard no more. I ain't seen nothin either. I ain't seen them all day. If they in there, they ain't come out. Ain't nobody seen them all day." Ellen Maben's tryin to keep her voice way down low. She don't want anybody hearin what she's sayin.

"What I hear is ain't nobody seen em," Al Johnson says.

"You think he dids it?" Ellen Maben's askin.

Al Johnson lowers his eyes, slowly shakin his head back and forth. Ellen Maben's silent as the dark while she's waitin for Al Johnson to stop that head shakin and say something.

"I don't know . . . don't know," Al Johnson's lookin back up and sayin.

"I seen them both go out of here. I remember it was just before that rain came pourin down. I seen both of them come out and goes up the alley. That didn't make no sense to me. That rain gettin ready to come down like it did and they's goin out in it. I tell you, that didn't make no kind of sense to me when I sees that," Ellen Maben says, then takes a quick look up and down the alley.

"I hears they goes to meet him."

Ellen Maben takes another quick look up and down the alley, then looks back down at Al Johnson and says, "I tried to be nice to them, you know, speak to them. But them, them kind of folks you can't be trustin. I ain't never seen a smile on that Willet's face. Now, he'd speak, but she wouldn't gives you the time of day."

Al Johnson gets to lookin down and shakin his head again.

"I'll tell ya," Ellen Maben's lookin up and down the alley and sayin at the same time, "if I sees them comin, Um gettin up and goin on in the house. I knows that Tommy Moses was never up to any good, but don't nobody need to be killed like that. Then just left up in some weeds. If I see em comin, Um goin in the house and lock my doors."

. . .

Mack Jack's up in his room, he's standin and lookin out his window. Sometimes he stares out at the lights he can see in other folks' window. Then he looks down at the streets he can see and just stares. He's turnin from his window, walkin back through his room. Slowly, he opens his door, closes it, and starts down the steps. Quietly he walks out onto the porch, looks up and down the dark street. Some folks are out on their porches that he can't see, ain't lookin for anyway. Jane Cook lives right across the street from Miss Alberta's roomin house. She's just sittin there, ain't thinkin about nothin, ain't lookin at nothin either. But if somethin moves, she watches it, tries to see what or who it is.

Some of that light from a far streetlight is fallin across that light blue shirt Mack Jack got on, makin it bright in the night. Jane Cook can't see Mack Jack's face, but she knows it's him comin out. She watches and waits just to see what way he's goin to go. She watches him come down his porch steps. She can see him standin silently on the sidewalk, see him lookin up and down the street. She watches him turn and start walkin up the street toward Bruston. She can see the bright blue of his shirt fade into the night, thinks of them dark blue eyes that dark man has, wonders when he's goin to play that horn again, then she wonders where he's goin. But he's gone now, out of her sight.

Mack Jack's slowly walkin up Tioga Street. The soft, slow, rhythmic sounds of his footsteps follow him. Other sounds come out of the night, snap at the soft sounds of footsteps passin. Some small yard dog is runnin along the inside of his fence, barkin at Mack Jack as he slowly walks by. He's not lookin at the dog, he keeps his head up and looks up Tioga Street. Other sounds come out of the dark: soft-talkin sounds come from porches; some baby's cryin. Its cries come out of a window, linger in the hot air as Mack Jack passes. Music and loud talkin gets in the air at the same time. Some man's callin after some woman that ain't payin him no mind. He's shoutin, "Hey . . . hey, come on back here." But that woman keeps goin, only leavin the clickin sound of her heels behind. That man goes on back into that beer garden folks call the Bucket of Blood. Even called it the Bucket of Blood before Mister Lewis took one of them double-barrel shotguns and blew Steven Brown's face nearly off his head in there. Folks say Mister Lewis told that Steven Brown to leave him be. But that Steven Brown couldn't listen. Mister Lewis went on home and got his shotgun.

Mack Jack's walkin past the Bucket of Blood. He ain't slowin and lookin in that open door. He's just lowerin his head a little bit when he walks through that sound of jukebox music comin out that open door. Tioga Street is one of them long streets, starts at Homewood Avenue and goes all the way up through Bruston. It don't stop until it gets to Wilkensburg, then it just ends. Mack Jack stops when he gets to the corner of Tioga and Bruston Avenue. Bruston Avenue folks are standin out on that corner. Them men that worked them daylong dirty jobs got clean-shaven and clean-lookin. Some of them Bruston Avenue women are standin out there, too. They know they're lookin good, got them short tight summer skirts on and their brightly colored blouses opened to show as much as they can. Tina Watkins sees Mack Jack comin, leans toward Rochelle Maxwell and whispers something, then she looks back at Mack Jack comin. Floyd Daye was one of them men standin on the corner. He sees them women whisperin, peekin past him. He's turnin his head and lookin over his shoulder, seein Mack Jack comin. That bottle of gin Floyd Daye got tucked in his back pocket is half empty. The other half of that gin is dancin around up in his head and gets his mouth sayin, "Well . . . Well . . . Well . . . If it ain't the Mister Horn-Playin Nigger. . . . Where's your horn, motherfucker? . . . Play me some horn, motherfucker . . ."

Quickly, Tina Watkins hisses at Floyd Daye, tellin him, "You better leave my sweet man alone." Now she's callin out to Mack Jack, "I know you're comin up here just to see me . . . with your fine self."

Them dark blue eyes of Mack Jack's are still starin at Floyd Daye. Slowly, he looks away to Tina Watkins. He's close enough to see that dark, tight skirt she has on, her legs and hips makin it fit to their curves. He can see the bright yellow of her blouse, her breast shapin the color of the blouse. He can see her face, dark brown in the night. He can see the red of her lips and smell her perfume as she comes toward him.

"Hey . . . Mister Horn-Playin Nigger. Where's your horn at?" Floyd Daye's yellin out.

Quickly, Tina Watkins is lookin back over her shoulder and sayin, "Floyd, why don't you shut up."

"Fuck you and that horn-playin nigger," Floyd Daye yells.

Tina Watkins spins around, shoutin, "Who in the hell you think you're talkin to, huh?"

Mack Jack slows, stops, and stares at Floyd Daye.

"Um talkin to you," Floyd Daye's shoutin.

"Kiss my ass," Tina Watkins yells and spins back around toward Mack Jack. She's lookin up in his face, smilin at him. But he's still starin beyond her; got his eyes on Floyd Daye. Quickly, she's sayin, "Don't pay that damn fool no mind."

"YOU CALLIN ME A FOOL? HUH? . . . YOU CALLIN ME A FOOL? WHO YOU THINK YOU CALLIN A FOOL?

HUH? I'LL WHIP YOUR AND THAT PUNK-ASS HORN-PLAYER'S ASS." Floyd Daye's shoutin and comin up behind Tina Watkins.

Mack Jack's keepin his eyes on Floyd Daye.

Some of them other men are callin out to Floyd Daye, tellin him, "Hey, man . . . hey . . . hey . . . come on, man, don't be startin no shit. That's Mack Jack, man . . . he's cool . . ."

Floyd Daye's hurryin his steps toward Tina Watkins, but that gin got some of them steps goin sideways instead of frontward. He's yellin ahead, tellin Tina Watkins what he's goin to do. She's spun back around and is tellin him, "You better get the hell on out of here."

"UM GONNA WHIP YOUR PUNK ASS, TOO," Floyd Daye's shoutin past Tina Watkins and tryin to get that shout up in Mack Jack's face.

"Come on, man . . . hey . . . don't be startin no shit," one of the other men is callin out.

Mack Jack's standin still, only his eyes are movin with every step Floyd Daye's takin. Tina Watkins's got her hands on her hips and her legs spread apart. She's shoutin at Floyd Daye, tellin him, "You better get your ass away from me."

"GET THE FUCK OUT MY WAY . . . UM GONNA WHIP THIS PUNK'S ASS," Floyd Daye's shoutin and pushin his way past Tina Watkins.

Mack Jack ain't movin, ain't takin his eyes off Floyd Daye either. Some of them other men are comin up behind Floyd Daye and tellin him to leave Mack Jack alone. Tina Watkins's shoutin, "Fool, what in the hell's wrong with you?"

Floyd Daye's a tall, lanky man, got that rusty pipe–colored skin and his black hair all slicked back. He's big, but he ain't as big as Mack Jack. That gin is tellin him he's as big as Mack Jack and to go on and get up in Mack Jack's face. Tina Watkins's just lookin at Floyd Daye. She ain't sayin nothin now, but her mouth and eyes are both wide open.

"UM GOIN TO WHIP YOUR PUNK-ASS." Floyd Daye's shoutin up in Mack Jack's face.

Mack Jack ain't movin, got his eyes right in Floyd Daye's. Some of them other men are tellin Floyd Daye to back off of Mack Jack. But he ain't listenin to them, he's still yellin up in Mack Jack's face.

"Hey, man, come on . . . come on, Floyd . . . this man ain't did nothin to you . . . come on man," some man's yellin at Floyd Daye and pullin at his arm.

"GET OFF ME . . . GET OFF ME, YOU HEAR?" Floyd Daye yells back at the man and jerks his arm away from him. Then he gets his face right back up in Mack Jack's, shoutin, "YOU A PUNK . . . YOU A PUNK-ASS."

"Hey, Floyd . . . Floyd . . . Floyd . . . he ain't bothered you man . . . come on, man" somebody's yellin and tryin to get Floyd Daye's arm again. But he keeps shoutin up in Mack Jack's face. He's so close, some of that spit flyin out his mouth is gettin on Mack Jack. That gin's tellin him to get a little closer. Then that gin don't know what to tell him. He's still up in Mack Jack's face shoutin. But that face ain't movin, them dark blue eyes ain't blinkin. They're lookin like they're glowin blue, makin Mack Jack's face look like some dark mask in the night. Then slowly, very slowly, Floyd Daye's seein some smile comin on Mack Jack's face. It ain't no pretty smile, none of them happy smiles. It's a cold smile. It's makin that gin up in Floyd Daye's head chill. It's makin him slow that shoutin down, makin him want to back away. It's makin him hear his name bein called, wantin to hear his name called and feel somebody pullin on his arm.

"Um goin to whip your ass," Floyd Daye's yellin as he's bein pulled away from Mack Jack. Tina Watkins's standin there watchin Floyd Daye bein pulled away. She's shakin her head back and forth and tellin him, "You almost got your ass whipped, fool."

Slowly, Mack Jack starts walkin again. But he's keepin his eyes on Floyd Daye. He ain't keepin that smile on his face, but it's still there.

"Where you going? . . . You ain't leavin, are you?" Tina Watkins's lookin up at Mack Jack and askin. But he's not turnin his head and lookin her way.

"Where you going?" Tina Watkins's askin again.

Slowly, Mack Jack takes his eyes off Floyd Daye. Tina Watkins sees that smile Mack Jack had vanish. But she's smilin now, walkin alongside of him and askin, "Where you going to tonight?"

Mack Jack keeps walkin slowly, Tina Watkins wraps her arm around his and leans up against him. She lets the sway of her hips rub against his side. She's whisperin up in his ear, "Where you going? Why don't you stay here and talk to me?"

Mack Jack leans her way, whispers something back in her ear. She smiles, pulls on his arm to lower his shoulder. She gets her lips on his ear, slides them, and lets them flutter over it while she whispers, "You can take me to nowhere with you, baby. Why don't you stay here and talk to me for a while?"

Mack Jack's gone, Tina Watkins watched him as he walked down Bruston Avenue and disappeared into the night. It is always dark down there where Bruston Avenue comes to that dead end. Ain't no streetlights down there and that weedy hillside goin up to the railroad tracks ain't nothin but a pile of darkness in the night. It's quiet down there if there ain't no trains passin. When they do, that train light brightens up the top of them high weeds before its rumblin sound shatters the stillness.

Mack Jack slows when he gets to the bottom of that hillside, stops, and stares up into them dark high weeds. Slowly, he turns around and looks back down Bruston Avenue. Then slowly, he turns back around and starts walkin up through the high weeds.

Except for the sounds of night bugs, it is quiet on top of the hill. A mild breeze blows over the empty tracks. Mack Jack stands along the side of the tracks, looks far off to where the tracks curve, comin around that bend from Wilkensburg. He's unbuttoning his shirt, lettin the mild breeze blow across his chest. Quiet moments pass before he turns and begins walkin along the dark tracks toward Homewood. Sometimes he walks with his head lowered, lookin down at the dark path along the tracks. Then sometimes he looks up, out over the hill. Them houses down there are dark except for them lights in the windows. It's quiet down there, them folks that might be sittin out on their porches talkin ain't talkin loud enough for them words to get all the way up on them railroad tracks.

Jason Pedder and Micky Hart been runnin that Washington, D.C., to Chicago 12:11 express train for years. They ran it with them big, old, dark gray steam engines pullin it. They like them big diesel engines they have now, ain't got all that stoppin just for water. They got that big, fast diesel runnin on that outside track, got it runnin on time, too. It ain't slowin down, don't have to as it comes around that Wilkensburg bend. That train light is brightenin up them dark tracks for them.

Mack Jack's got his head lowered, lookin down at that dark path he's walkin on. But in that dark he's seein it ain't hot like the night. It's cold, not that chilly cold that makes you shake. It's that soft cold tells you it's nice and you belong in it. You can become nothin in it, don't have to be anything ever. Didn't have to be anyway.

But that dark cold is shakin now, that big diesel comin fast on that outside track is makin it shake. That train light is shinin on something bright blue along the side of the tracks. Jason Pedder is liftin his head and leanin forward in his seat to see what that bright blue is. Micky Hart's lookin, too, then he's hearin Jason Pedder mutterin, "What's that damn nigger doin that close to the tracks? . . . Shit."

That big train horn's blowin, tryin to make more noise than that big rumblin-soundin diesel. That silence that was restin up around the tracks is up and gettin its ass out the way from all that noise comin. That horn-blowin sound is burstin out of the dark air, findin its own space in the night. Some of them folks sittin down on them dark porches never pay them night trains no mind. They just stop their talk until them trains pass and they can hear what they were talkin about. But that loud horn blowin got them lookin up at the tracks, wonderin why that train's makin all that noise this time of night.

Mack Jack's still got his head down, lookin at that dark path he's walkin on. But that horn blowin is gettin in his ear, got its low, long groanin sound slow-dancin up in his head. It's got him gettin his head up, feelin that ground beneath his feet shakin. It got him lookin back over his shoulder, seein that fast light in the night comin. It's gettin closer, shinin in his eyes. Slowly he's steppin away from the path, gettin near them weeds alongside of it. Them weeds are shakin, too. That loud-comin rumblin sound is pushin that hot air in front of it away, makin it blow like some hot wind up in Mack Jack's face. He turns from it, lowers his head, and slowly starts walkin again.

That train gone now, even them loud clickity-clackin echo sounds it left behind have gone on and left, too. That silence took its time gettin back up along them tracks. It's back now, and Mack Jack's walkin in it. But that horn sound is still up in his head. It's stuck there, don't want to go nowhere. It ain't a train horn no more; it's makin music. It's makin Mack Jack make some sounds in his head. It's makin him want to stop walkin, turn and look out over that hill, play that horn to all them little lights in the night. But that horn sound is gone now, got out of Mack Jack's head and went on to play someplace else. Mack Jack can't hear it no more, his fingers ain't playin nothin but the dark.

·   ·   ·

Them folks down Gus Goins's ain't heard that train passin. That jukebox playin in that front room ain't lettin them hear no train goin by. Folks that ain't dancin to that jukebox music is sittin in them chairs and listening to it. Bill Lovit's sittin in that front room on one of them foldin chairs in there. He keeps tryin to sit up straight, but that wine he's been drinkin keeps makin him lean off that chair. He done fell off once, didn't even know he had fallen off until folks started to pull on him tryin to get him back up. Olinda Harris was so busy dancin when Bill Lovit fell on the floor, she didn't even see him until she almost stepped on him. Then she just stepped away, caught up with that beat and kept dancin. Buster Willie from the hill is in there watchin her dance. She knows it, too. Buster Willie don't come back to Homewood since he moved up on the hill where they got them good nightclubs. Got them places that Charlie Parker would be at playin. But when Buster Willie does come back to Homewood, he comes back clean, always lookin good. Olinda Harris wants him lookin at her. She's makin sure she's shakin her butt his way.

Al Johnson's back in that back room playin cards. Pete Turner's lookin at him, waitin on him to make his play. Al Johnson ain't ready to throw a card down and pick another one up yet. Pete Turner got a grin on his face, and the longer Al Johnson takes, the bigger that grin's gettin. Wendell Hill and Gene Holland are playin them cards, too. Wendell Hill's grinnin, too. He knows the same thing Pete Turner knows. He knows Al Johnson ain't got a card worth a dime in his hands. Pete Turner lets a little laugh come out his mouth before he says to Al Johnson, "You want us to go on home . . . come back tomorrow nights? . . . You think that's be enough time for yous to make up your mind?"

Al Johnson ain't sayin nothin, ain't takin his eyes away from his cards either. Pete Turner laughs and keeps laughin as he's tellin Al Johnson, "You ain't got nothin . . . And you ain't gettin nothin. I can see why you ain't doin nothin . . . But yous givin me your money . . . and I likes that . . ."

Then Al Johnson's lookin over at Pete Turner and sayin, "How you know what I have, huh? You ain't even found out how fat, black, and ugly you are yet. You ugly motherfucker . . . now you know . . . but you still don't know what I got."

Al Johnson's lookin back at his cards and tryin not to laugh at what he just told Pete Turner, but he ain't tryin too hard.

Them cards he's holdin ain't changin at all. He still don't know what one to throw away and what one he better keep.

Carl Hughes knows what he has to say and better say it quietly. He's over in the corner of that card-playin room talkin to Lucille Briggs. He's sippin on that glass of bourbon he's got, takin his time and quietly sayin what he got to say. He's tellin Lucille Briggs what he heard up in that hardware store he works at up on Homewood Avenue. He knows he's the only Colored that done heard what he heard. He knows what the white people talkin about. Lucille Briggs got her a drink, too.

"They think they know who killed Tommy. They got a description of somebody that come in the Shamrock lookin for him. They knows Tommy was goin to meet this man the same night he gets killed."

Lucille Briggs is quiet; she wants to listen. But she's thinkin, too, busy addin up in her mind what Carl Hughes's tellin her and what she done already heard bein whispered. Now she's whisperin, tellin Carl Hughes, "I'll tell you, I think it was Jeremiah. And I wouldn't be surprised if it was. They ain't been seen since, ain't nobody seen em comin or goin."

Dicky Bird was inside, up in that front room watchin them folks dance. But it got too hot for him, he needed to get some air. Now he's out on that back porch of Gus Goins's talkin with Bobby Rose. Bobby Rose ain't happy and he ain't thinkin about what Dicky Bird got to say. He knows Olinda Harris is back in there dancin and ain't payin him no mind cause that Buster Willie's sittin back up in there. Bobby Rose is leanin up against that porch post, smokin a cigarette and starin out into the night. Dicky Bird's sittin on one of them chairs and eatin that sandwich Gus Goins made for him. He's got a mouthful of that sandwich, but he's still talkin.

"Ah gots to go on up the junkyard. Ah needs me some of that two-inch pipe . . . Just a bit of it . . . Mister Ellis says Ah finds him some, he give me somin for it . . ."

Bobby Rose takes a big drag on that cigarette, blows that smoke out into the dark, then says, "Hope you find it."

"Theys got it up there . . . Ah finds it."

"Hope you do."

"Ah gots me one of them electric kind of lamps ta-day . . . Yes, sir, finds me a good lamp. Finds it up there in Wilkensburg. Comes across it the first thing . . ."

Bobby Rose ain't thinkin about no lamp and don't want to either. He gives Dicky Bird a little grunt sound and looks off into that dark yard. Then, when he hears all them dogs startin to bark, he gets to tryin to see out in that dark alley. Dicky Bird's still talkin, sayin somethin about that lamp he found. But now, Bobby Rose couldn't hear him if he wanted to. Them alley dogs are barkin like each one of them got a cat in the corner. Gus Goins's chickens done woke up and got to squawkin, too. That dark alley is startin to light up. Bobby Rose can hear them cars comin now. Quickly he steps away from that porch post, gets up on his tiptoes, and tries to see out in that alley.

Dicky Bird done stopped chewin on that sandwich and got to tryin to see out in that alley, too. He don't know what's wrong, but somethin tellin him somethin wrong.

"SHIT," Bobby Rose yells out. Dicky Bird still ain't seen nothin yet. He's tryin to see what Bobby Rose done saw.

"COPS . . . COPS ARE COMIN," Bobby Rose yells and runs off that porch so fast he makes it shake. He's still runnin, trippin on stuff he ain't seein, until he gets to that big side fence. Now he's climbin over that fence so fast he ain't even feelin that nail rippin at his pants leg. Dicky Bird can't see nothin, cept for all them lights out in the alley. But he knows he's seen enough. He's up from that chair and hurryin on into the house. He knows he has to tell Gus Goins them policemen are comin.

Al Johnson can't see Dicky Bird hurryin through that door, but he can hear that hurryin sound and looks back over his shoulder. Pete Turner sees Dicky Bird comin through that door, don't need to look twice to know somethin's wrong.

"POLICEMEN'S COMIN . . . THEY'S OUT THERE," Dicky Bird's yellin as he's comin through the door.

"SHIT . . . GETS THE MONEY OFF THE TABLE," Al Johnson's yellin and grabbin for his money.

"GODDAMN IT," Pete Turner yells and starts grabbin for his money, too. Wendell Hill don't give a damn about that couple dollars he got on the table. He's up and runnin into that front room for that other door. Folks in there dancin to that loud jukebox music don't know why Wendell Hill's bumpin them out of his way. Pete Turner's runnin through that room now, yellin, "RAID! . . . POLICE OUT BACK! . . ."

Gus Goins was back in his kitchen when Dicky Bird come back there and told him the police are comin. He knows he can't run, knows he got to get that big wad of money out his pocket and get it someplace them cops can't find it. Quickly he's gettin that money out his pocket, stickin it inside of one of them dead chickens he got layin on the sink. Then he's takin that chicken and puttin it in a big pot of water.

Al Johnson ain't movin. He knows if those cops are out in the back, they'll be out front, too. He's still sittin at that card table, but actin like he ain't never seen a card in his life when that back door comes flyin open.

Big Lenny Boughner's pushin that door open, shoutin, "ALL RIGHT . . . ALL RIGHT . . . GET YOUR HANDS OUT YOUR POCKETS AND GET YOUR ASSES UP AGAINST A WALL . . . GODDAMN IT . . . MOVE!"

Next thing Al Johnson sees is so many cops comin through that door he can't count them. One of them is snatchin at his arm and shoutin, "GET YOUR ASS UP."

That jukebox is still playin. But them folks ain't dancin. Most of them are tryin to follow Wendell Hill and Pete Turner out that other door. But as hard as they are tryin to get out that door is as hard as they're bein pushed back in. Victor Blaire is one of them cops that loves to use his hittin stick. He got his stick up and yellin, "WHERE IN THE HELL DO YOU THINK YOU GOIN? . . . GET BACK IN THERE!"

Wendell Hill knows he can't get no farther. He's tryin to back up, but he ain't backin up fast enough. That stick of Victor Blaire's is comin down through the air so fast it's makin a swishin sound. Then it's soundin like it's a baseball bat, smackin the hell out of some baseball. Wendell Hill's head is burstin open, blood gushin out the crack in it and runnin down over his face. He's fallin down; Pete Turner's tryin to get him back up. Victor Blaire's got that stick back up and yellin, "GET BACK IN THERE . . . GET IN THERE . . ."

"ALL RIGHT . . . ALL RIGHT . . . KEEP YOUR HANDS OUT YOUR POCKETS . . . GET UP AGAINST THE GODDAMN WALL . . . ALL OF YOU . . ." Lenny Boughner's yellin as he comes into that front room. Them cops that were shovin and pushin folks back through the other door are pushin them up against the walls. That jukebox is still blarin. Lenny Boughner snatches a whippin stick from one of them other cops. That glass coverin that jukebox is shatterin, pieces of it flyin everywhere. But that music is still playin, that drum beat is still makin that floor bounce. That jukebox is dead now, ain't got a heartbeat left in it. Lenny Boughner's smashin its little record-playin arm, too.

Blood's still comin out of Wendell Hill's head, rollin down his face and drippin on his shirt. He's tryin to stay up on his feet, but he keeps fallin down. Pete Turner's tryin to hold him up. Victor Blaire's got his stick up again, gettin ready to swing it at Wendell Hill again. Pete Turner's yellin, "DON'T HIT HIM NO MORE . . . DON'T YA HIT HIM AGAIN . . ."

Victor Blaire's face wasn't red, but it's red now. His lips are drawin back over his teeth and he's yellin, "YOU BETTER SHUT YOUR FUCKIN MOUTH . . . ONE MORE WORD OUT OF YOU . . . I'LL BUST YOUR FUCKIN HEAD WIDE OPEN . . . YOU BETTER KEEP THAT NIGGER UP AGAINST THAT FUCKIN WALL . . ."

Gus Goins heard that splatterin sound of his jukebox bein broken up. He's comin out that back kitchen, goin into that front room. One of them cops starts grabbin at his arm, tellin him to get up against the wall. He's pullin away, shoutin, "THIS IS MY HOUSE . . . WHAT THE HELL'S GOIN ON HERE? . . . YOU CAN'T COME IN HERE BREAKIN MY STUFF UP."

Lenny Boughner sees Gus Goins comin in that front room. He's watchin him lookin at his jukebox all smashed up. Gus Goins looks up, looks over, and sees all that blood comin down Wendell Hill's face. He looks over to Lenny Boughner, askin, "What you doin this to me for? We ain't givin you no trouble here . . . Why you doin me this way for, Captain?"

Lenny Boughner gets a little smile on his face, says, "I had a complaint about you, Gus. Somebody complained you were

breakin the law. Yep, they said you had some gamblin goin on
here and sellin some illegal alcohol. That's a little problem,
Gus. I'm goin to have to search this whole place, look for
evidence. If I find any evidence, I'm going to have to make
some arrests. Looks like you have a little problem here."

.   .   .

Mister Allen was havin a good sleep. He didn't even have any
dreams runnin through his head that he had to look at, until
some dog got up in his mind with that barkin. Then that
poundin and yellin got up in his mind, too. Mister Allen was
wishin that dream would go on away, let him sleep in peace.
But it wasn't goin nowhere. Every time Mister Allen thought
that dream left him, it came back. He's got his eyes open now,
knows he ain't asleep, and wonderin why he's still dreamin
about them dogs barkin and all that poundin. Then he's hearin
somethin he knows ain't no dream. He's hearin them dogs
barkin; that poundin ain't stopped. But he's hearin that yellin,
"POLICE . . . POLICE . . . OPEN UP."
        Mister Allen's awake now, puttin his robe on as he's hur-
ryin down them steps and gettin to that front door. He's openin
that door slowly, peekin out, and seein all them police cars in
the alley. He's stickin his head farther out that door. He's
lookin down the alley and seein all them policemen up on that
Jeremiah Henderson's porch. He can see them tryin to break
down that door.

· SEVEN ·

The sun was comin up, but it was comin up slow, takin its good old time lightin up the road. That white line runnin down the center of the road was still just a long gray streak. A light rain was fallin, just enough to have them windshield wipers goin back and forth real slow. Every once in a while some roadside signs showed up in the car lights. Jeremiah watched for them, and the last one he saw read JACKSONVILLE 25 MILES, WILMINGTON 79 MILES.

Except for them big trucks comin up the northbound side of the road, makin that quick whiffin sound as they passed, the road was quiet. Willet wasn't lookin out the window: there was nothin to see. One side of the road looked like the other, high, dark trees standin in the dark. Sometimes there were open fields, maybe some early light on in some farmhouse. But most of the time, just stuff in the dark that she was tired of lookin at. She's sittin with her head leanin back against the seat. Sometimes she's lookin down at the dashboard, looks for a while, then looks back out at the dark road.

Way above the dark road, that slow sun keeps comin up. Them long gray streaks runnin down the center of the road are gettin a little brighter. Jeremiah's lookin at one of them road signs, sees what it reads. He turns back and looks to the road, sighs, and says, "We almost there."

"I know," Willet says quietly.

"We ought to be there in about a half hour," Jeremiah says.

"I know," Willet says, leanin up in her seat and reachin in her purse. Quickly, she gets a cigarette out, lights it, then starts feelin around in her purse for somethin.

"You sure you want to go back?"

Willet keeps diggin around in her purse.

"You think she'll let you see him?"

"I'll see him," Willet says.

"Do you think she'll let you?"

"I said I'll see him," Willet says as she slowly, carefully takes her hand out of her purse. She's lookin down at what she's holdin, twistin it around in her fingers.

Jeremiah's quiet, lookin off to the sides of the road. He can see out in them far fields he's passin. That slow comin-up sun was brightenin up them fields. Browns, greens, soft yellows are makin them fields pretty to look at. But that ain't what Jeremiah's lookin at that's makin him keep lookin out in that field he's passin. It's them other colors he sees, pale tattered-lookin colors. Some mule-drawn shabby brown wagon is out in that field. Dark folks with them pale-colored overalls already got their backs bent over pickin at somethin. Jeremiah looks back at the road, sighs, and says, "Damn, they're out there working in that field already."

Willet looks out at the field, then slowly looks back down into the car. She stares into the shade in her open hand, looks into the small glows of yellow and the little sparkles of white. She stares silently for a moment before sayin, "This is the one I like."

"Huh?" Jeremiah's askin.

"This is the one I really like. It got diamonds in it."

"Huh . . . huh?" Jeremiah's askin as he quickly looks over at Willet.

"His ring . . . I really like this one."

Jeremiah looks back to the road sayin, "Them rings are worth a lot. We can get a lot of money for them."

"I'm goin to keep this one."

"What are you goin to keep it for?"

"I just want it."

"Why?"

Willet looks over to Jeremiah and stares silently. "I'm keepin it."

Jeremiah's drivin slower, lookin around more. Some big sign on the side of the road reads WELCOME TO WILMINGTON. The road ain't empty no more, other cars are behind and in front of him. There's even a few folks out walkin alongside the road. Soon, that road ain't a road no more, it's turned into a big wide street, got traffic lights at the corners. Jeremiah's sighin, sayin, "Well . . . we here."

Willet's leanin up in her seat, lookin out the window. A slow smile comes to her face for just a moment. Jeremiah's askin, "What way do I go now?"

"Just keep goin straight down here," Willet says, leaning back in her seat. "We have to go all the way down until we get to Front Street, then we turn there. We have to turn right, and that will take us out to Snake Town."

"Snake Town," Jeremiah says quickly, with a little smile on his face.

"Yes, Snake Town," Willet's sayin, rollin her eyes at Jeremiah.

"You never said anything about Snake Town. You always talked about Wilmington. You never said anything about a Snake Town."

Willet's silent.

Jeremiah laughs a little. "How come they call it Snake Town?"

"They just do, that's why," Willet says, then looks out the window.

Downtown Wilmington had them big tall buildings. That early-mornin sunlight was only lightin the top of them. That darkness the night was leavin behind was still hangin on the side of them tall buildings and lurkin in between them. Folks hurryin to their early-mornin jobs were startin to fill up some of them sidewalks. Raymond Weavers was hurryin, settin up his newspaper-sellin stand on that corner of his. Early-mornin folks wouldn't recognize that corner if Raymond Weavers wasn't out there tryin to sell them a paper. Two young women with waitress's uniforms on are talkin with each other as fast as they're walkin. They're hurryin by Raymond Weavers and his newspapers, ain't payin him no mind. Some fat man with a straw hat on and a tight white shirt tryin to fit around his belly is hurryin across the street. He's lookin at that big, dark, new car goin by, tryin to see who's in it. Raymond Weavers sees Bill Marks comin and gets a paper ready for him so Bill Marks don't have to slow down too much. Bill Marks's always in a hurry to get his telegraph office open. Raymond Weavers is callin out, "Good mornin there, Bill. Looks like a nice day comin up here."

Bill Marks already got his nickel out and some good words ready to say. He's tellin Raymond Weavers, "Good mornin, Raymond. You have yourself a good day today."

Ain't too much about them Wilmington early mornins Raymond Weavers don't know. He knows who's goin to be comin by and when they're goin to be comin. He don't have to look at no clock to see what time it is; he can watch the way them shadows slide down off them buildings. He knows when it's time for that mornin traffic to start gettin heavy and them folks in the cars stoppin for their papers. That light at his corner is turnin red, he's lookin at them cars stoppin, seein that big new car he can't remember seein before. He's watchin that young Colored fella drivin that car and wonderin where it's goin. Now he's seein them Yankee plates on that car and givin it a real long look.

Willet's sittin up in her seat tellin Jeremiah, "You have to turn at this corner."

Jeremiah's lookin at that corner where he has to turn and he sees that old paper-sellin white man starin at him. Raymond Weavers keeps lookin. Now he's wonderin why that Colored boy's starin at him. He's tightenin up his face, makin it stern-lookin. But he ain't turnin it away.

Jeremiah's mutterin, "What the fuck are you lookin at?"

Raymond Weavers's seein that nigger sayin something at him. He doesn't see no smile on that boy's face. And doesn't like the look that nigger's givin him.

Jeremiah's still starin.

That red light's turnin green.

"Go on, the light's green," Willet's sayin.

Slowly, Jeremiah's lookin away from that old white man starin at him. But he can still see that man's face in his mind. He's mutterin, "White motherfucker."

"What?" Willet's askin.

"That old man over there likes to look too much."

Willet leans forward, looks over at Raymond Weavers, sees him starin at them. She leans back in her seat, slowly says, "So . . . let him look."

Jeremiah's pushin down on the gas pedal and turnin that corner. He's on Front Street now, it has them shoppin stores and tall buildings, too. But that street look don't last too long before it becomes some old road again.

Willet's got her window down some, and that mornin air is rushin into the car. It's blowin her hair, blowin in her face. But it can't blow the silence away from her eyes. She's lookin out at what she's passin by. That old half-fallin-down barn is still in that field; it ain't fell down yet. That old, big droopy-lookin tree still looks like some big old man standin on a hill. And that air rushin in her face ain't changed its mornin smell. Slowly she's turnin away from the window, lookin at Jeremiah and quietly sayin, "You have to slow down. We have to make a turn up there. There's a sign up there."

Jeremiah's slowin the car down, lookin and then seein some little sign sayin STONEY TOWN 3 MILES, with an arrow pointin which way to turn. He's turnin the car onto some narrow road. It's got them big trees growin along its sides, makin it all shady. "I thought you said Snake Town."

"Snake Town's behind Stoney," Willet says quietly.

Stoney Town only had that one narrow road goin back to it and comin back out of it. It was sorta hidden back there beyond all them big tall trees. Real old folks say Indians used to live back up in there, but ain't a feather left of them now. Everybody past the age of twelve that lived in Wilmington knew where Stoney Town was. Some folks would only whisper about it and hoped their God wouldn't hear them. Sailors off them ships pullin into Wilmington that ain't never been to

Wilmington in their lives didn't have a problem findin Stoney Town. And they didn't have a problem findin them little back streets, even at night. Them drinkin and dancin joints back there always had their pretty bright lights on. That Red Star dancin joint was always full. And them Stoney Town nighttime women were always in there. Sometimes some of them sailors would get to actin up too much, wantin to break things up. Sheriff Elmer would have to go back there and get them out. He'd have to stick them in that jail of his, keep em there til mornin, charge them for their keep.

Sheriff Elmer didn't let no trouble get on that front street of Stoney Town. He made sure them good-actin folks didn't have to be bothered with them back street ways. That front street was called Dilworth Street. It had a few shoppin stores and them other kind of shops that decent folks needed. But Dilworth Street didn't go too far before it got to the creek, and it stopped right there at the creek bridge. Most folks didn't need to go any farther. Just the Colored folks. That creek didn't have a name, and if it did, nobody knew what it was. They just called it the creek, but everybody knew what that other side of the creek was called.

Jeremiah's drivin slow. Ain't no signs sayin to, but he knows he better not go fast. He's lookin around at them shops on Dilworth Street, sees that jailhouse sittin on that street, too. He sees some of them early-mornin folks givin him a good long look. But he ain't givin them that long look back.

Willet's sittin quietly, sometimes lookin out the window, then lowerin her eyes. She's lookin up now, seein the dark brown handrails of the creek bridge stickin up at the end of the street. She can see the ground beginnin to slope toward the creek. She can't see the creek, dosen't need to. She knows it's there, same mucky color it's always been. Softly she's tellin Jeremiah, "We have to go across the bridge . . . Snake Town's over there."

That creek wasn't wide, no wider than a good hop, skip, and a jump. It wasn't too deep either, three or four feet at the most. That bridge was old, put up for them horse- and mule-pulled wagons. It shakes, leaves them rattlin, clingin sounds echoin in the air when one of them cars or field trucks goes over it.

Jeremiah's drivin slowly over the bridge, tryin to see what's on the other side. He can see that dirt road startin, see it curvin through some brownish green wet-lookin land. Early mornin sunlight is shinin through them trees and light brown, skinny, stick-lookin things growin out of it. Then that sunlight's fallin across that still, murky brownish green water. It's makin it shine like dark, still satin.

Willet's lookin over the handrail of the creek bridge, starin down at the water. She looks up the creek as far as she can see before she slowly turns and looks out to the dirt road. Quietly she says, "We'll go to my sister's first."

Snake Town wasn't too far from the creek bridge, right up that dirt road. It wasn't on a map nowhere. On them official papers it wasn't nothin but a part of Stoney Town, come under Sheriff Elmer's jurisdiction. But folks in Stoney Town didn't see it that way. They didn't do a lot of thinkin about Snake Town. Most Stoney Town folks sorta thought wasn't nothin past the creek cept Coloreds and snakes. But some of them Stoney Town young men would wait til the sun would go down to sneak across that creek. And some of them Snake Town women knew they were comin.

Daytime, Snake Town looked like something the sun was

mad at. It got so mad it burned everything all dark, made them shanties look like they were made of cinders. Them shanties that weren't out the road some were built real close to one another. Each shanty had its own little worn-out path gettin back to it from the road. Them Snake Town children would run up and down them paths all day long. Weeds never did have a chance growin up under their feet. But them Snake Town dogs would spend most of their time lyin up under them porches, stayin out of that sun beatin down on everything. Most folks, cept for them real old ones, be gone most of the day. They'd have to get out of Snake Town to get some money, cause there weren't no money in Snake Town to get. They'd have to go to them fields, get that pickin-field money. Or maybe get them some little money from doin some chores for them Stoney Town white folks.

Nighttime it could get real dark in Snake Town. That one electric line runnin out there didn't go too far. Most folks still had them oil-burnin lamps tryin to light up the dark. Sometimes there would be so many night bugs flyin around them lamps that light comin from them couldn't get past to light up nothin cept them bugs. Folks sittin out on them sittin porches doin that nighttime talkin about the day would just go on and talk past the dark to that face they couldn't see.

Down that Snake Town road some, wasn't much of Snake Town left. But folks went down there anyway, needed to go, could find their way down there in the dark. Daddy Jake had his place down there, had him a place for folks to come, get them somethin to drink, and dance to that music playin down there. Come Sunday mornin, folks would go down that road, too. They'd have to go down there to get to that hope they couldn't find all week. Reverend Bell would be down there in that A.M.E. church passin out that hope. That church was painted white, always gleamed in that sunlight. Old folks say that church been down there since slavin days.

Rustin Hampton had already gone to them pickin fields. Had to; needed to feed them children him and Lulu got. Lulu would have been gone, too, cept that child she's carryin now is too close to comin. Just tryin to get herself up in the mornin was hard enough. She couldn't be bendin down all day long in them pickin fields. Them other children she has are up, been fed, and are out playin in that yard of hers. But that noise they're makin ain't makin her mornin no easier. She's sittin at that cookin-room table, tryin not to think about them clothes she got to get washed and them children yellin for her, too. She knows she needs a little time fore that day come and take every minute she got. She can't keep no silence in her mind for them children callin for her. She's yellin out that screen door, tellin them children to stop all that hollerin. But she's still hearin, "Mama . . . Mama . . . look. Mama . . . come look, Mama."

She's up and lookin out through that screen door, seein that big new car pullin up and stoppin out in front of her yard. It's takin its time drivin up in her mind and tellin her it's there. Them children are still yellin, "Mama . . . Mama . . . look, Mama."

That car door is openin now. In Lulu's mind, it's openin even slower than it is. That dark hair she can see is slowly gettin to her mind, bringin back time gone by. But it ain't bringin that time back fast enough to tell her what her eyes are seein. She keeps lookin.

"Mama . . . Mama . . . who's that? . . . Who's that, Mama?" them children are yellin.

Them children are still yellin, but Lulu's stilled in her own silence. Her eyes are seein things her mind ain't certain she's seein. Some little feelin is tellin her to keep lookin, start hopin. She can see a face now, see it lookin up to her home. That little feelin she got is tellin her what she's feelin ain't goin away, it's just comin. Quietly, slowly, she's pushin that screen door open and steppin out onto her sittin porch. Softly, she's utterin, "Lord have mercy . . . My God."

"Mama . . . Mama . . . Mama," them children keep hollerin. But that silence is still in her mind. That kind of silence that makes any sound seem too far away to hear. Slowly, she's steppin out onto the porch, walkin through them hollerin sounds of her children. She's walkin to the edge of her porch, that early-mornin sunlight is gettin in her eyes. But she ain't squintin, couldn't if she wanted to. She's starin, tryin to make her mind tell her what she's seein is there, come back.

"Mama . . . who's that, Mama?"

"Hush," Lulu's tellin the children. But she ain't takin her eyes off what she's seein.

Willet's standin silently at the side of the car. She's lookin up the yard path, past the children starin and pointin at her, to the woman she sees.

Jeremiah's sittin in the car, lookin out the window and up at that shack-lookin house. He's seen them children in the yard; now he's watchin that woman slowly comin down her porch steps. He can still hear them children yellin, but he's lookin at and feelin the silence on that woman's face. But that silence ain't there no more, that woman's yellin, callin out, "Wil . . . Lord! Oh my God, Wil!"

Lulu's comin down her steps, now she's startin down that dirt path, she's tryin to walk fast, tryin to run. That pale blue nightgown she has on is flingin loose, trailin behind her. She keeps callin out, "Wil! Wil, oh my God!"

Willet's still standin silently beside the car. She's watchin her sister comin to her. She's reachin up to her eye and wipin away a tear before it even comes. Slowly she begins to take a step toward her sister. Then quickly she's feelin the mornin air gettin in her face, blowin her hair back as she's hurryin through it, runnin as fast as she can.

. . .

That mornin sun is lightin up the alley, but today that mornin talk is all about last night. Folks are already out on them porches tellin all they know about what they'd seen and heard them policemen doin. Mister Allen's talkin, too. He's tellin Ellen Maben, "Don't need to have that kind of trouble around here. That kind of trouble just bring more trouble, don't needs that around here."

Ellen Maben's sayin, "It scared me, yes it did. I knew as soon as I seen all them policemens out here . . . As soon as I seen them . . . I knew they come for that Jeremiah and that girl . . . It scared me, wakin up and hearin all that poundin . . . Didn't know what that was . . . Thought somebody tryin to break in my house . . . Tell me it was on fire or something."

Ellen Maben's still talkin, tellin Mister Allen what she thinks. But sometimes she stops real quick, looks over her shoulder, and gives that far alley a good look. Mister Allen's keepin his eye on that alley, too. Ellen Maben's sayin, "I hope they catch them . . . put them in jail and get them away from here."

Bill Lovit can't remember anything Dicky Bird's tellin him he should. He can't even remember how he got himself back to that shed of his. He's sittin up on the side of that bed he got in there and lookin over at Dicky Bird, wonderin what Dicky Bird's talkin about. That sun ain't high enough yet to get some light into that shed. It's all gray in there. Dicky Bird's sittin on one of them wooden boxes Bill Lovit calls a chair. He had to come in there and shake Bill Lovit awake, got tired of standin in that burnt-out lot callin for him. He's tellin Bill Lovit how Pete Turner and Al Johnson had to rush Wendell Hill to the hospital. He's sayin, "Theys get him out of there . . . Soon as them policemens leave out of there . . . theys gets him down to the hospital . . . Theys say he had to go see a doctor . . . Couldn't nobody but a doctor be able to stop all that blood comin out of his head."

Bill Lovit still ain't rememberin nothin. The only thing he knows is every time he wakes up, he's someplace else and don't know how he got there. He's lookin at Dicky Bird and askin, "How he doin?"

Dicky Bird's sayin, "I ain't heard . . . I gets out of there myself. I had to get myself out of there. Gus wasn't fit to be doin no talkin to. Theys bust his place up like that . . . I goes on and gets me some sleep. Then I gets up and comes down here . . . I ain't heard nothin yet . . . I figure the way he looked, he's got to be still down there at the hospital."

Dicky Bird's still talkin, but Bill Lovit ain't even tryin to listen no more. He's leanin over, lookin around that piece of plywood floor he got in that shed. Ain't a bit of that early sun gettin that floor light enough to see what he's lookin for. But he's still lookin and now he's reachin down and feelin around that floor. Dicky Bird keeps talkin. He ain't askin Bill Lovit what he's lookin for: he already knows.

Bill Lovit's fingers touch what he's been lookin for. Quickly he's tryin to get his fingers around the neck of that bottle of wine. He's got it now and is sittin back up on the side of his bed. He ain't got to look at it to see how much he got left. He can feel how much he got by just holdin that bottle and he knows he got enough for a good mornin swig. He's openin that bottle and singin, "Wait til the sun shines Nelly . . . And the clouds go driftin by . . . Wait til the sun shines Nelly . . ."

· · ·

Tommy Moses's mouth ain't open no more. His eyes are closed, too. His mama had Mister Hopewell go down that city morgue and get her son out of there. She told Mister Hopewell, "You goes down and gets Tommy for me . . . Gets him a nice suit and puts it on him . . . puts him in a nice shirt. And . . . and . . . and puts a nice tie on him. I wants him to look nice."

Mister Hopewell still got Tommy Moses in that back room of his undertaker shop. He's got Tommy lookin just like his mama wants to see him. Mister Hopewell lives up over his undertaker shop, but he ain't come downstairs yet. He's havin him another cup of coffee and waitin for that sun to get a little higher. Then he's goin to get that coffin he got Tommy Moses in and roll out to that hearse of his. He knows Tommy Moses's mama's waitin on him to bring Tommy on up there to her house for that wake-sittin time. She told him, "You brings him on up here . . . Brings him to his home . . . I wants him here with me just one last time."

Gus Goins is up, been up and cussin out everything he sees. He's already got that front room of his cleaned up. It took him a good time to get Wendell Hill's blood washed off of everything it got on. That broken glass from his jukebox got all over the place, too. He had to get all that cleaned up. He tried to clean up that front room without lookin over at that jukebox and seein it all busted up. He didn't want to see that, see that record-playin arm all broke up and knowin he's got to spend some money real quick to get him another jukebox. He knows it's Friday mornin: Friday night is comin.

Gus Goins's out in that backyard of his gettin them chickens fed and tryin to make up his mind which ones he's goin to cook up for the night. That big white rooster he's lookin at is lookin back at him, givin Gus Goins that kiss-my-ass look. And it's been peckin at him too much for one bad mornin. It was back in the corner of that coop, but it ain't there no more. Gus Goins's got it by its feet. It's bein carried upside down, flappin its wings so fast it's blowin dirt up off the ground. When it ain't clackin, it's stretchin and twistin its neck so it can peck up at Gus Goins's hand; peck at his legs, too. Alley dogs, even them ones way up the alley hearin all that noise that chicken's makin, get to barkin. All that noise ain't makin Gus Goins happier. He was goin to take that chicken over to his choppin block, whack its head off there. But he's quickly grabbin that chicken by its neck, twistin and yankin it around. That chicken's head's comin off real quick, its neck ain't nothin but a handful of shredded, bloody chicken meat. Them wings are still flappin, but Gus Goins ain't hearin no more of that clackin.

That early sunlight is tryin to get in Mack Jack's room again. But it's fallin weak, endin up in that dark shade like it always does. Mack Jack's lyin on his bed watchin that light comin through the window. Sometimes he closes his eyes to it. But when he opens them back up, that light is still there. Slowly, he's gettin up, sittin on the side of his bed. He's leanin over, got his elbows on his knees and his face down in his hands. His eyes are closed and he don't have to see that day tryin to get in his face. It's quiet: them children ain't out playin and fillin up the mornin with all that noise yet. But that silence in Mack Jack's head ain't quiet. It's whisperin, tellin him it's there, ain't goin nowhere. When it ain't whisperin, it's laughin. Then sometimes it gets real quiet, lets Mack Jack think it's let him be. Then, it starts laughin again.

Mack Jack's up from his bed and standin at his window. That sunlight gettin on his face is makin his dark skin silky brown. Them dark blue eyes he has are lookin down from that sky to the tops of them dark houses. Lookin at how them roofs are shaped and them chimneys stickin up to nowhere. That silence is still in his head, whisperin and tellin him it's still there; ain't nothin there cept it.

· EIGHT ·

Everybody livin in Snake Town knew that big new car was sittin in front of Lulu's house and they knew who came in it, too. All them Snake Town children been all around it, tryin to peek up and see in its windows, too. Lulu's oldest child, Sheldon, told all them children, "That's my aunt Wil's car. That's her car. She's come to visit me. She comes from all the ways up north, all the way down here from Pittsburgh . . ."

Some folks were out on their sittin porches stretchin their necks to get a look over at Lulu's house. When they weren't doin that lookin, they were doin that whisperin back and forth. Dorothy Webb was out on her sittin porch whisperin across that yard path runnin between her house and Pauline Russell's house. "Ah ain't seen her yet. She's ain't come out since she went in. She's wit a man . . . Ah ain't seen him either."

Pauline Russell's lookin over at Lulu's house. She's shakin her head back and forth and sayin, "Ah wonder what she come back here for . . . Ah ain't never thought Ah see her again."

That coffee Lulu made ain't hot no more. But Jeremiah's still sippin on it. He's sittin at that table in the cookin room feelin the weariness from the road weighin his mind down. He's sittin quietly, ain't said nothin since he came into the house. Willet and Lulu are sittin at that table, too. Willet's coffee cup is still half full. She ain't touched it in a while, she's smokin a cigarette and starin down at the dark wooden table-top. Lulu's talkin, been talkin real fast sometimes. She's been tellin Willet about her children and when she had them. She's talkin about her marryin Rustin Hampton, too. But when she does, she don't talk as fast and looks down at that tabletop, too. She's up now, goin over to that cookin stove and askin, "Ya all want some more coffee? Ah gots plenty."

Jeremiah shakes his head no. Willet looks at her cup, smiles a little, and says, "You can pour me some."

Lulu's sittin back down at the table. But she ain't talkin now. She's just holdin her cup of coffee in her hands and starin into it. Except for the sounds of them children playin out in the yard, it's quiet. Lulu knows she got to say somethin, ask some-thin. But she keeps starin down into her coffee cup.

That smoke comin from Willet's cigarette is slowly floatin through the small cookin room. Then it's slowly seepin through the little holes in the screen door. Sometimes, Willet raises her eyes from the table, looks through that smoke, and stares. That far-off blue in the sky and the green tops of them trees she's seein ain't nothin but blurry colors in her mind. She's lookin back down at the table now and quietly askin, "Have you seen him?"

Lulu sighs, but she ain't sayin nothin. She lets that silence keep its peace. Softly, Willet's askin, "Does Mama and Papa still have him?"

Lulu sighs, looks up at Willet, then looks back down at the table. Slowly, she begins to speak into the silence. "Mama has him, Wil . . . Wil, Papa . . . Ain't nobody knew where ya were. Ain't nobody knew . . . Papa been dead three years this spring . . . He had one of them strokes, got all crippled, then he has another one and dies . . . Wil, ain't nobody knew where ya were to sends for ya . . . Mama's fine, she got Mason. He's gettin big, looks just like you . . . Mama . . . She . . . Ya know how Mama is."

It's silent for a moment, even the sound of them children playin seems to stay away from the moment. Willet's starin down at the table, that dark wood and coffee cup are as still as the look in her eyes. Lulu's sayin, "Wil, Mama ain't goin to want ya comin around. Ya know how she is. She ain't goin to want that."

"I don't care what Mama wants," Willet mutters softly.

Lulu sighs.

Jeremiah stirs in his seat, then takes a sip of his cold coffee. Willet keeps starin down at the table. That dark wood she's starin at ain't nothin she's seein.

Lulu's softly sayin, "Wil . . . Wil, ya gots to think of Mason . . . Mama's only what he knows . . . Papa gone and he don't know nothin but Mama . . . Mama don't tell him nothin, she says he don't need to be knowin."

"He ain't Mama's child. He's mine," Willet says.

"He don't know nothin, Wil."

"He don't need to know. I know for him. That's my child and I know it and I'll never forget it."

"Mama loves that boy, Wil."

"His mother loves him, too."

"Mama ain't told him nothin. He don't knows ya."

"He will. I'm his mother and Mama ain't goin to keep me away from him."

"Ya ain't been back since ya up and left."

133

Willet looks up at her sister. Lulu's lookin back at her, silently starin into her eyes. Willet looks back down at the table, softly sayin, "I'm back now."

"Wil . . . Mason's bout six or seven years old now. He ain't goin to know nothin about ya. He was just a baby when ya left out of here. Mama . . . Mama all he knows . . . Since Papa gone, Mama ain't got nothin but him, too."

Willet's askin, "What's he look like?"

Lulu's smilin, sayin, "When he was littler, he was so pretty he look just like a little girl. Mama wouldn't let Papa cut his hair. He got that long dark curly hair. It's so pretty. Anybody can see he got your eyes and all. Every time Ah see him now, looks like he done grown up another inch."

Willet's still starin down at the dark table. But her eyes are brightenin, a little smile has come to her face and lingers there.

Lulu's sayin, "Mama don't let him out of her sight. She keeps him from doin all that runnin. He loved Papa. Couldn't get him off Papa's lap when he was a baby. Wil, Mama take good care of him."

That little smile on Willet's face slowly goes away. Lulu's gettin up from the table, goin over to the cookin stove. She's lookin over her shoulder, sayin, "Ah knows ya all hungry. Lets me get somethin on for ya. Got plenty here."

Them little rattlin echoes of them pots bein moved around on the cookin stove stay in the air for a moment. Lulu's tryin to hide the sound of her deep sighs in all that rattlin noise. Jeremiah's tryin to lean back in his chair, get comfortable. Willet's lookin up, back out through that screen door. She's still starin out at the far greens and blues she can see. Lulu's lookin back over her shoulder, askin, "How longs ya stayin, Wil?"

Jeremiah looks at Willet. But she's still starin out the screen door. That clangin noise the pots were makin is gone. Lulu's lookin back over her shoulder, waitin on Willet to answer her. But she ain't seein nothin but a silent look on Willet's face. "Wil," Lulu's askin, "how longs ya stayin til?"

Willet's lookin away from the screen door, givin Lulu a quick stare. Jeremiah's watchin her, waitin on her to answer Lulu. But she's not sayin anything, just slowly lookin back down at the table. Lulu's turnin away, puttin a little grease in one of those pots. She's startin to hum some soft song about her Jesus. Willet's lookin up and askin, "Mama make Mason go to church all the time?"

Lulu's lookin back over her shoulder and sayin, "Ya know Mama, Wil. She ain't missed a day of church since ya been gone. She come early wit Mason, make sure he there for Sunday school and all. Ya should see him all dressed up. He's the cutest little thing ya wants to see."

Willet's still lookin at Lulu, seein her quickly turn away. Lulu's hummin that song about her Jesus again, but she knows it ain't his eyes she feels starin at her back. Slowly, Willet's turnin, lookin at Jeremiah and sayin, "I want to go see him now."

Jeremiah's lookin at Willet; she's starin at him. Lulu ain't hummin no more. She's turnin from that cookin stove and sayin, "Wil . . . Wil, ya can'ts go there. Mama ain't goin to lets ya see him."

.   .   .

Tommy Moses is laid out in his mother's house. Mister Hopewell brought him on up there as soon as he could. He had to find him some extra help to get that coffin carried up in Tommy Moses's mother's house. He needed him some big men. He knew Tommy Moses wasn't goin to get no lighter carry him up them porch steps at his mama's house. Tommy Moses's mama was waitin for him. She told Mister Hopewell, "Just puts him over there in fronts of the mantel. Puts him there where Ah laid his daddy. Lord have mercy . . . now my baby's here."

Ethel Smith been livin next door to Tommy Moses's mama for years. Since she came up from Memphis in the spring of nineteen fifteen. She used to hold Tommy Moses when he was just a baby. She's watchin Mister Hopewell open up that coffin and sayin, "He looks nice . . . He looks nice . . . He looks just likes he sleepin."

Tommy Moses's mama ain't sayin nothin. She's standin real still. Ain't nothin movin on her cept them tears rollin down her cheeks. Mister Hopewell's tryin to say some nice things in a hurry. He knows he got to get on out of there and get down to Saint Francis Hospital. Jackson Kemp is down there, passed on durin the night. Alice Kemp wants him to go on down that hospital and get her husband's body. Mister Hopewell knows he's goin to have a busy day. He already got Althea Chambers layin up his shop, waitin on him to get her embalmed and lookin nice.

Folks don't see much of Reverend Sneed, but know him when they see him. Can't help but look up at him, he bein way over six feet tall. He got that dark yellow skin, almost the same color as all them gold teeth he got in his mouth. But he carry himself fine, always got that preacher collar on and that black preachin suit. He wears that big black hat, too. Folks see him comin, they try to straighten themselves up, too, try to get their heads and shoulders up like his. They try not to talk too long with him, feel like them beady eyes he has is lookin right through them. They got to keep lookin away, don't want him seein all down in their souls. They don't want to be lookin at that Bible he always carryin and thinkin about the last time they opened up their own.

Dicky Bird's finally got Bill Lovit out that shed. They're pushin them wagons up Tioga Street. That noise them wheels are makin is chasin the quiet out of the mornin. Bill Lovit ain't lookin or carin about where he's goin. Dicky Bird's talkin to him. But he ain't listenin. With all that noise them wagons make, he couldn't hear anyway. But that noise, and the fact that Bill Lovit ain't listening, ain't never stopped Dicky Bird from talkin. But he's gettin quiet now, wishin he'd have pushed that wagon a different way. Dicky Bird's seein Reverend Sneed comin down Tioga and knows the Reverend done seen him comin up. He's slowin that wagon down, knowin he's got to stop and say some real nice things. Bill Lovit's wonderin why Dicky Bird's stoppin, he's lookin out over his wagon. Now he's stoppin, too, and sayin real nice, "Good morning, Revernt." But he don't know that early-mornin wine got him yellin what he's sayin.

Dicky Bird's noddin his head and sayin, "Good mornin there, Revernt. Looks like a nice day comin here."

Bill Lovit's yellin over what Dicky Bird's sayin and tellin the Reverend, "Been meanin to come by and see you, Revernt. Yes, sir. Been meanin to come by and talk to you."

Reverend Sneed's in a hurry, got him a few things to do before he goes on and gets him some sleep. He's just gettin off from that nighttime job he has. He works that midnight shift, gots him the top three floors of one of them downtown big office buildings to keep clean. He wears his preachin suit down to work; wants folks to see who he is before he changes into his cleanin clothes. But come Sunday, he's in his shoutin church. And folks say nobody can preach like that man.

Bill Lovit done pushed his wagon over to the sidewalk, smilin and waitin for the reverend to near. Dicky Bird's still out in the street behind his wagon, don't want to get too close to that preachin man. Reverend Sneed knows he got to stop, say somethin, knows he just can't walk on by like he wants to. He ain't that close to Bill Lovit yet, but he don't have to get close to know Bill Lovit ain't got a sober thought in his head.

"Revernt, you just the man Um lookin for this mornin. Yes, sir. I was goin to stop by and sees you anyway. Yes, sir, I sure was," Bill Lovit's tellin the reverend.

That noise them wagon wheels were makin is still rattlin around up in Reverend Sneed's head. He ain't heard a word of what Bill Lovit's been sayin. But he's tryin to pretend like he did. He's nearin Bill Lovit and lookin down at him, sayin, "Well, Mister Lovit, how are you this mornin?"

Bill Lovit's smilin, lookin up and sayin, "Yes, sir, I was comin by to see you. Yep, I was just thinkin about it . . . Tellin myself, I got to go see the revernt. Yes, sir, I was."

Dicky Bird ain't sayin nothin, ain't got the slightest idea of what Bill Lovit's talkin about. Reverend Sneed's sayin, "It's good to see you this mornin, Mister Lovit. It's good to see you too, there, Dicky Bird."

"It's mighty fine seein ya, Revernt," Dicky Bird says back, then goes on and looks down at the ground.

Bill Lovit's tryin to keep himself straight standin, but that early-mornin wine don't like that straight standin. It wants to sway back and forth, have a good time while it's up in Bill Lovit's head. Reverend Sneed's still in that hurry, but Bill Lovit ain't rushin. He's rockin back and forth now, tryin to keep his head up. But it's done started bobbin up and down. Spit's startin to run down his chin at the same time he's tryin to get them words out his mouth. His head's down now and he's lookin at that gold cross hangin down from Reverend Sneed's neck. He's quiet now, just starin at that cross. Reverend Sneed's sayin, "Mister Lovit, I'm goin to have to be on my way here. Gots some errans here . . . Why don't you come to Sunday service? We can talk after service . . . The Lord can turn everything around. Come on in Sunday."

Bill Lovit ain't tryin to look up, ain't even lookin at that cross anymore. He's lookin down at the ground and mutterin, "I ain't gots my children no more, Revernt."

Mister Allen ain't been out on his porch yet. He's still in that front room of his, listenin to and starin at that radio in there. Mister Allen don't like what he's hearin come out that radio, don't like it at all. Mister Allen ain't never heard of no Korea, but he don't like what he's hearin about it. It sounds like that man in the radio is talkin about war comin. He's tellin Mister Allen that them North Korean Communists done attacked South Korea. He's tellin Mister Allen that President Truman is goin to send American troops over there and stop them North Koreans from spreadin that Communism. He's sayin them Russians done gave them North Koreans weapons. Mister Allen likes Mister Truman, thinks he's a straight-talkin man, but he don't like them wars. That man in the radio is still talkin, sayin how General Douglas MacArthur is in command. Mister Allen's still starin at that radio, but he ain't seein it all the time he's lookin at it. Sometimes he's seein his brother, Luther, still young-lookin. He can see him the last time he saw him. See him wavin with that army suit on. Now he's seein his mama cryin when they told her that Luther ain't never comin back, that theys buried him over there in France.

Them children are already out in the alley hollerin and carryin on. Ellen Maben's sittin out on her porch. When she ain't watchin them children, she's lookin up and down the alley. She wants to see who might be comin fore they see her. Her husband, Jimmy, done told her, don't be worryin about Jeremiah and that girl comin back here. He said, he might be crazy, doin that killin. But he ain't stupid enough to come back here.

Ellen Maben's lookin over at Mister Allen's porch, wonderin where he's at. She ain't seen him all mornin. She's still wonderin where Mister Allen is when she sees somethin movin way up the alley. Her eye ain't told her mind what it saw but her mind's tellin that eye it better hurry up and find out. She's lookin up that alley, now she's yellin to them children, "YA GET UP OUT THAT ALLEY . . . COME ON . . . GET OUT THE ALLEY . . . GET YOURSELF UP ON THE PORCHES."

Them children are stoppin that playin, lookin up at Ellen Maben, then turnin and lookin up the alley. Some of them see them cars comin and one of them sees them red lights on top the cars. They start yellin, "POLICEMEN'S COMIN . . . PO-LICEMEN'S COMIN."

Ellen Maben's up out of her chair, she's leanin over that porch rail and keepin her eyes on them police cars comin. They're comin fast, gettin closer. She's yellin at them children,

"YA ALL GET OUT THE ALLEY . . . GETS YOURSELFS UP ON THE PORCH . . . YA HEAR ME? . . ."

The children are backin away from that alley, gettin up on them porch steps. The closer the police cars's gettin, the bigger their eyes are gettin. They done heard about how Pucky finds a dead man, sees him all bleedin. That hush talk their mamas been whisperin about ain't no secret to them. They heard that whisperin, know them policemen's lookin for Mister Jeremiah and Miss Willet.

Them police cars is gettin closer, slowin up. Ellen Maben's backin away from that porch rail, gettin herself closer to her door. Mister Allen's heard enough about that Korea, don't need to hear no more to know another war's comin. He's up out of that chair, turnin that radio man off. But that war comin is still up in his mind, ain't let him have no peace. He's hearin his own sigh and feelin some silence he shouldn't be feelin. It's quiet; them children ain't makin that noise. Now Mister Allen's hearin some cars comin down the alley. He's goin to that door, pullin it open, and slowly peekin his head out. He can see Ellen Maben standin back by her door, see them children gettin up on their porches.

Them police cars are comin fast. Them back alley dogs are barkin, some are chasin the police. The cars ain't slowin down. They're runnin over that old broom handle that's been lyin out in the alley for days. That broom handle's crackin, throwin that crackin sound up in the air with them dog-barkin sounds. Some of them children that's standin on their lower porch steps are gettin up on them higher ones. Mister Allen don't like to see them children gettin scared; he don't like that. Them cars don't have to be comin that fast and that look Mister Allen's gettin on his face is sayin that. He's openin that door all the way, steppin out on his porch, starin at them cars comin.

Them cars are slowin down, then stoppin real fast. Them wheels are skiddin across the alley bricks. Ellen Maben's watchin them stop in front of Jeremiah Henderson's house. She's seein them policemen gettin out the cars. They're pullin them guns out and runnin up Jeremiah Henderson's porch steps. Mister Allen's watchin them, too. Can hear the sounds of them pushin that door open again and the shouts of, "POLICE . . . POLICE."

Lenny Boughner ain't runnin up them steps. He's standin next to his police car, lighting up a cigarette and lookin up and down the alley. Them police that went into Jeremiah Henderson's house are comin back out, shakin their heads, and shoutin down to Lenny Boughner, "Ain't no sign of them, Captain."

Quietly Lenny Boughner's lookin up and down the alley. Now he's lookin up at Ellen Maben and Mister Allen standin on their porches. He's walkin over toward their porches. Them children are watchin every step he's takin. He's lookin at them, sees their big eyes watchin him. Slowly, he smiles and gives them a quick wink of his eye.

Ellen Maben ain't takin her eyes off Lenny Boughner. She's watchin him get closer and closer to the bottom of her porch steps. Mister Allen's watchin him, too. Them other back alley folks heard all that noise and shoutin. They came out, got on their porches, too. That noise is gone now, can't nobody hear nothin cept the sound of Lenny Boughner's footsteps nearin Ellen Maben's porch.

Mister Allen's watchin, tryin to listen, too. Them other policemen have come back down Jeremiah Henderson's steps. They're standin around their cars. Lenny Boughner's lookin up at Ellen Maben askin, "Lady, have you seen those two people that live in that house there? Have you?"

Ellen Maben's lookin down at Lenny Boughner, sayin, "No, sir, I ain't seen em. I ain't seen em at all."

"Do you know those two people that live there? That girl, her name Willet?"

"I know her name is Willet. That's what she say it was. But I don't know her well. She ain't speak to me."

"Her last name Mercer?"

"She ain't never said. Didn't tell me. I ain't never ask her either."

Mister Allen's tryin to hear every word he can hear, see everything he can see. Them other back alley people are stretchin their necks over their porch rails. Some of the children have eased themselves off their porch steps and lookin at them police cars. Lenny Boughner gives that alley a quick up-and-down look, then looks back up at Ellen Maben, sayin, "Well, they goin to have a little problem when I find them. You see em around here again, you call the station, let us know."

Mister Allen's watchin them police cars drive away. They're not down at the end of the alley before the hum of that hush talk fills the air. The children are back in the alley playin. But them folks that were on them porches ain't back in their houses. They're comin off them porches and goin over to Ellen Maben's porch steps.

Mister Allen's done heard and seen all he needs to know. But he's still standin on his porch, thinkin he needs a little bit of that fresh mornin air. Now he's lowerin his head, starin down at some dark shadow hidin down in the corner of his porch. He's liftin his head and goin on back into the house. That war comin done got back into his mind.

. . .

One of them long coal-carryin freight trains is comin around that Wilkensburg bend. That big gray locomotive engine pullin it is blowin its horn, lettin anything that might be in its way know it can't be doin no stoppin. Them big heavy coal cars are rockin back and forth on the tracks, makin that rumblin noise. It's around that curve now, comin down into Homewood. That noise it's makin is gettin into folks' windows, makin them speak up a little louder if they want to be heard.

It's quiet in Mack Jack's room. The train is gone. But it's still runnin through his mind, makin all that noise. It won't get out and give him back that stillness he had in his head. He's up, lookin out his window, starin out at them tops of houses he can see. But he don't stare too long before he turns, goes back to his bed, sits back down on its side. That rumblin noise is still in his head. He's up again, goin to that window and lookin out. His clothes are still lyin on the floor beside his bed. That sunlight comin through the window is gettin on his bare chest, makin his dark skin shine. He's away from the window again, standin in the corner of the room. That sunlight cannot touch him now: he's as dark as the shade he's standin in. But he's lookin out of the shade, starin at the light comin through the window. Now he's reachin down, pickin up his clothes. He's puttin his clothes on. But that rumblin sound is still runnin in his mind. He's goin out of his door, stoppin in the bathroom. He's pissin in the toilet, watchin the yellow stream of piss splash into the water, makin noise. He's flushin the toilet, it's makin that loud gushin sound. It's still makin that sound, it's swirlin around in his head. But he can see his head, his face in the bathroom mirror lookin back at him. He ain't turnin away from it, he's starin at it. He's starin past the darkness of its skin, into the blueness of its eyes. That gushin sound is still swirlin around and around in his head. But them eyes ain't movin. They're lookin into themselves.

It's quiet, been quiet, one of them quiet mornins for Miss Alberta. She's sittin on the porch of her roomin house. Edmund Yates is sittin out there, too. He's got that shawl over his shoulders, his chin is down restin on his chest. His eyes are closed, but his mouth is wide open. That sunlight is fallin on his face, but it can't get down into them deep wrinkles. They're dark in the light, dark wriggly lines runnin forever across his face. Sometimes he breathes, gets a little air, then sits and waits for the next breath to come. Miss Alberta's talkin to him, always does. She tells him everything she got to say sometimes. She knows he ain't listenin, maybe can't even hear her. But that don't make her no never mind, she talks to him anyway.

Miss Alberta's hearin footsteps comin down her stairs. She knows whose footsteps they are. She's been waitin on them and knows she will hear them comin through her hallway, comin out onto her porch. She's lookin over to Edmund Yates, then rollin her eyes to the sound of them footsteps she hears comin and whisperin, "He's comin. I hear him comin now . . . I don't know who he thinks I am."

Ain't nothin on Edmund Yates movin or makin a sound. He ain't hearin a word Miss Alberta's sayin. Some fly's buzzin around his open mouth, but he ain't payin it no mind either.

"Just who he think he is? Hum." Miss Alberta's mutterin as she hears them footsteps gettin closer.

Edmund Yates ain't openin an eye.

Mack Jack's at the bottom of them steps now. He's comin through that dark hallway. He's pushin that screen door open and steppin out onto the porch. Edmund Yates doesn't even know he's there. Miss Alberta's tryin to pretend she ain't heard him comin.

Mack Jack stops, stands in front of the screen door. He's takin a whiff of the freshness that's left in the mornin air. Now he's lookin over at that old man. Edmund Yates's chin ain't movin from that spot on his chest it's restin on. Miss Alberta's lookin up at Mack Jack, waitin on him to look her way. Slowly he's turnin his head, she's watchin him, sees him lookin at her, smilin at her with his eyes. But it's a quick smile that turns away from her as he begins to walk by. Miss Alberta ain't smilin, she's callin out to him, askin, "Where's you goin?"

Mack Jack slows, but he ain't turnin around and lookin back. He's just shakin his head back and forth real slow. Miss Alberta pokes her mouth out some and says, "We gots to talk here some."

Mack Jack stops at the edge of the porch, but he ain't turnin around. He's standin there in his own silence.

"I needs to talk to you."

Mack Jack's lookin back at her over his shoulder.

"I gots to have my money."

Mack Jack's silent.

"You ain't givin me nothin for the room all month, now."

Mack Jack's silent.

"I gots to have my money. I tries to be nice about it,

but you can't be stayin here without payin. I can't have thats."

Slowly Mack Jack's turnin his head, lookin off, and starin across the street.

"I needs my money."

Mack Jack's silent. Miss Alberta's got her mouth poked out. She's starin at the back of his head, waitin on him to turn around and look at her. He ain't turnin and she's sayin, "It's Friday . . . I wants my money come Monday mornin. You hear me? I wants my money. I don't have my money, you got to finds you someplace else."

Oliver McCray's comin up Tioga Street, got that Friday mill money in his pocket. He's done worked all night and ain't thinkin about nothin cept gettin home, gettin him some sleep. His eyes don't want to wait til he gets home, they half-closed already, til he sees Mack Jack comin down the street. Oliver McCray is gettin that good-mornin smile on his face and callin out, "Hey, man, what you up to this mornin?"

Mack Jack's nearin Oliver McCray, lookin at him. Oliver McCray is stoppin, sayin, "Where you headed this time of the mornin?"

Mack Jack ain't slowin down. He's lookin at Oliver McCray but ain't sayin nothin, just lookin. Oliver McCray's eyes are gettin real big; he's watchin Mack Jack just walk on by. Oliver McCray's mutterin, "You silly-ass motherfucker."

Gladys Lymon is out in that front yard of hers, always is in them nice mornins. She keeps that yard of hers lookin nice, keeps them weeds away from her roses. She's bendin over til she hears the sound of them footsteps comin down the sidewalk. She's straightenin up, lookin to see who's comin. She likes to give folks a "good mornin" when they pass. Most folks that ain't in no hurry stop and tell her how pretty her flowers are lookin. Mack Jack ain't stoppin. She's callin out, "Good mornin . . . How are you?"

Miss Alberta sat on her porch for a while, told Edmund Yates everything she was thinkin about Mack Jack. She told him, "He better has my money come the first thing Monday mornin."

Edmund Yates is still sittin on that porch. Miss Alberta got up and went on into the house. That mornin ain't quiet no more, since all them porch-sittin folks are out on their porches talkin back and forth. Them children are playin them ball games in the street. Edmund Yates got his chin up and his eyes open. All that noise them children are makin, he ain't hearin at all. Some little cool mornin breeze was blowin, blew across his face, but it stopped. He's waitin on it to blow again.

· NINE ·

That high Snake Town sun was gettin real hot. That high noon hour was gettin close. The tops of them shanties were gettin to look like they were bakin. That heat comin down on them was so hot you could see it simmerin. Them dogs that had any kind of sense at all crawled up under them sittin porches and tried to find them some shade. But them little barefoot, big-eyed Snake Town children ain't never paid that heat no mind. Old folks watchin them doin all that playin out in the sun would sit back in whatever shade they could find and just shake their heads. But them old folks and anybody else sittin out on them sittin porches that can see Lulu's house ain't thinkin about them children now. They're stretchin their necks and starin through that glarin hot air at Lulu's porch.

Willet's out on Lulu's porch. She's standin at the edge of the porch, leanin up against one of them porch posts. Folks lookin at her know she ain't lookin back at them. They can see she's got her head down and ain't looked up since she's been standin there. All that noise them children are makin ain't gettin nowhere near that silence around her. She's got her arms folded across her breast. Her head is gently leanin against that post she's up against. If she looks up, it's only with her eyes.

Jeremiah's still in that cookin room, and that weariness

from the road won't get out of his mind. Lulu's sittin at that table talkin to him, but he ain't sayin much back. Sometimes he doesn't want to say anything back at all. Lulu's askin, "Ya gots people up in New York?"

Jeremiah's noddin his head yes and sayin, "Yeal, I got my brother up there."

"Your mama ain't up there, too?" Lulu's askin.

"No, she's still livin in Jersey. She lives in Newark."

"That's where ya be bornin and all?"

"Yeal . . . Yeal, I was born there."

"Your daddy up there?"

"No, ahh . . . No, he ain't up there."

"Oh," Lulu's sayin quietly and tryin not to let her eyes drift. She doesn't want to look out through that screen door. But she's lookin anyway, takin a quick peek at Willet standin out on that porch. Then she's lookin back at Jeremiah and sayin, "Ah likes to get out of here, too. Goes up there somewhere. Rustin keep sayin he's goin to take us on up there. He says he's goin to take us up there to Detroit. His sister be up there. He say he's goin to get one of them jobs makin cars. But he's been sayin that."

Jeremiah ain't sayin nothin.

Lulu's quiet for some long moment, too. Slowly she's turnin her head, lookin through that screen door and softly sayin, "Wil gots to know Mama ain't gonna want her seein Mason. Mama's goin to have a fit if Wil goes out there."

Jeremiah's turnin his head, lookin out that screen door. Lulu's askin, "Ya works in one of them mills up there?"

Jeremiah's turnin his head, lookin at Lulu. Now he's lookin down at the table and sayin, "Yeal, I worked in the mill."

Lulu's lookin back at Jeremiah and askin, "When ya gets that new car? That's one of them brand new kind, ain't it?"

Quickly Jeremiah's sayin, "I got that a couple months ago. It runs good. It's a Buick."

"It's real nice."

"It runs good," Jeremiah's sayin and lookin back out that screen door.

That sunlight is hot on Willet's face, but she ain't feelin it in her mind. She's starin down at that dirt path comin to the porch, but she ain't seein it in her mind. Them folks that can see her still got their necks stretchin out lookin at her. Sometimes she sees them, sees their dark faces in the shade, but her mind wanders past them.

· · ·

It wasn't as noisy down that Snake Town road past the church and Daddy Jake's. There wasn't too many folks livin down there, but it was just as hot. Della Stucky was goin down that road, was hurryin down there, too. That big straw hat she had on was keepin some of that sun out her eyes and off her head. But that walkin-fast sweat was still rollin down her dark brown face. She's done passed that A.M.E. church, looked its way, could hear that Sunday mornin singin in her mind. But that singin didn't stay in her mind too long. She hurried on past that church and kept thinkin about what she was carryin in her mind. The farther she was gettin down that road, the heavier them thoughts she had in her mind was gettin. She's hurryin around that dark shady curve in the road, knowin she ain't got far to go.

Everybody in Snake Town and most of them folks in Stoney Town had known Vergil Mercer. Folks say he was a quiet-walkin man, carried himself well wherever he went. He was a big tall man, had them high cheekbones and that dark, tree bark–colored skin. Vergil Mercer liked to keep to himself, didn't like nothin that wasn't respectable. He had him some land out there past the church, had him two mules to work his own plantin fields. Folks say all that workin by himself is what bring that stroke down on him. They say all that age he had on him couldn't take all them long days no more.

Gertrude Mercer was one of them young, high-yellow, good-lookin Wilmington women. Vergil Mercer went on up there to Wilmington and kept on goin up there til she come back to Snake Town with him to be his wife. Folks wondered why that pretty woman be wantin to come down from Wilmington to live in Snake Town, when most folks they knew were tryin to get out. But after them years kept comin and goin, folks stopped that wonderin, don't even talk about it no more. Gertrude Mercer had her ways, too. Some folks said she carried her nose too high. And when she had them girl children, she acted like they were too good to be around them other Snake Town children. But everybody knew that woman could sing. Come Sunday mornin down at the church, folks say when she got to singin, even them birds outside would shut up and listen. Sometimes she could get to shoutin, too, be tellin her God and everybody else about the troubles she has. But folks don't talk about Gertrude Mercer's girl Willet, they just whisper.

Della Stucky's around that curve in the road and still hurryin. She has her head up, lookin to see if anyone's out on that far porch she can see. But she can't see nothin cept the stillness and the shade on the porch. She's hurryin, turnin off the road and up the long yard path.

Out behind Gertrude Mercer's home, it is always quiet in them fields. In the trees along that side fence, the shade hides secrets. Some brown little pullin wagon's been pulled back under them trees. It's in a small clearin beneath some low-hangin branches. It's got things in the back of it, a shiny empty tin can, a big empty glass jar, some stuffed soft ball with the stuffins hangin out of it, and a small brown-shell turtle. That turtle's got its head stickin out of its shell. That turtle's takin a few slow steps, then stoppin and lookin around. It knows it can't get up over that little wagon rail keepin it in. But it moves close to it, stares at it, then slowly turns from it and moves toward the shiny tin can. It can see the shiny reflection of its old man's–lookin face starin back at it. Quickly it's pullin its old man's face and its old wrinkled legs back into its shell. It's bein picked up out of the wagon and gently bein placed on the ground. It's hearin the sounds of a soft voice callin to it, but it ain't stickin its face back out of its shell. That soft voice keeps callin at it, "Toby . . . Toby . . . Toby."

That turtle's slowly stickin its head out of its shell, lookin around. That shade in that small clearin is cool, dark. Only a few streaks of the sun's rays are gettin down through them low-hangin branches and thick leaves. Mason Mercer's standin next to his little pullin wagon, lookin down at that turtle. His eyes are big, bright brown. That little bit of sunlight comin down through them leaves is makin that black curly hair of his shine in the shade. He ain't got no shirt on, them hard back-bendin times ain't come down on him yet. His skin is still soft, tender. His skin was light, creamy color, but the hot summer

Snake Town sun has made it golden brown. He's quietly watchin the turtle; it ain't movin. He's whisperin to it, callin it by that name he gave it. He's tellin it, "Come on, Toby . . . Come on, Toby, sticks your head out more. Come on."

Gertrude Mercer gets up before that sun comes up. She gets the chickens and the two mules fed. Then she gets out in them fields of hers, gets that pickin done for her day. That food she ain't pickin for herself, she gets it ready to sell, make her some dollars for what else she needs. But come that high noon time, she likes to get in the house, get her quiet time. She's got that chair in the back room she sits in, reads her Bible, whispers to her God. Sometimes she gets up, looks out that window, makes sure Mason ain't too far out of her sight. She's lookin for him now; can't see him or that little wagon he pulls around. But she's hearin her name bein called.

Della Stucky's comin up that long yard path. She's lookin up to that shady porch and callin out, "Yew-hew . . . Yew . . . Sister Gertrude . . . Yew-hew . . . Sister Gertrude . . . Yous in there? Yew-hew."

Gertrude Mercer's turnin away from her back window. She's knows Mason ain't far, probably done pulled his little wagon up under them trees. She's hurryin out of that back room, goin into that front room. She's tryin to look through that screen door to see who's callin for her. That "Yew-hew, Yew-hew," she's hearin is quickly tellin her who's callin for her. She's openin that screen door and goin out onto the porch. Della Stucky sees her, quickly calls out, "Yew-hew . . . Sister Gertrude."

Gertrude Mercer's slowly walkin to the edge of her sittin porch, she's watchin Della Stucky hurryin up that path. She knows that fast walkin ain't bringin nothin but trouble. She can see Della Stucky's face beneath the brim of that straw hat she's wearin. But she can't see her eyes, she keeps lookin, tryin to see what them eyes might be gettin ready to tell her. She can't wait to see Della Stucky's eyes. She's callin out, "What's the matter, Sister Della?"

That sun is beatin down on Della Stucky's head. She's keepin her face down, hurryin toward them porch steps. Gertrude Mercer's standin at the top of them steps. She's still waitin on Della Stucky to look up, tell her what she's hurryin to tell her. Except for the sounds of Della Stucky's footsteps comin up that path, it is quiet. But it ain't quiet in Gertrude Mercer's mind. She's callin up to her God, tellin him, Lord, please don't bring no more troubles here.

Della Stucky's slowin, tryin to get some of that breath back she done lost to all that hurryin. She's takin her time comin up them steps. Gertrude Mercer's watchin her, askin, "Is somethin the matter, Sister Della?"

"Ah hads to come on here," Della Stucky's mutterin, comin up them steps.

"Somethin done happen?" Gertrude Mercer's askin.

"Ah hads to come, soons Ah sees it, Ah hads to come," Della Stucky's mutterin, tryin to get her a good breath. She's up on that porch now, but her head's still lowered. Gertrude Mercer's lookin, waitin to see her face. Quickly she's askin, "Somethin the matter, Sister Della?"

Slowly, Della Stucky's lookin up, sighin and whisperin, "Willet's comes to Lulu's. It be her. Ah sees her."

Slowly Gertrude Mercer's lowerin her head, bringin up her hand to her brow. Her other hand ain't movin; it's hangin loosely at her side.

"It be her, Ah sees her."

Gertrude Mercer ain't takin her hand down from her eyes. She's closed herself and ain't sayin nothin.

"It be her. Ah sees her out on the porch. She comes in one of them big cars. Children say some man brings her. He be theres, too. Ah sees her . . . It be her, Ah knows that."

Gertrude Mercer's takin her hand down from her eyes. She's rushin down them steps and hurryin around to the back of her house. She's lookin out over them fields.

It's still quiet and cool back in the shade of them trees along the side fence. That turtle done crawled up under some bush, but Mason knows where it's at. He ain't let that turtle get out of his sight. He's down on his hands and knees, peekin under that bush. He's whisperin at that turtle, tellin it, "Toby . . . Toby . . . Yous get back here . . . Yous hear me? Come on, Toby."

"MASON . . . MASON . . . MASON . . . WHERE ARE YOU? YOU COME HOME. MASON . . . COME HOME." Gertrude Mercer's yellin out over them fields.

Della Stucky's walkin back up that Snake Town road. She's takin her time, don't need to be doin no hurryin now. She passed that church, heard that singin in her mind again, got to hummin along with it. Them porch-sittin folks that's watchin her comin know where she's comin from. Most folks ain't left their porches. The ones that can see Lulu's house keep lookin over there. Willet ain't on that porch anymore. They watched her leanin up against that post til she jerked her head up, looked at them real hard, then turned and went back into the house. But they can still see her; that look she gave them is lingerin in their minds.

Lulu's children keep runnin in the house wantin to eat and bringin that playin noise with them. Them little girls she has been peekin at Willet, lookin at her hair and wantin her to look back. Sometimes Willet looks up, smiles, then quietly lowers her head. Lulu's been chasin them children back outside, tellin them it ain't eatin time. Then she sits quietly at that table and waits on Willet to say something, anything. Jeremiah's quiet, too. When he ain't lookin down at that table, he's lookin out through that screen door.

Lulu's starin down at her hands, that are holdin that cup of cold coffee. She ain't drinkin that coffee no more, just holdin it. She's feelin Willet lookin up and starin at her. Slowly Lulu raises her head, looks at Willet, and hears her sayin, "Lulu, I'm goin out there now. That's my child Mama got."

Jeremiah keeps lookin out through that screen door. Lulu's lookin at Willet and ain't sayin nothin. But Willet ain't lowerin her eyes, she keeps starin at Lulu as she says, "I'm goin out there now."

Lulu's sighin, lookin back down at that coffee cup and sayin, "Wil, ya can'ts do that. Thinks of Mason."

"I am."

.   .   .

Lenny Boughner's quiet, he's sittin in that office of his down at Number Five Police Station. He got his door closed because he don't want to be bothered. That little radio was on, but he's turned it off. One of them cigarettes he smokes is burnin in the ashtray. That smoke from it been curlin up into the air. But he ain't thinkin about that cigarette burnin. That quick tappin on his door is makin him flinch. He's lookin at that door and yellin, "Yeal, come on in."

Clifford Valansky is comin through that door in a hurry.

He's always in a hurry, got them fast ways about him. He likes bein a policeman, always got his uniform clean, got starch in his shirts, too. He ain't through the door all the way before he's sayin, "Got somethin on that Moses murder."

"Huh?" Lenny Boughner's askin.

"Got somethin on them two."

"What?"

"That Henderson did a little time up in Sing Sing. Armed robbery, larceny, name it, he likes it. We got a Newark address on him."

"What about the girl?" Lenny Boughner's askin as he smashes that cigarette out in the ashtray.

"We think she's this girl they had down Number Two. They had her down there a couple times, shoplifting, resisting arrest. Yeal, we think it's the same girl. We got a last name on her, Mercer, Willet Mercer. Looks like she's from North Carolina, Wilmington area."

"What about the car, it show up yet?"

"No, no sign of it."

"All right, wire New York, give them a make on that car. And wire Wilmington, just in case."

"What do you want them on: stolen car, suspicion of murder?"

"Yeal."

Clifford Valansky went as fast as he came. Lenny Boughner's lighting up another cigarette and lookin at that little radio of his. It ain't on, but he keeps starin at it. Now he's turnin and lookin at that picture he has on his desk. The eyes in that picture are lookin back at him. Them two little girls in that picture look just like their mother. Their mother has her arms around them and is smilin, lookin out of that picture at him. He's sighin, seein days and nights in his mind he doesn't want to think about again. Dead men's faces he ain't forgot about, callin his name, callin him back. He doesn't want to hear them callin his name, doesn't want to hear that radio talkin about another war.

Clayton Bass is old, seen them seventy-eight years go by slow and hard. That time bent his back and that walkin up them porch steps to give Tommy Moses them last respects ain't did nothin but put pain in his eyes and all over his face. He's lookin down at Tommy Moses and takin them big, long, deep sighs. Tommy Moses's mother is standin next to him. She ain't got too far away from that coffin all mornin. When ain't nobody else there cept her, she goes over and stands over that coffin, ask her God why Tommy went the way he went. Sometimes she reaches over into the coffin and gently touches Tommy Moses's face. It ain't cold to her.

Clayton Bass is still lookin down at Tommy Moses, but he's talkin now, mutterin, "Ah knew this boy's daddy, knews him well. Good man. Ah hates to see him goes. When Ah hears abouts this boy, it breaks my heart to hears it. Ah thinks about his daddy. Lord's got them both up theres now. He calls ya, ya gots to come."

Tommy Moses's mother is quiet. Clayton Bass's voice wasn't nothin in her ear cept some soft mutterin sound. He's still talkin, sayin, "Ah has to come on up here to gives my respects."

Clayton Bass is gone now. Tommy Moses's mother is alone again. It's quiet. The sounds of children playin out on the street are comin through the open windows. But them sounds slow, stop, stay away from that coffin and let Tommy Moses's mother have her silence.

Bill Lovit's gettin tired of pushin that cart. He's tellin Dicky Bird he needs some rest. Dicky Bird don't like that stoppin durin the day. He knows he got to find him enough good stuff he can get a couple dollars with. And he knows he ain't found nothin worth a dime all mornin. He's wipin the sweat from the back of his neck, lookin at Bill Lovit and sayin, "Ah gots to gets me somethin fore this day gone."

Bill Lovit ain't payin any mind to Dicky Bird. He's pushin his cart up into some empty lot. Dicky Bird's still tryin to get that sweat off his neck. He's takin some quick peeks up at that sun, too, tryin to see how much day's gone by. He knows if Bill Lovit gets to sittin down for a minute, he ain't back up for an hour.

Bill Lovit sees some shade next to that big high fence at the back end of that lot. He's leavin his cart set and gettin over to that shade. Dicky Bird's tryin to figure what he should do. He knows it's Friday and he always likes to have him a few more dollars come them weekend days. Bill Lovit ain't tryin to figure out nothin, not even where to sit himself down beside that fence. He knows that big piece of cardboard is lyin over there by that fence. It's been lyin over there, got that damp air smell comin out of it from all that rain that done soaked it. But Bill Lovit ain't thinkin about no damp air smell. He's already sittin on it, leanin back up against that fence. That bottle of his is up, too, and that little bit of wine he got left in it is flowin down his throat.

Dicky Bird's pushin his cart up into that empty lot, too. He still ain't figured out what he should do, he just got tired of doin that figurin. That wine bottle ain't empty yet. Bill Lovit's holdin it up, shakin it, and can see that little last drop swirlin around in it. He's goin to try and get that last little drop, too. He's got that bottle up again, got his head tilted back as far as he can get it. The bottom of that bottle is pointin straight to the sky.

Dicky Bird don't like that sittin down durin the day. But he's sittin down anyway and leanin back up against that fence. That shade he's sittin in is coverin his face, coolin that sweat on the back of his neck. He's starin out into that empty lot, seein them little pieces of broken glass glitterin in the sunlight. Bill Lovit's mumblin, "Gots to gets me some."

Dicky Bird ain't thinkin about what Bill Lovit said. He's lookin out in that empty lot and thinkin about that dollar he ain't gettin as long as he sits there. Bill Lovit's squirmin around, tryin to get his hands in every pocket he has and mumblin, "I hads me a dollar, I know . . . I know I had some money. I put me a dollar in my pocket. Keeps it in there. I know I had it in there."

Dicky Bird's lowerin his eyes away from that bright sunlight heatin up that empty lot. He's lookin down into that shade around his feet, lookin at things he ain't thinkin about. Bill Lovit's still squirmin around, diggin in his pockets. He ain't findin what he's lookin for. That bottle he got lyin out in front of him is tellin him it's empty. He ain't never no more gettin anything out of it. He don't like what that empty bottle and his empty pockets is tellin him. He's pullin his hands out of his pockets and makin some quick groanin sounds. Dicky Bird ain't payin him no mind, he's still lookin down into the shade. That bottle is lyin near Bill Lovit's feet. He's kickin at it and tellin Dicky Bird, "I needs me a dollar."

Dicky Bird's silent.

"Lets me hold a dollar?" Bill Lovit's askin.

Dicky Bird's keepin his head down, but he's sayin, "Ah ain't gots it."

"Don't tells me that. You got to got somin. You got fifty cents. I know you got somin."

"Ah tell ya now, Ah ain't gots it."

"You got somin."

Dicky Bird ain't sayin nothin, he's keepin his head down. But Bill Lovit ain't shuttin up. He's sayin, "I knows you got somin. You knows I gives it back. Come on, we can goes down Gus's. Gets somin down there."

Dicky Bird's jerkin himself up from that fence. Bill Lovit's lookin at him and askin, "Where you goin, huh?"

Dicky Bird ain't answerin, he's walkin out of that shade. Bill Lovit's callin after him, sayin, "Where's goin? You just goin to leave me here?"

"Ah ain't got no time to be sittin. Ah gots my work. Ain't got time for that drinkin. No, sir, ain't got time for it," Dicky Bird's shoutin back over his shoulder.

"You thinks you too good for me. You think you too good. Let me tell you somin. I gots my dignity. I got my respects. Go on and go."

Dicky Bird ain't lookin back, he's gettin his cart and pushin it out of that lot. Bill Lovit ain't lookin at him no more, he's lookin down at that empty bottle. Them sounds of Dicky Bird's wagon wheels rollin over that lot is fillin up the air. But them sounds are gone now and Bill Lovit got that bottle back up to his mouth.

Folks up on Homewood Avenue got them sidewalks filled up doin that shoppin. Them folks that ain't goin in stores are stoppin and lookin in windows. Joey Deluca got that fruit stand there at Homewood Avenue and Kelly Street, right across from the five and dime. Folks can hear him tellin what he got for them a half a block away, know it's him before they get close enough to see him. They know he'll have that white fruit-stained apron on, tied around all that fat belly he got, that red handkerchief tied around dark gray hair he got. He's holdin a handful of peaches in one hand and a half a watermelon in the other. He's chantin, "COME GETS YOUR PEACHES . . . GET YOUR PEACHES . . . GOT YOUR MELONS HERE, TOO."

Folks walkin by that fish market that don't want no fish hurry on by. Try to get past that stink before it gets too far up their noses. Them kids that got their wagons out in front of grocery stores, waitin to haul some groceries, got them sidewalks all cluttered up. Folks got to zigzag through them. But when they see Blinky comin, twirlin that policeman's stick, they get the wagons out the way and behave if they weren't.

Friday is Rita Block's shoppin day. She lives in one of them big mansion-lookin houses on the other side of the tracks. She loves to stop and do that talkin, too. Gloria Spillman saw her comin; wished she hadn't. But she knew Rita Block seen her comin, too. They're doin that talkin now, out in front of Isaly's ice cream store. Rita Block's sayin, "My oldest, Debbie, is having her second. She's out in California. She's expecting in August."

Gloria Spillman's gettin ready to say somethin back. But she ain't now. Rita Block got her mouth open, but she ain't sayin nothin either. She's glarin at the back of Mack Jack, who just walked between them, almost bumped them out the way. And didn't say pardon me.

Mack Jack ain't stoppin to look in the windows. He's

walkin down Homewood Avenue with his head up high. But he still looks like he ain't seein nothin he's lookin at. That high sun is makin the blue in his eyes look brighter and his dark skin look darker. Folks that ain't never seen him before don't want to do that starin, but they got to do that lookin.

Mack Jack's turnin off Homewood Avenue, going down Kelly Street. Joey Deluca's tryin to sell him some peaches, tellin him about them melons he wants to sell, too. He's holdin them peaches up for Mack Jack to see, but Mack Jack ain't lookin. Kelly Street doesn't go too far from Homewood Avenue before it ends at that wide Washington Street, where all them big trucks keep goin by. But Mack Jack's goin farther than Kelly Street goes. He's crossin that big wide street, walkin between them trucks whizzin by.

Mack Jack's in East Liberty now, he's walkin up Meadow Street. It ain't too far from Elmira Avenue, but folks that live on Meadow Street try to stay as far away as they can from that Elmira Avenue. Some of them Meadow Street folks are on their sittin porches, tryin to enjoy any quiet time that comes by. Clyde Boykin's sittin out on his porch readin that *Sun Telegraph* newspaper. He got them bifocal readin glasses down at the end of his nose. But everytime he can hear somebody walkin by, he got to lower that paper, look out over them glasses to see who it is. He doesn't want good folks passin to think he ain't speakin, too busy to be polite to them. He's lookin over his glasses at Mack Jack walkin by. Now he's slowly puttin that paper back up in front of his eyes, pretendin he ain't seein nobody.

Mack Jack slows, stops when he reaches Elmira Avenue. He's lookin up and down the avenue. Some of them Elmira

Avenue young men are standin across the street. One of them is lookin at Mack Jack and whisperin to the others. The ones that weren't lookin are turnin their heads and lookin, too. Mack Jack turns and starts walkin up the avenue. The young men across on that corner keep watchin him.

Shorty Fletcher ain't much taller than one of them fire hydrants stickin up at one of them Elmira Avenue corners. He got one of them real big heads. Folks say he got one of them water heads, must have been born like that. They say that's why he act like he ten instead of that thirty he must be by now. He's out in front of that Satin Club, doin one of them sweepin-up jobs he got. Folks see that broom handle stickin way up in the air lookin like it's movin by itself, til they look down and see Shorty Fletcher pushin it. Some of them Elmira Avenue kids like pickin on him. They wait til he ain't lookin, throw some empty can at him, call him a big watermelon head, then they run. They know he can't catch them, them short legs he has be movin real fast. But it still take him forever to get twenty feet up the street, and them kids be around the block by then.

Shorty Fletcher just about got that sidewalk all cleaned up. He got all them empty bottles and the rest of that dirt swept up into a big pile. He's lookin down at that pile smilin, but that smile comin off his face real fast. His eyes are gettin big watchin them feet he's seein knockin some of them bottles away from his pile. He's lookin up, way up, and yellin, "What you do that for, huh? You see my pile, you seen it there. Why you do that for?"

Mack Jack's slowin, lookin down at that little man yellin up at him.

"What you do that for, huh?" Shorty Fletcher's yellin up at Mack Jack. But Mack Jack ain't sayin nothin back and that ain't makin Shorty Fletcher's smile come back on his face. He's snarlin like one of them little street dogs gettin ready to snap. Slowly Mack Jack's stoopin down, pickin up them bottles he kicked away from that pile and puttin them back. He's lookin at Shorty Fletcher and whisperin something to him. That smile is comin back on the little man's face.

That sunlight out on Elmira Avenue doesn't get back in them narrow walkways between some of them buildings. Folks got to always walk through that dark shade to get to them outside steps back there. Them steps go up to the upper floors of them buildings. All kinds of folks live up there in them rented rooms. But them folks livin up there can always tell when somebody that don't live up there is comin up the steps. They stick their heads out of doors or peek out their windows to see who it is. They don't need no law comin up there and gettin in their business. Them steps ain't squeakin right and Salina Amos ain't expectin nobody comin to see her while the sun's still up. She's grabbin that money on the table, stickin it down in her panties, and wrappin her nightgown around her real tight. The squeaky sounds of someone comin up the steps is gettin closer. She's tiptoein to her window and peekin out through those dark maroon curtains she has coverin that window. She knows can't nobody be lookin in on her and nobody can see her peekin out. She's seein someone comin, stares at that dark sweaty face until it gets to her landin. Now she can only see the side of it as it passes. But she ain't gettin away from that window. That face done passed, but it's still stuck up in her mind. She can't see it anymore, but she can hear the sounds of footsteps going up to the next floor. But them steps are still squeakin wrong.

Bella lives up on that next floor. Folks that know her, don't know her last name and ain't never asked. But they know she lives up on that top floor and keeps to herself up there. If they do see her, it ain't for long. But they stop what they might be doin, watch her til they can't see her no more. Some of them Elmira Avenue men that see her passin can't take their eyes away from her. They see that tall, dark, red-skinned woman with them bright eyes and that long black hair hangin all the way down her back. In their minds they try to see how long her legs are that she keeps covered with long skirts. She lets them look, doesn't turn to them whispers she might hear. But the men just whisper, they don't give her that, "Hey, Baby" talk. They keep them whispers quiet, lower their heads if they think she's goin to look their way. But them Elmira Avenue women don't bother doin that lookin anymore, but they still do that whisperin. Salina Amos does a lot of that whisperin talk. She tells them other women just what she thinks of that so-called Bella. She tells them, "I can hear her up there doin that chantin she does. She's piculiar. And that cat she got up there is just as piculiar-actin as she is. I don't like them black cats. That thing sits at my window and looks at me, have to get a broom after it."

Salina Amos is still listening to the sounds of them steps squeakin and wonderin who's goin up them stairs. Except for the sunlight comin through that back room Bella's in, it is dark. But that light comin through the window can show her what she's starin at. It can show her the grain in that small piece of dark wood she's carvin up. Half of that small piece of wood is lookin like a dark face in the night. Its eyes are big, bulgin out of the wood as if they are starin into darkness. That cat is lyin on the table that Bella's sittin at. It is watchin the sharp knife she has in her hand chip and cut into the wood til it hears them steps squeakin. Quickly it's jumpin off the table, disappearin into the darkness along the lower walls of the room. Bella hears the sound of the stairs squeakin, the sound of footsteps nearin her door. But she keeps chippin and cuttin into the wood.

Little bubbles of sweat are slowly runnin down Mack Jack's face and droppin on his shirt. He's standin at Bella's door, slowly and lightly tappin on it, then waitin in silence for it to open. The black cat is in a dark corner, it meows. Salina Amos is still by her window, listening to the tappin she can hear and wonderin who that man is. But Bella knows, knew from the way the steps squeaked, who was at her door. She's layin the knife down on the table, gettin up from her chair, and walkin toward the door.

The door is opening and Mack Jack's lowerin his eyes away from Bella's. She's starin silently at his face, but Mack Jack ain't lookin up. Softly Bella's sayin, "You look a pity. Come in here."

Slowly Mack Jack steps inside and stands silently. Bella closes the door, walks past him. He follows her into the kitchen; it is cool, shady, and dark in there. That ceiling light bulb ain't on and them curtains at the windows are keepin that sunlight out. Mack Jack stops in the center of the kitchen, slowly looks toward that light tryin to get through them curtains. Bella is goin to the sink, but she stops, turns around, looks at Mack Jack. He ain't looked away from them windows. Softly Bella's sayin, "Sit down."

Mack Jack's turnin to the sound of her voice. He's lookin at her eyes starin at him.

"Sit down, I'm goin to get you a glass of ice water. Sit down," Bella says and keeps starin at Mack Jack til she sees him lower his eyes from hers.

Mack Jack looks around the kitchen, sees a chair in the far corner of the room. He goes to the chair, sits, but leans over and stares down at that linoleum-covered floor. Them dark colors, blues, browns in that linoleum sorta swirl around them brighter colors of reds and yellows. Mack Jack's lookin at the brighter colors, them darker colors all look the same gray in the shade. Some of that sweat rollin down his face is drippin quietly down onto the floor. Bella's droppin ice cubes into a glass of water. That soft clatterin sound of the ice cubes dangles in that dark shade Mack Jack's sittin in. He's lookin up and leanin back in his chair. Bella's bringin him the glass of water, handin it to him. It is cold in his hands. He's holdin the glass, lookin up at her as she reaches, touches, slowly begins to rub her hand over his sweaty forehead. Softly she's tellin him, "Go on, drink the water."

Mack Jack's lookin down at the glass of water and bringin it up to his mouth. He's drinkin the water, takin slow, long gulps. Bella's gently rubbin the side of his face; it is still hot and sweaty. Her hand is slidin through the sweat, her fingers are touchin the side of his mouth. Very slowly she's rubbin her thumb over his lips, around the smooth top of the glass, and into his mouth. Mack Jack's lowerin the glass away from his lips, cold water is drippin down his chin. Bella is rubbin her thumb over his tongue, takin her other hand and caressin the back of Mack Jack's neck. He's closin his eyes, lickin at her thumb. That black cat's sneakin into the kitchen, goin into one of the shaded dark corners. Bella's movin closer to Mack Jack, gently pressin on the back of his neck, pullin his face against her stomach and whisperin, "Where have you been?"

Mack Jack's silent.

That black cat's in the dark corner starin out at Mack Jack. Its dark green eyes glow out of the darkness. Mack Jack's lowerin his face into Bella's stomach, slowly lickin and suckin on her thumb. She's leanin over and whisperin into his ear. She's askin, "Why haven't you come to see me?"

Mack Jack's silent.

· TEN ·

Sometimes that Snake Town heat could shut folks up, have them sittin quietly til it goes away. Them folks that can see Lulu's house is still doin that, rollin their eyes at it. Della Stucky's back from down the road and tellin Gertrude Mercer what she had to tell her. Folks that had seen her goin down the road knew where she was goin. When they seen her comin back from down the road, they knew where she had been. They didn't have to wonder what she told Gertrude Mercer, but they were wonderin what Gertrude Mercer told her. Della Stucky's sittin out on her porch. She ain't told nobody where she went, but everybody knew.

That old mirror hangin up on the wall in Lulu's back room is dull. It don't show faces back the way it used to. Willet got a pan of water sittin on the table beneath the mirror. She's washin her face, tryin to get all that makeup off it. She keeps lookin in that mirror, wipin at her face with that washcloth. But that mirror ain't showin her the face she wants to see. That makeup's comin off, but some of that age time put on her face ain't comin off at all. She's combin her hair now, combin it down and lettin it hang down over her shoulders. But she keeps lookin in the mirror, lookin into her own eyes.

Lulu's children have been fed, they ain't runnin back and

forth into the house botherin her. She's sittin quietly at the table in that front room. Sometimes she says something to Jeremiah, but when she does it don't take too long before that silence between them comes back. When Jeremiah ain't liftin his head and takin them quick glances out through the screen door, he's lookin down and starin at that table he's sittin at. Now he's lookin up, Lulu's lookin up, too. Willet's comin out of that back room. The bright yellow dress she has put on brightens up the room, makes everything around her look dark. Jeremiah's lookin at the dress, then lookin up at Willet's face. He sees her eyes and lowers his head, looks back down at the table. Lulu's still lookin up, lookin up from the dress and starin at Willet's face. But Willet ain't lookin back at her. She's goin to the table, pickin up her pack of cigarettes from it, and quickly puttin them in her purse. Lulu's watchin her, waitin for Willet to look back at her. But Willet ain't lookin back, ain't sayin nothin. She's pickin her purse up from the table and quickly walkin to the door. Jeremiah's lookin up now, watchin her. Lulu's sighin, callin out, "Wil . . . Wil."

Willet ain't stoppin.

Quickly, Lulu's gettin up from the table, pushin her chair out of her way and goin to the door, sayin, "Wil, ya can't be goin down there now. Ya hear me?"

Willet's openin that screen door.

"Wil . . . Wil," Lulu's callin.

Willet's steppin out on the porch.

"Wil . . . Wait, Wil . . . Lets me go down and talk to Mama. Lets me go down first, tell her ya here. Wait, Wil," Lulu's at the door callin out.

Della Stucky's got her head up and is lookin out of the shade of her sittin porch. She's watchin everything she can see goin on over at Lulu's house. That Dorothy Webb and Pauline Russell got their heads up, too, lookin.

Willet's goin down the steps.

"Wil . . . Wil . . . Ya can'ts go down there now. Wait, Wil," Lulu's at the edge of her porch, sayin.

Willet's goin down the path.

Them children that were doin that runnin and playin done stopped, shut their mouths. But their eyes are wide open and watchin that woman with the pretty yellow dress on.

Jeremiah's up from his chair, he's at the door lookin out at Willet goin down the path. Lulu's steppin down them steps, yellin out, "WIL . . . WIL . . . DON'T GO DOWN THERE NOW. WAIT."

Willet slows, quickly looks back over her shoulder.

"WIL . . . WAIT."

"NO," Willet shouts back at Lulu.

Della Stucky hears that shoutin, leans back into the shade. Them children keep lookin, the ones that are on that path the woman with the pretty yellow dress is comin down, get out the way.

"WIL . . . WIL . . . COME BACK," Lulu's callin.

Jeremiah's standin out on the porch now. Quickly, he's lightin a cigarette, blowin the smoke out his mouth, and watchin Willet go down the path.

That Dorothy Webb and Pauline Russell ain't takin their eyes off of anything they can see. They're watchin Willet come down that path. Quickly, they're lowerin their eyes now, tryin to get them away from that hard stare Willet's givin them.

Lulu ain't sayin nothin no more. She's standin on her steps watchin Willet get to the end of her path and start down the road. Jeremiah ain't sayin nothin either. He's puffin on that cigarette, blowin smoke out his mouth and lookin at them folks he can see that are watchin Willet.

Lulu's turnin and lookin up at Jeremiah sayin, "She can'ts goes down there . . . She can'ts."

Jeremiah sighs, shrugs his shoulders, looks out to the road, and watches Willet.

Lulu's sayin, "Mama ain't goin to lets her see Mason."

Jeremiah takes a long drag on his cigarette, lowers his eyes from the road, and stares at Tommy Moses's car sittin down there at the end of the path.

Lulu's sayin, "With Papa dyin, Mama ain't needed Wil comin back here."

Slowly, Jeremiah looks away from the car and back to the road. But he ain't lookin down the road at Willet, he's lookin up the road. Lulu's back up on the porch. She's lookin at Jeremiah, but he ain't lookin back at her. She's turnin from him and lookin out at the road; she can still see Willet going down the road. Slowly Lulu's bringin her hand up to her forehead and wipin at the sweat she feels rollin down it.

That road is hot but Willet ain't lettin that heat comin down on her head get in her mind. She's walkin fast, the skirt of that long yellow dress is makin them swishin sounds. Some of them small, hot-time bugs are tryin to fly up in her face. Quickly, she's bringin her hand up and slappin them out of her face. When she ain't lookin down the road, she's got her head down and lookin at the ground. That old white-painted church ain't too far down the road. Willet can see it in her mind, but she doesn't want to look up and see it. She's pushin it out of her mind, but it keeps jumpin back in it. That old white-painted church is there now. It ain't in her mind, it's down the road and she can see it. That high steeple with the cross on top is stickin up in the sky. But she ain't lookin up no more, she's lookin down at that road. She's passin that church, keepin her head down and eyes away from it. That road ain't got no faces on it, no voices comin up out of it. But she's seein faces, hearin voices in her mind that won't get out. Faces that ain't smilin at her, just starin. That church is empty now. But them faces she's seein are in there, been there, ain't never left. Them voices are in there, too, still whisperin around her.

Nate Crawford knew that Snake Town road, knew every inch of it. He didn't have to look up to see where he was goin or where he was. He didn't even look up when he had to spit some of that tobacco out of his mouth. He'd just squirt it through the side of his mouth. That one tooth he had left didn't stop that tobacco from gettin out. He's been haulin anything he can haul for folks up and down that road since before he can even remember. Sometimes when folks see him passin with that mule wagon of his, they don't speak. They figure he's either sittin up in that wagon asleep, drunk, or dead. One or the other they don't want to be doin no disturbin. Them mules he got pullin that wagon know that road, too. Don't like nothin on it that ain't supposed to be there. They're flinchin their ears and startin that side-steppin. They don't like that bright color they see comin down the road. That side-steppin they're doin is joltin that wagon. Nate Crawford had his head down, but it's bouncin up. His eyes were half closed, but he got them wide open now tryin to see why his mules ain't actin right. He's seein that fast-walkin, good-lookin woman with that bright dress on comin his way. He's pullin back on them reins, gettin them mules to slow down and go off to the side of the road.

Willet's nearin them mules, givin them a quick look and walkin off to the side of the road. She ain't thought of that old mule wagon man in years. She ain't lookin up to see his face, but that face is back in her mind already. It's done wiggled its way through all that time she ain't thought of in years. She ain't slowin down or lookin up. But them mules have stopped and she's hearin, "Hey theres . . . Yous ahh . . . Yous ahh."

Willet's slowin, lookin up at that old man and seein that same face that was already in her mind. It ain't lookin no different than the last time she saw it.

Nate Crawford's tryin to get them words out his mouth and keep that tobacco juice in at the same time. He's lookin down at Willet and sayin, "Ah knows yous. Yous ahh . . . Yous been gone from heres."

Willet ain't sayin nothin. Them little flyin bugs are tryin to get up in her face again. That sweat stink comin off them mules is already got up her nose. She's smackin at them bugs and lowerin her eyes away from that old man.

"Yous ahh Mercer. Ah knows yous, yous that Mercer girl. Yous thats one that goes from here."

"That's who I am. I'm Willet."

"Ah knows it. Ah knows it as soons as Ah gets a good looks at ya. Yous Vergil Mercer's girl. Ah knows it soons Ah gets me a good looks at ya. Yous the ones that goes."

Willet's rollin her eyes up to that old man lookin down at her. He's got a smile on his face, but she ain't smilin back. He's still tellin her who she is, but she ain't listenin now. He's sayin, "Ah knows yous. Yous back ta be with yous mama?"

"I got to go now," Willet says quickly.

Nate Crawford still got that smile on his face. But he ain't got nothin to smile about. Willet's gone, walkin on down that road. She ain't lookin back, but that old man is still in her mind. He's brought her daddy's face back and put it in her mind, too. She can see it lookin at her, she's lookin down at that road, but her daddy's face ain't left her mind. She ain't got to look up to know that dark shady curve in the road ain't too far.

Gertrude Mercer's tryin to sit quietly in that front room of hers. But she can't. Mason's in there, too, and he doesn't want to be. She's tryin to make him sit in that chair at the table, keep him there when she goes to the window and looks out. But he keeps wantin to get up, go back outside. He's squirmin in that seat, sayin, "Mama Gert, can'ts Ah goes back out?"

"No, you just sit, rest yourself now," Gertrude Mercer's sayin, then sighin and lookin toward her window.

Mason's sittin, holdin a half-full glass of tea in his hands. That ice that was in it done melted. That tea ain't cold no more, but he's still takin sips of it. When he doesn't have that glass up, he has his head down. But he keeps rollin up his eyes and givin Gertrude Mercer them quick stares. She up now, standin by her front window and lookin out at the road. That road's empty, been empty since she watched Nate Crawford takin his haulin wagon up it. She's hearin a sudden noise, flinchin, turnin back to Mason and yellin, "Didn't I tell you to rest yourself? Sit back down in that chair."

Mason had slowly eased himself up out of his chair. But he's quickly sittin back down. He's lowerin his head again and slowly rollin his eyes back up at Gertrude Mercer, mutterin, "Ah wants to go out. Ah wants to go out."

"No, you hear me?" Gertrude Mercer says, then hurries to the door and closes it.

Mason lowers his eyes, pokes his mouth out. Gertrude Mercer's lookin back out of the window. She's lookin at where that road comes curvin out of the shade. Them big trees along that part of the road won't let her see in that shade beneath them, but she's lookin anyway.

Mason's sittin quietly in that chair. He has pushed the glass of tea away from him and ain't lookin at it either. He's starin at Gertrude Mercer's back. That sunlight comin through the window ain't lightin her back. It's dark, still against the light.

Willet's eyes are lowered, starin down at the ground as she walks. She does not have to look up or look ahead to know the road is curvin. All them tree branches hangin out over the road makes it darker and lookin like it's goin into the night. She's in that dark shade beneath them trees now. The air is cooler, sounds of faraway birds singin seem farther away. But she ain't thinkin about them birds singin. She's lookin up now, tryin to see around the curve of the road.

Mason's squirmin in that chair again. That chair is makin them little squeaky sounds. Gertrude Mercer's starin out at that road. Sometimes she lowers her eyes, looks down at some of the sunlight caught in the cracks of her porch boards. She tries to let her thoughts rest there before she does that lookin up the road again. But that squeaky noise comin from that chair ain't lettin her thoughts rest. She's turnin around and lookin at Mason. He ain't lookin back at her, he's squirmin around in his chair and pokin his mouth out. She's sayin, "Sit still in that chair and rest yourself."

"Ah wants to go out, Mama Gert."

"No, I said."

Mason ain't movin around in that chair no more, but big tears are startin to come out of his eyes and roll down his face. Gertrude Mercer's turnin again and lookin back out that window. That road is still empty, but she keeps lookin. Sometimes she forgets what she's lookin for. But them feelins she got that's makin her doin that lookin won't go away. Squeaky noises are comin from that chair again. Mason's squirmin around in it, whimperin and mutterin, "Ah don't want to stay in here sittin down."

"HUSH CHILD. HUSH." Gertrude Mercer's yellin, but she ain't lookin back over her shoulder at Mason. She's keepin her eyes on that road where it comes around the curve. There's some bright color movin up in that shade. She's watchin it, tryin to tell herself she ain't seein nothin. But them feelins she has is tellin her it's there. That day that she didn't want to come has come, like she knew it would. She's starin at that bright movement comin through the shade. She got sweat on her forehead, but she's feelin cold comin in her: that kind of cold that freezes a thought, won't let it move and become somethin new, goes back to bein somethin old. Mason's doin that whimperin, but she ain't listenin. She ain't sayin nothin, ain't lettin no sound take away that silence she needs.

Willet has stopped. She's standin in the shade of the road. She's bringin her hands up and puttin them on her hips. She can see out of the shade that house sittin back off the road. It's lookin like it always does in her mind, cept now it's lookin back at her. It's makin her feel it's starin at her, waitin on her; been waitin. Slowly she's lowerin her eyes away from the house, lookin down at the ground.

Gertrude Mercer doesn't need to see more of what she's seein to know what she's lookin at. That feelin she got, had always had, is tellin her what she's seein. It's bringin a face she can't see out of the shade. It's puttin that face up in front of hers. It's makin her look at that face, won't let her push it away. She's whisperin up to her God, tellin him to give her

179

some mercy. Mason's whinin, squirmin around in that chair. Them sounds he's makin is scratchin on that silence she's tryin to keep her feelings in. She's hearin that whinin now, but she ain't takin her eyes off that far dark curve of the road.

That half glass of warm tea sittin on the table is lookin all blurry to Mason. He's starin at it through them big tears bubbled up in his eyes. Some of that sunlight comin through the window is gettin on that table, shinin in that half glass of tea. It's makin that dark brown tea look brighter, look dark, pretty red. Mason's pushin that glass of tea farther away from him. His mouth is poked out, he's breathin through his nose. Them snifflin sounds he's makin keep gettin louder. He's mutterin, too, sayin, "Ah don't wants to sit here."

"HUSH CHILD, HUSH NOW," Gertrude Mercer's yellin over her shoulder. Them sounds of Mason's moanin ain't goin away. But they ain't gettin in her mind now. Slowly, she's backin away some from the window. But she ain't takin her eyes away from that road.

Willet's comin out of the shade, walkin slowly. That sunlight is gettin in her eyes, but she ain't lowerin her head. She's starin at that house, feelin it starin back at her.

Gertrude Mercer doesn't need to look out that window no more. She's got her head down, starin at the dark wall beneath the windowsill. She knows she got to look up again and look out that window. But she knows she's goin to see the same thing she already lookin at in her mind. She's closin her eyes, but she's still seein Willet comin in her mind. She can see that walk of hers ain't changed none. That hair is just as long as it was.

"Mama Gert . . . can Ah goes out now?" Mason's mutterin.

Gertrude Mercer's silent.

Willet's hands are loosely hangin down at her sides and slowly movin with each step she's takin. But her eyes ain't looked away from that house. She's tryin to see through that porch shade and into them dark-lookin windows.

Gertrude Mercer got her head up again and is lookin out that window. She can see Willet's face now, feel her eyes starin at the house.

Mason's squirmin in that chair again. Them squeaky sounds are crawlin over that stillness Gertrude Mercer's tryin to keep her mind in. She's turnin away from the window and quietly walkin over to Mason. He ain't lookin at her; he's still starin at that glass of tea through them tears he has in his eyes. She's reachin over to Mason, then gently rubbin his back. He still ain't lookin up at her, but he's mumblin, "Cans Ah goes out now?"

"No, child," Gertrude Mercer says softly, but keeps rubbin her hand over Mason's back.

Willet has turned off of the road and is startin up the long yard path. In her mind, she can see her daddy sittin on the porch, her sister chasin after her in the yard, hear her mama callin after them. But her eyes ain't seein nothin but the shade on that porch. Some birds up in them faraway trees are singin. Each step she's takin is leavin a soft trailin sound behind her. But she ain't hearin nothin, just feelin that silence she's lookin at.

Mason's lowerin his head, whimperin and sayin, "Mama Gert . . . Mama Gert . . . Um bein good. How comes Ah can'ts goes out? Toby's in the wagon. Ah have to goes get him."

Gertrude Mercer's sighin, puttin her arms around Mason, and pullin him closer to her.

"MAMA . . . MAMA . . . MAMA," Willet's callin out as she nears the porch steps.

Gertrude Mercer pulls Mason closer to her. But he's quickly raisin his head and sayin, "Mama Gert, somebody's come."

"MAMA, IT'S ME. IT'S WILLET."

"Mama Gert, who that?" Mason's askin.

Gertrude Mercer's silent.

"MAMA . . . MAMA, IT'S ME, WILLET."

Mason's tryin to look toward the window. Gertrude Mercer can hear the sound of footsteps comin up the porch steps.

"MAMA . . . MAMA, YOU IN THERE?"

"Mama Gert, somebody's comin."

"Hush child. Hush."

"MAMA . . . MAMA . . . YOU IN THERE?"

"Mama Gert, somebody's there."

"Hush now." Gertrude Mercer's whisperin and tryin to bring Mason closer to her. But Mason's squirmin around and tryin to look toward the window. His eyes are big. Them tears in them ain't rollin down his cheeks no more. They're just stayin big bubbles in his eyes.

Slowly, softly, Willet steps up onto the porch, then stands silently starin at the closed door. That porch board she's standin on had squeaked. But that squeaky sound is gone now and she can't hear nothin else. She's whisperin, "Mama . . . Mama, you in there? It's me . . . It's Willet."

Silence.

"MAMA . . . MAMA," Willet's yellin at the door.

Quickly Gertrude Mercer's puttin her hand on Mason's cheek and turnin his face to hers. She's lookin in his eyes and whisperin, "Now you do as I tell you. Mama Gert got to go out there and tells her to go away from here. You stay right here in this chair. Don't you dare get up. You stay right here. You hear me?"

Mason's lookin up into Gertrude Mercer's eyes and askin, "Mama Gert, she callin ya Mama. Why she callin ya Mama? Who she be?"

"Never mind, you hear me? You stay in here and don't you dare get out of this chair. Mama Gert goin to make her go away."

"MAMA . . . MAMA," Willet's callin toward the door. Suddenly it's openin up. Gertrude Mercer comes out of the house and slams the door closed behind her. Silently she stands in front of the door. She's starin at Willet. Her dark eyes are as still as the shade she's standin in.

Willet's starin back into her mother's eyes.

"What do you want here?" Gertrude Mercer's askin.

Willet's silent.

"What do you want?"

"I come back, Mama," Willet says softly.

"You ain't got nothin to be comin back here for. Nothin," Gertrude Mercer's sayin.

"I got somethin to be here for, Mama."

"No, you don't."

"Mason's mine, Mama."

"You ain't fit to have nothin."

"Mason's mine, Mama. I want to see my child."

"Get out of here."

"No, Mama. No."

"GET OUT OF HERE. YOU AIN'T FIT TO SEE NO-BODY HERE. GET OFF MY PORCH," Gertrude Mercer's yellin.

"THAT'S MY CHILD, MAMA," Willet yells back.

Mason ain't movin from that chair, but he ain't takin his eyes off the door. He's starin at it and listenin to hear his name called again. He can hear all that yellin but he can't see nothin cept that dark side of the door he's starin at.

"YOU AIN'T SEEIN HIM. YOU AIN'T SHOWED A CARE FOR HIM AT ALL. YOU AIN'T FIT TO SEE HIM. GO ON AND GO BACK TO WHERES YOU BEEN," Gertrude Mercer's yellin.

Willet's lowerin her eyes away from her mother. She's lookin down at them porch floorboards and starin at dark cracks runnin through them. Tears are comin to her eyes, then slowly runnin down her cheeks.

Gertrude Mercer is raisin her chin, holdin it high. But she's starin down at Willet. That silence on her face is makin it still, like it ain't never smiled or laughed or changed with time.

Slowly Willet's raisin her head, lookin at her mother, and whisperin, "Mama, Mason's my child. Ain't nothin that did happen or nothin that is ever goin to happen to change that. I just want to see him. That's my child, Mama."

Silence.

That porch board's squeakin, Willet's slowly steppin back on it. Now she's standin still but lookin past her mother to the closed door. Them tears comin from her eyes are fallin down on her yellow dress, makin little gray spots. But she ain't lowerin her eyes away from that door.

Gertrude Mercer ain't movin, she's keepin her chin up.

Willet wipes the tears from her eyes, calls out, "MASON . . . MASON . . . MASON."

"GET OUT OF HERE . . . YOU HEAR ME? GET OUT OF HERE," Gertrude Mercer's yellin.

"MASON . . . MASON . . . MASON," Willet keeps callin.

Mason's gettin up out of that chair. He's wipin the tears from his eyes, but he ain't lookin away from that door. He's hearin that yellin on the other side of the door. But he's listenin for his name to be called again. Some feelin is gettin in him, it's makin his little mouth droop open and his eyes get real big. But it ain't tellin him what he's feelin. Slowly he's walkin toward that door.

Gertrude Mercer's steppin away from that door. She's gettin up in front of Willet, yellin, "YOU AIN'T SEEIN HIM. YOU AIN'T NEVER SEEIN THAT CHILD. GET OUT OF HERE."

Willet's starin back in her mother's face, yellin, "I AIN'T GOIN, MAMA. I WANT TO SEE MASON, MAMA. I WANT TO SEE HIM. YOU CAN'T STOP ME, MAMA."

"YES I CAN. THAT CHILD DON'T KNOW WHO YOU ARE . . . AND HE DON'T NEED TO KNOW. YOU AIN'T NO GOOD TO YOURSELF. YOU AIN'T NO GOOD TO HIM."

Slowly, Mason's sneakin that door open enough for him to peek out through that screen door. He's tryin to look around Gertrude Mercer's back, see who's callin his name.

Willet's yellin at her mother, tellin her, "YOU DON'T KNOW WHAT HAPPENED, MAMA. YOU DON'T KNOW. DON'T NOBODY KNOW."

"WILLET, YOU AIN'T GOIN TO SEE HIM. NOW, GO," Gertrude Mercer yells.

Willet ain't yellin nothin back. She ain't lookin at her mother no more. A softness has come to her eyes, but them tears are still drippin out of them and rollin down her cheeks.

Gertrude Mercer sees that sudden softness gettin in her daughter's eyes. She sees Willet lookin around her and at that door. Gertrude Mercer's turnin around and lookin at that door.

That screen Mason's lookin through is dark and it's hidin his long black curly hair behind its dark little holes. But it can't hide them big light eyes lookin out of them.

"CLOSE THAT DOOR. CLOSE IT. YOU HEAR ME?" Gertrude Mercer's yellin at Mason.

Willet's starin at the big bright eyes behind the dark screen. She can see them lookin back at her.

"CLOSE THAT DOOR, MASON," Gertrude Mercer yells.

Softly Willet calls out, "Mason . . . Mason."

"MASON, CLOSE THAT DOOR," Gertrude Mercer yells again.

Mason's steppin back from that outer screen door and closin that big dark door. Willet's watchin him til she can't see him no more, but she silently keeps starin at that door.

. . .

That Snake Town sun can get real high, get up there and seem like it ain't movin, ain't goin to move. Folks don't look up at it, don't have to, don't even think about it bein up there. That heat comin down tells them that sun ain't moved. And if some time went by, it was that slow time. That time that didn't never change anything.

Jeremiah's sittin out on Lulu's porch steps. He's lookin out at that Snake Town road. Sometimes he looks down that road as far as he can see, waits to see if he can see Willet comin back. Then he looks up that road, sighs before he looks over to Tommy Moses's car.

Them children ain't stopped their playin. That hollerin and runnin up and down them yard paths ain't makin that silence folks sittin in go away. Dorothy Webb and Pauline Russell are still out on their sittin porches, but they ain't doin that back-and-forth talkin, just that quiet lookin down at that road. Della Stucky's sittin on her porch watchin that road, too. Sometimes she rolls her eyes over to Lulu's porch to see if that man's still sittin on them steps. Then she rolls her eyes back to that road.

Lulu's sittin in that cookin room of hers. She knows she don't be needin to be out in that sun. That child she's carryin is hangin low and she knows she don't need that heat takin her strength away. She's sittin at that table starin down at things she ain't seein. Cept for them playin sounds comin through the windows, it's quiet in that cookin room. But it ain't quiet in Lulu's mind. She's hearin that slow time passin by, draggin every moment it takin away. But it ain't bringin what she's waitin for. Willet ain't back from down the road yet.

· ELEVEN ·

Mister Allen's standin at that back door of his. He's lookin out through his screen door. If them dogs ain't barkin, it's quiet out in them back alley yards. That high afternoon sun ain't doin too much heatin up in them yards. It sorta just makes all them big shadows out of them row houses fall all zigzaggy over everything in them yards. Mister Allen ain't thinkin about what he's lookin at anyway. That kitchen radio he got is on and ain't lettin him think of nothin else cept it. That radio is tellin him what Harry S. Truman goin to do about that Korea. Mister Allen don't want to hear that war talk. He knows he can turn the radio off like he done a few times already. But he knows he just would turn it back on again and that war ain't goin to stop just because he wants it to.

Mister Allen's turnin away from that door and lookin over at that radio. It's started playin that soft music again and it's givin Mister Allen some of that thinkin time he's been wantin so he can think about somethin else. He's turnin that radio off and mutterin, "Hum, don't need another one. Just had one."

Ellen Maben's out sittin on her porch, been sittin out there most of the afternoon. When she ain't talkin to folks goin by, she's leanin back in that chair and lookin up and down that alley. She's lookin over at Mister Allen's porch when she hears that front door of his openin. She's waitin til he steps out on his porch, but she ain't givin him a chance to sit down before she's yellin over, "Where you been, Mister Allen? Ain't seen you since this mornin."

Mister Allen don't feel like that hollerin back and forth talk. But he's puttin a smile on his face anyway and sayin, "Been in there listenin to that radio some."

Ellen Maben's watchin Mister Allen, givin him a chance to sit down. He's sittin now and she's askin, "Oh, you listenin to that Korea stuff on there?"

Mister Allen yells back, "It ain't lookin too good over there."

Ellen Maben's shruggin up her shoulders and sayin, "I ain't never heard of no Korea til I heard them start talkin about it. Tell you the truth, I gets tired of listenin to them talkin about it. That's all they were talkin about when I was listenin this mornin. Next thing you know, they goin to want Colored to go and fights, too. Don't make no sense, havin another war."

Mister Allen ain't tellin Ellen Maben what he's really thinkin. He's still got that smile on his face and tellin her how he thinks President Truman knows what to do. He ain't tellin her he's thinkin she's simple-talkin and he wish she leave him be.

Ellen Maben's sayin, "Got enough trouble around here without folks goin someplace they ain't never heard of to find some more. That's what I think."

Mister Allen sighs, looks up at the sky, wipes at his brow, and says, "This heat can get to you."

Ellen Maben takes a quick look up at the sky, looks back over to Mister Allen and says, "I gots me some ironin to do. But I ain't gettin that iron out til it cools down here some."

Some of that quiet time Mister Allen was waitin on came by. It even let him sit for a while and think that Ellen Maben was goin to let him have some peace. But he's hearin her sayin, "I hear they havin his funeral tomorrow."

"Hum?" Mister Allen's sayin, raisin his chin and lookin over to Ellen Maben. She's lookin back at him and sayin, "They buryin Tommy Moses tomorrow. Miss Lampkin come by here a little while ago. Says she was up on Homewood Avenue. She say she sees Ethel Smith up there. Ethel tells her they buryin him tomorrow. She says Ethel was over to see him, says he looks real nice. She told Miss Lampkin that he didn't look like he was killed the way he was. Said he look real nice."

Mister Allen knows he got to say something back. He's still tryin to think about what he's goin to say. But now, he got to stop that thinkin and listen to Ellen Maben tellin him, "I sure be glad when they catch them, put them both under the jail. Ain't no tellin what they do to somebody next. I keeps my doors locked."

Mister Allen ain't sayin nothin. He's thinkin about and seein Tommy Moses in his mind. He knows Ellen Maben's lookin at him, waitin on him to say something back. But he ain't sayin nothin, just slowly shakin his head back and forth.

Ellen Maben's askin, "You think they goin to catch em soon?"

Mister Allen stops shakin his head and gets to noddin it and sayin, "Law gets them. That law will gets. Can't runs too long from the law."

Ellen Maben's sighin and takin some real long looks up and down the alley. Mister Allen's wonderin if they got that soft music still playin on the radio.

Them chickens out in Gus Goins's yard ain't doin all that

squawkin. Most of them went on and got up in them coops and ain't payin nothin no mind. Al Johnson's hurryin past them chickens and callin out, "Hey Gus . . . Gus."

Gus Goins is in that kitchen of his. That white rooster he yanked the head off of ain't got a feather left on it. It's soakin in a big pot of water settin in the kitchen sink. Gus Goins is standin over that sink, lookin and yellin out the window, "Yeal, I'll be out in a minute."

Al Johnson hurries on up on that back porch of Gus Goins's and sits down on one of them chairs. He ain't sittin there too long before he's yellin out, "Bring me somethin out when you come, somethin cold. It's hot out here."

"Where you think you at, nigger? Some damn resort you done seen in the movies?" Gus Goins yells back out of the window.

"Yeal, um on the Riviera," Al Johnson yells back.

"Shit, sounds like to me that the only Riviera you goin to find your black ass on is goin to be in Korea," Gus Goins yells out.

"Fuck that shit," Al Johnson yells at that window, then leans back in his chair.

Gus Goins is comin out onto his porch with two glasses of lemonade in his hands anyway. Al Johnson's lookin up at him and askin, "What's that?"

"Lemonade."

"Lemonade. I don't want no damn lemonade," Al Johnson's sayin, but takin one of them glasses out of Gus Goins's hands anyway.

"You better take it. You ain't gettin nothin else for free," Gus Goins's sayin and sittin down.

Al Johnson's gently shakin his glass, watchin and listenin

to the ice rattlin against the glass. It's makin them little clangin sounds. He's still starin in that glass and listenin to that ice rattlin. But he's sayin, "That shit over there ain't lookin good."

"Huh?" Gus Goins says.

"That shit goin on in Korea."

"I ain't worried about it. I ain't goin nowhere," Gus Goins says, then laughs a little. "Shit, I ain't goin back over there for nothin. I spent two and a half years over there. I ain't givin them another day. I'm too old for that shit again, but you ain't. Truman's goin to get your ass."

"How you figure?" Al Johnson's sayin, then sippin some of that lemonade he's been holdin.

"I ain't got to figure nothin cept Um too old and you ain't."

Al Johnson's still sippin that lemonade. Gus Goins takes a sip of his lemonade, then says, "Shit, they had us on that Okinawa. Them Japs didn't want to give that up for nothin. They were all up in them damn caves. We had this one boy with us, Calvin was his name. I think he was from California someplace. One of them Jap mortar rounds come in and hit that boy right on his head. Shit, wasn't enough left of that boy to fill up a potato sack with. Shit, I ain't goin nowhere."

Al Johnson's quiet for a moment, then asks, "Anybody hear anything about Wendell? Why they have to beat him in his head like that?"

Gus Goins shrugs his shoulders, takes a quick sip from his glass and says, "Just be glad it wasn't you. I had to get me another box in there. That cost me money, now."

Al Johnson quickly says, "I hear they're buryin Tommy tomorrow."

"You goin?" Gus Goins asks with a little laugh.

"Nigger ain't meant nothin to me. As far as Um concerned, Jeremiah did some folks a favor," Al Johnson says.

"Yeal, but . . ." Gus Goins says, then lets his thoughts drift into silence.

"But what?" Al Johnson's askin.

"Shit like that ain't good for business. You know that. Shit like that don't do nothin but bring the law around. Don't need that shit," Gus Goins says.

"Where you think they hidin? Ain't nobody seen em at all."

"I don't care where they at. Just as long as that damn Boughner keeps his ass out of here."

"They catch them sooner or later."

Gus Goins is silent for a moment, then says, "You know I always got to protect my business. Can't have them comin in here, breakin my place up."

Al Johnson takes a quick sip from his glass, then almost at a whisper says, "Yeal, Gus, I understand that. I would have done the same."

.   .   .

Them night clubs down on Elmira Avenue don't wait til dark to open their doors and let that music out into the air. Sweet Man Sam's already in that Satin Club with that guitar of his. He's sittin up on that stage, got his eyes closed and that guitar of his makin rhythms outta that music he's feelin up in his mind. Vann Irvis is up on that stage, too. He's behind them drums, beatin them soft and slow. Kenny Douglas is up on that stage, too. He's got that trumpet in his hands, but he ain't playin it.

He's just swayin back and forth in his chair, lookin over at Sweet Man Sam. But Sweet Man Sam ain't lookin back. He still got his eyes closed and his fingers dancin with them guitar strings. Charley Lennwood is up on that stage, too. But most folks listenin to that music can't see him, don't have to know that's who's playin that piano. Folks that can see him done stopped wonderin about how that wee little man can play that big piano. Some folks laugh, say he ain't nothin but fingers. But they shut that laughin up when he's playin.

Kenny Douglas is bringin that trumpet up to his mouth, closin his eyes, tiltin his head back. He got folks waitin to hear that horn blowin. It's blowin. His hot breath is twistin and curlin through it, turnin into that music folks want to hear. They're listenin to it, lettin it blow in their ears. It's got their eyes closin, got their heads noddin, got them poppin their fingers and tellin Kenny Douglas, "Yeal, man . . . You got it, baby . . . You got it."

Ain't too much of that hot afternoon sunlight gettin through them dark curtains hangin over Bella's windows. But that sound of music comin up off of Elmira Avenue ain't havin no trouble at all gettin through them windows. Mack Jack's in that back room of Bella's, lyin on her bed. The sound of that music is in his mind, been in there. That soft drum beat is softly tappin against his feelings. But the sound of that horn in his mind ain't soft. It's sharp and slicin through his feelings, makin him close his eyes, then quickly open them up again and stare up at the dark ceiling. His shirt is off, been off. Bella made him take it off. She's lyin beside him on that bed. She's rubbin her hand over his bare chest, sometimes lettin her nails scratch lightly over his skin. She has her face nestled against his shoulder, close to his neck. She's whisperin to him.

Her lips are flutterin against his skin. She's sayin, "You need me now."

Mack Jack's silent.

Bella's whisperin, "You wants me, don't you?"

That horn ain't blowin now, but that soft drum beat ain't went away. Mack Jack's closin his eyes, waitin on that horn to blow again. Bella's slowly rubbin her hand up over Mack Jack's chest to his neck, then over his face. Her fingers are gently glidin over his cheeks, his lips. She's whisperin, "You need me."

That horn's blowin again.

Bella's lowerin her lips to Mack Jack's neck, kissin and lickin at it. Some low, long, slow moan is seepin up from Mack Jack's throat, his eyes are closin. Bella's slidin her lips up over his chin, whisperin, "You mine, ain't you?"

Sweat is startin to come out of Mack Jack's face, chest. It's makin his skin slippery. Bella's fingers are makin little circles in the sweat. She's closin her eyes, whisperin, "Say you want me."

Quickly Mack Jack's grabbin Bella by her shoulder, rollin over and bringin her beneath him. He's lookin down at her, starin into her eyes. Her blouse has come open, her breasts are bulgin out her brassiere. She's lookin up into his eyes, her lips are perched open, but she's silent.

Mack Jack gets up, goes and stands by the window, then stares out through the dark curtains. His penis is hard, throbbing. Bella's softly callin out, "Come back."

Mack Jack's silent.

That horn's stopped blowin, but the soft sound of that drum beatin's comin through the window. Bella's sayin, "You need me, come back here."

Mack Jack's feelin something touch his leg. He's seein that black cat leanin against his leg lookin up at him. It meows and scoots away. Bella's whisperin, "You can't go away again. You need me."

Mack Jack's raisin his head and lookin back through them dark curtains. Some of that sunlight gettin through the curtains is fallin on his face. It's makin his face warm, makin that sweat on his forehead roll down his face.

Bella's whisperin, "You need me. I can take care of you. You don't need anybody. You know I'll take care of you."

Mack Jack turns from the window, slowly goes to the foot of the bed. Bella's lookin up at him, watchin for him to look at her, waitin for him to come closer. Quickly that black cat comes from the shadows, jumps up on the foot of the bed and lies at Bella's feet. It's starin at Mack Jack, watchin him take his shirt from the bed post. Bella's sayin, "You can't go again."

Mack Jack's puttin on his shirt.

Bella's sayin, "Why are you leaving again? I'll take care of you. I know what you need. Don't I always give you what you need?"

Mack Jack stops buttoning his shirt and looks at Bella. He watches her get off the bed, near him. She's close, touchin his face with her hand and askin, "Where are you goin?"

Mack Jack's turnin from Bella and walkin out of that back room. She's followin him, sayin, "You ain't got nobody cept me, just me. You can't leave me. I can take care of you. You need me."

Mack Jack keeps walkin toward the door.

Them Elmira Avenue folks that can't wait for the sun to go down to do their business know how to work them doorways. They stand back in the little bit of shade they can find, wait for that business to come their way. They always got something to sell and keep their eyes open for something they can get for nothin. Percy Witaker can lean back in the shade of them doorways. Ain't no smile ever on his dark, smooth face til he see somethin he needs. Then he can step out of them doorways, give that sweet salesman smile to somebody passin. He's steppin out of that doorway, smilin and sayin, "Hey, man, hey. You need a little today. Got somethin here."

Mack Jack's slowin, lookin toward that man comin out of the doorway and walkin up to him. Percy Witaker sees he got an ear listenin to him and some eyes lookin his way. Quickly, he looks up and down the avenue, then looks back at Mack Jack and whispers, "Hey, man, you lookin for somethin good? I got the best stuff on the set. You want a little bag, man?"

Mack Jack's lookin into Percy Witaker's eyes.

Percy Witaker whispers, "I got some good stuff, man."

Mack Jack looks away from Percy Witaker, then slowly walks away. Percy Witaker whispers, "Hey . . . Hey, man."

It's quiet out in front of the Satin Club. Ain't nothin left of the sound of music cept them smiles on folks comin out of there. Kenny Douglas got that trumpet of his in its case. He's standin out in front of the Satin Club, got his handkerchief out and wipin at that sweat on his forehead. Sweet Man Sam's standin out there, too. His face ain't nothin but sweat. He ain't thinkin about that sweat rollin down his face. He's tryin to get that cigarette he got hangin out of his mouth lit. He's got that match struck, but he can't get his hands still. They keep shakin, makin that flame wiggle away from the tip of that cigarette. Kenny Douglas is turnin to Sweet Man Sam and sayin, "Hey, man, get a look at who's comin. Ain't that Mack Jack?"

Sweet Man Sam doesn't look anywhere til he gets that cigarette lit. Now he's blowin the smoke out of his mouth, lookin up and sayin, "Yeal, man, that's him."

"Hey, Mack Jack," Kenny Douglas is callin out.

Mack Jack slows, then stops, looks at Kenny Douglas and Sweet Man Sam. Kenny Douglas says, "I heard you were back in town. Damn, man, ain't seen you since Saint Louie."

Mack Jack shrugs his shoulders.

Kenny Douglas says, "Yeal, man, it was Saint Louie. Yeal, man, it was at the Candle Light. Yeal, man, you were playin with Micky Jay. Where you been hidin, man?"

Mack Jack's lookin down at the ground and shruggin his shoulders. Kenny Douglas gives Sweet Man Sam a quick look, then looks back at Mack Jack and says, "Yeal, man, I heard they took your music. That's some rotten shit. I heard that whole album Micky Jay did up in Chicago was your stuff. Man, that's some rotten shit he pulled on you. Yeal, man, I heard about that."

Mack Jack's still lookin down at the ground. Sweet Man Sam says, "Hey, we goin around the corner. You know, to get nice. I got to get nice now."

Kenny Douglas says, "Yeal, man, why don't you come on with us?"

Reese Street ain't no wider than an alley. It's one of them little streets that runs off Elmira Avenue. Folks that don't have to don't go down Reese Street. They say they don't need to be walkin down into nothin but trouble. Half of them old-time apartment buildings on Reese Street done just about fell down anyway. Them folks livin on Reese Street got their ways and ain't none of them ways is right. Sweet Man Sam's walkin fast; he ain't waitin on Kenny Douglas and Mack Jack to catch up with him. Them Reese Street folks sittin on them stoops looked real hard to see who was comin. But as soon as they saw Sweet Man Sam and Kenny Douglas, they sorta figured that man with them was all right, too.

Walker Healey got him one of them first-floor apartments in one of them fallin-down buildings. Reese Street folks know he don't live there, just do that little business of his there. Most folks don't even know his name is Walker Healey. They just call him Mixer; been callin him that. But they know when he's there, that long Cadillac car of his be sittin right out front. Mixer's big, got to stoop down to look through that peephole he's got in his door. He's peepin through that peephole and at the same time he's yellin, "Yeal, who's that?"

Sweet Man Sam's tappin on Mixer's door and yellin through it, sayin, "Hey, it's Sweet Man. Open up."

Mixer ain't openin that door yet. He's still peepin through that little hole and yellin, "Who's that wit you?"

"Kenny, and we got Mack Jack with us. Mack Jack's all right, he's with us. Come on, man, open up," Sweet Man Sam's yellin through that door.

Mixer's crackin that door open, gettin him a good look through that crack. Sweet Man Sam's tellin him, "Come on, man, open up."

Ain't nothin in them rooms Mixer got on that first floor cept some old raggedy chairs and some old blue couch with its stuffin comin out. It's dark in there. Mixer got all them windows covered up with anything that will stop somebody from seein in. That air in there smells like it's been in there a long time. It smells like it got a lot of summertime sweat stuck in it. Sweet Man Sam ain't thinkin about that stink gettin up in his nose. He's hurryin on through that door. Kenny Douglas hurryin through that door, too. Mixer ain't watchin them pass; he's got his eyes on Mack Jack. Kenny Douglas is lookin back over his shoulder and sayin, "This is my man, Mack Jack. He's all right, man. Yeal, Mack Jack's fine, plays that sax like nobody can."

Mixer keeps his eyes on Mack Jack passin him, then he peeks out on that street before he closes and locks that door back up. Sweet Man Sam's already back in the back room, sittin on one of them chairs and rollin his shirt sleeve up. Kenny Douglas is sittin on that big couch and tellin Mack Jack to take him a seat, too. Mixer's sayin, "Yeal, what you need, huh?"

Sweet Man Sam's sayin, "You know what I need, baby."

Kenny Douglas is smilin, sayin, "Yeal, man, I gots to get good, real good. Gots me another set to play tonight." Then he's lookin at Mack Jack and sayin, "Just wait. Mixer's stuff is nice. It's goin to have you up there past the motherfuckin moon. Yeal, man, you goin to be up there past the moon."

Mixer's lookin at Mack Jack and askin, "You gots your money, now, don't you?"

Kenny Douglas is sayin, "Hey, man, I gots it."

There's some half-burned down candle sittin on some little table by the couch. Mixer's leanin over, lighting the candle. Mack Jack stares into that little flame startin to flicker. Sweet Man Sam's sayin, "Yeal, man, light it up. Yeal, let there be light."

Mack Jack's still starin at that candlelight. Kenny Douglas is lookin at him and sayin, "Yeal, man, I heard you stayin over in Homewood. You know, keepin low for a while."

Mack Jack looks at Kenny Douglas, then looks back at that candle burnin. Kenny Douglas says, "That was some shit Micky Jay pulled. I didn't think he was like that. Everybody knew that was your music, didn't have to listen ten times to know that. Yeal, man, I heard you got down about that, stopped playin."

Sweet Man Sam's sayin, "Some dudes get close to that big-time recordin money, they change up on you. Micky Jay good with that bass. But he's bad with business. It's a wonder ain't nobody cuts his throat by now."

Sweet Man Sam ain't thinkin about Micky Jay no more. He ain't thinkin about nothin but what he's watchin Mixer do. Mixer's gettin what he needs, puttin it on a spoon. Sweet Man Sam's starin at that spoon, lookin at that nice brown powder in it. He's smilin now, sayin, "Yeal . . . Yeal."

Mack Jack's starin at that spoon, watchin it bein held over that candle burnin. He's watchin that little flame get bigger, try to curl up from around the bottom of that spoon. Kenny Douglas's lookin at Mack Jack and sayin, "Mixer got the best shit around, man. Yeal, just wait til you get your hit. You going to be fine, man."

Sweet Man Sam's holdin that spoon over the candle, he's watchin that little bit of water he put with that nice brown powder. He's smilin, waitin and watchin for that little bit of water to get hot. He wants to see that nice brown powder melt. It's melting.

. . .

Some of them Snake Town children playin out on that road done stopped that runnin and hollerin. Them ones that are keepin that playin up are stoppin now and lookin down the road, too. Willet ain't seein them children lookin down the road at her. She's walkin up that road, but her head is down and she ain't lookin at nothin but that ground she's walkin on.

Jeremiah's been lookin up and down that Snake Town road. But now he's only lookin down, watchin Willet comin. Della Stucky's sittin back in the shade of her sittin porch, but she got her chin stuck up tryin to see what them children are lookin at. She can see past them now, but she's not puttin her chin back down. Dorothy Webb went into her house to get herself something to drink. She's comin back out on her porch, but she ain't sittin back down. She's standin in the shade of her doorway watchin Willet walk through them children standin on the road.

Lulu's standin out on her porch. The silence of them children made her come out of that cookin room of hers to see where that silence was comin from. Them children Willet's passin know to keep that silence. Them dried tears they can see on that pretty woman's face is tellin them there's something they should be quiet about.

Slowly Jeremiah's steppin down them steps and walkin down the yard path. Willet ain't too far from him now. He can see her face, her eyes still lookin down at that ground she's walkin on.

Willet's passin Tommy Moses's car, but she ain't lookin at it. She's lookin up at Jeremiah as he nears her, askin, "What happen? Did you see him?"

"I saw him. Mama wouldn't let him come out, but I saw him lookin out the door," Willet says, then lowers her eyes and goes on up the path.

Lulu's watchin Willet comin up them porch steps. She can see her face when Willet gets up on the porch, but she ain't sayin nothin to Willet. She's just watchin her pass and go into the house.

Jeremiah's comin up them steps now. Lulu's lookin at him, he's lookin at her. But they ain't sayin anything to each other; they're just doin that lookin. Willet's in the shade of that cookin room. She's sighin as she slowly sits down at that table. Lulu's comin back into the house, but she ain't sayin nothin to Willet. She's sittin down at that table, too.

Them children done started that playin and hollerin again, but that noise they're makin ain't gettin into the silence in Lulu's cookin room. Jeremiah's quietly standin in the doorway lookin at Willet. She's gettin the pack of cigarettes out of her purse. Lulu's sittin still, got her head lowered and tryin to keep her eyes down, too. But she keeps glancin up, lookin across the table, seein if she can see them feelins on Willet's face. Willet's lightin her cigarette, blowin the smoke out of her mouth, and watchin it float away. Softly Lulu's askin, "What did Mama say? Did she lets ya see him?"

Willet looks at Lulu, then looks down at the table and says, "I saw him. Mama wouldn't let me see him, but I saw him peekin out the door."

"What Mama say to ya?" Lulu's askin.

"It don't make no difference what Mama says. That's my child and she can't say nothin to change that," Willet says, then slowly brings the cigarette up to her mouth, puffs on it until it glows red.

Jeremiah sighs, turns around, and looks out at the road. He looks at them children playin, them women sittin on their porches starin at him. He looks at Tommy Moses's car, sighs, turns back around, and slowly goes to the table. Lulu looks up at him, then watches him sit down. She waits on him to look at her, but Jeremiah ain't lookin at nothin cept the dark top of that table. Lulu looks at Willet and says, "Wil, ya got ta give Mama some time."

"I don't have time to give Mama. I can't stay down here just to give Mama some time," Willet says.

Lulu says, "Wil, this is ya home. Ya can always come back here."

Willet's lookin across the table, starin into her sister's eyes. Lulu ain't lookin away, she keeps lookin at Willet's face. That little piece of time caught between them can't go noplace. It's movin now, Willet's lowerin her eyes and lookin back down at the table.

Jeremiah looks up, looks at Willet and softly says, "We gots to get out of here. We can't stay too long."

Willet looks up, stares into Jeremiah's eyes, then slowly looks back down at the table. Jeremiah sighs, gets up from the table, and goes to the door. He stands in the doorway, lookin out at the road. Lulu's still lookin at Willet, watchin her stare down at the cigarette she's holdin. Softly Lulu says, "Mama needs time, Wil."

Willet's silent.

Lulu says, "Ah goes see Mama, Wil. Ah goes down tomorrow and tells Mama ya just want to see Mason fore ya have to goes. Maybe Mama listen ta me some."

.   .   .

Ain't no more shade left on Gertrude Mercer's porch, but she's out there sittin on it. That sunlight ain't gettin in her eyes, cause she's sittin with her head down. Mason's out in the front yard, pullin that wooden wagon of his around. Sometimes them little squeaky sounds comin from them wagon wheels makes her look up and out into that yard.

That turtle got its head back up in its shell and ain't stickin it out for nothin. It's in the back of Mason's wagon, bouncin around like a rock every time Mason pulls the wagon over a bump. But Mason ain't lookin back at that turtle, talkin to it, or thinkin about it. When he ain't lookin out at the road, he's takin quick peeks at Gertrude Mercer sittin on the porch. But he's too far away to see them tears comin out of her eyes.

Gertrude Mercer's lookin up now, wipin her eyes with that apron she's wearin. She's takin a quick look up at the sky, lookin to see how far that sun got to go fore it starts to lowerin and takin the day away. But that sun's tellin her it ain't goin nowhere soon.

Mason's hearin Gertrude Mercer callin him, tellin him to come to her. He doesn't want to go to her, but he's goin anyway. He ain't lookin where he's goin and he ain't hurryin. He's walkin real slow, got his chin just about hangin down on his chest. Gertrude Mercer's watchin Mason nearin them porch steps. She knows he ain't lookin up at her, so she's lifted her head to look off to where the road begins to curve.

Mason's lookin up them porch steps and askin, "Ah have to comes in again?"

"Just for a while, child," Gertrude Mercer says. Then she smiles a little and says, "You can come back out in just a bit."

Slowly, Mason's comin up them steps, but he's keepin his head down. Gertrude Mercer's holdin that door open for him. But she ain't watchin him pass, she's lookin off to where the road curves. That dark shade there never goes away. It's still there when Gertrude Mercer turns from it and goes into the house.

Mason didn't have to be told. He's sittin on the chair at that table. He still got his chin hangin down close to his chest. He's keepin his head down and ain't lookin across that table at Gertrude Mercer. She had pulled a chair out from the table as quietly as she could and sat down in it. Mason still ain't lookin at her, but she's lookin at him, tryin to see his eyes. Softly she's callin his name now.

Mason ain't lookin up, doesn't want to hear his name called no more. He don't want nobody hollerin at him. He don't want to talk no more. He's lookin down, got his eyes half closed. Mama Gert's tellin him to get up and come to her. But he don't want to. She's callin his name, but up in his mind he's hearin the woman Mama Gert was hollerin at. He's hearin her callin his name. He's still seein her face and wonderin where she's gone.

"Come here, child, come on over here to Mama Gert. Come on now," Gertrude Mercer's sayin and tryin to keep them tears she feels in her eyes from comin out.

Slowly, very slowly, Mason's lookin up.

Gertrude Mercer's holdin her hand out to Mason and softly sayin, "Come on over here. Come on, now."

Mason's gettin up, but he's keepin his head down as he goes to where he's been called. He can't see it, but he feels Gertrude Mercer's hand touchin him, slidin up and down his back, pullin him closer to her. He's in her arms now, feelin her breath against his cheek. She's whisperin to him, tellin him, "I didn't mean to yell at you. You ain't did nothin to be yelled at for this day."

Mason's closin his eyes, leanin against Gertrude Mercer's shoulder. She's sighin, whisperin, "You just don't know, child . . . You just don't know, baby."

Mason ain't sayin nothin, Gertrude Mercer's pullin him closer and rockin him a little in her arms. But Mason still ain't sayin nothin, don't know how to say what he's feelin anyway. Gently Gertrude Mercer's slidin her arms from around Mason's back. She's puttin her hands on his shoulders and lookin at his face. Mason's keepin his head lowered. She's got to see his eyes and she's whisperin, "Look up to me, now . . . I got to tell you somethin, child . . . You got to know somethin . . . You hear me?"

Mason ain't lookin up.

Gertrude Mercer's whisperin, "Look up here, now. I got to tell you somethin. I got to tell fore somebody else tells you. I can't keep you in these yards forever. Now you look at me."

Slowly Mason's lookin up.

"You're just a child," Gertrude Mercer whispers, then sighs. Mason's still lookin in her eyes. Softly, she's sayin, "That was your mama that come here. . . . That was your mama, child."

Mason's lowerin his eyes, keepin them down. But, slowly, he's lookin back up and askin, "Jesus bring her back?"

Gertrude Mercer's sighin, closin her eyes. She's silent for a moment before openin her eyes and whisperin, "No, child, Jesus didn't bring her. She ain't goes to Heaven likes I told you. I just told you that . . . but . . . but . . ."

"Is she come see me again?" Mason's askin.

Gertrude Mercer looks down past Mason's eyes lookin up at her and becomes silent.

· TWELVE ·

Dicky Bird knows he got a long way to go, but he ain't hurryin none. He's got him a smile on his face and a cart full of stuff he knows he can get a couple dollars for. He's way up in them Wilkensburg hills, comin down one of them alleys up there. Some of them backyard dogs think he's passin just to give them something to bark at. Dicky Bird ain't payin them no mind, even them dogs that try and climb up over their fences to get at him. They ain't makin him push that cart no faster and ain't gettin that smile off his face. He can see that sun ain't too far from settin and he can be back to Homewood before it does.

Bill Lovit can always find him a couple dollars somewhere. He ain't lookin for nothin else. He's got what he wants. That cart of his is pushed up in them high weeds behind Mott's place. Mott got him that good kind of business, knows somebody wantin a haircut can always find him there in that basement of his. If he ain't there, folks just wait. They know he ain't went too far on that one leg of his. Mott don't talk about it much, but everybody that knows him knows what happen to that other leg of his. They know it got blown off in that first big war. Mott don't talk about that, but he always got some good talk for everything else. Some menfolk that don't even need a haircut do that stoppin by for that talk. As soon as Mott heard Bill Lovit callin his name and stumblin down his basement steps, he knew once Bill Lovit got down them steps it would be a long time fore he went back up. Bobby Fulton, Norm Jenkins, and Oscar Scott's down in that basement, too. Mott's up on that high chair of his, workin them scissors and clippers on Norm Jenkins's hair. Bobby Fulton and Oscar Scott done come to get their hair cut, too. But they ain't in no hurry and thinkin about that waitin they're doin. Bill Lovit's sittin in one of them waitin chairs, but he ain't waitin on nothin. Half of that new bottle of wine he got has been gone and if he ain't talkin, he's sippin on the other half. He's talkin now, got some of that wine in his mouth drippin down his chin. But he ain't thinkin about that. He's tellin everybody what he thinks about that Korea they have been talkin about. He's sayin, "Um . . . Um . . . Op . . . demistical . . . Gots to be demistical. Mister Truman, now he's demistical. Gots to be."

Oscar Scott got one of them big bellies. When he sits, he got to keep his legs spread open, give that belly somewhere to hang. He's laughin and that belly is just a-shakin down between his legs. Now he's lookin over at Bill Lovit and sayin, "Oh, ya optimistic. Shit . . . Ya some optimistic . . . Um-hum."

"Yes, sir . . . Yes, sir . . . I am," Bill Lovit says, then shakes his head yes and keeps shakin it.

Mott's keepin them scissors clippin around Norm Jenkins's ear. But he's sayin to Oscar Scott, "Now lets the man have him that there optimistic if he wants it."

Oscar Scott laughs, says, "Nigger don't even know where Korea be."

"Yes, I do. Yes, sir, I knows where Korea be. Don't you be tellin me I don't know where Korea be. I knows," Bill Lovit says.

Oscar Scott's belly is doin that shakin. He's lookin over at Bill Lovit, laughin and askin, "Oh, ya know where it is? Just where is it then?"

Bill Lovit ain't thinkin about Korea now. He's got that bottle up and is gettin him a quick sip. Bobby Fulton's sittin over in that chair in the corner. He ain't sayin much, never does. He's tall and thin, got that dark yellow-colored skin. His face is real skinny-lookin and them light brown eyes he got ain't too far apart from each other. He's lookin up at Mott and sayin, "I know theys be sendin for me. I didn't want to go last time, but I figure I goes before they sends for me. They sends me down to South Carolina for that trainin. They tells us we can't goes into town, gots to stay on base there. But these two boys goes and sneaks out one night. I just knew one of em. He was from over there in Jersey. But theys goes into this town lookin for girls, you know. They finds them boys next day. You know them white folks down there hangs the both of em. Hangs them up in the same tree and leaves them hangin. The MPs has to goes out there and cuts them down. I knows they be sendin for me again."

Bill Lovit's puttin the cap back on that bottle of his, then wipin off his mouth with his hand and sayin, "I knows where Japan is. Yes, sir."

Dicky Bird's just about where he's been wantin to be and still got that smile on his face. He's got them couple dollars he thought he was goin to get and that sun ain't even down yet. But Dicky Bird knows there ain't too much left of the day, knows it's time to get him somethin to eat. He done looked up, seen that low-hangin sun. But he don't need that sun to tell him he's hungry.

Gus Goins is sittin out on that back porch of his. The cool evenin air got him leanin back in that chair of his and not carin about nothin. Them chickens out in his yard ain't doin all that runnin around. The ones that ain't already climbed up in the coop are just doin that slow walkin and peckin at the ground. Them chickens doin that slow walkin and peckin ain't payin that clankity rattlin noise they're hearin no mind. Dicky Bird's pushin that empty cart of his up into Gus Goins's yard. Gus Goins ain't thinkin about Dicky Bird til he hears somebody callin his name. He didn't know he had his eyes closed til he had to open them to see who was callin him. Dicky Bird's comin up them steps sayin, "Looks like ya gettin a little nap here. Ah need me one, too. Yes, sir, went on up there to Wilkensburg, has me a good day."

Dicky Bird's still tellin Gus Goins about Wilkensburg. But Gus Goins isn't listenin. He's lookin up at the sky and tryin to figure out what time it is. When he sees that sun is just about down, he knows that Friday night is goin to get up on him soon. Dicky Bird done took him a seat, but he's still talkin about Wilkensburg. Gus Goins knows he ain't got time to be carin about Wilkensburg. He got to get that cookin started.

Dicky Bird's still sittin out on that porch. Ain't nothin left of that sun cept a glow in the far sky. But Dicky Bird ain't thinkin about that time goin by. The only thing he's thinkin about is how good that chicken Gus Goins is cookin smells. That smell is comin out that open window right onto the porch and right into Dicky Bird's nose. The more of that smell gettin in his nose, the hungrier he's gettin.

Al Johnson's comin up through Gus Goins's yard and Pete

Turner ain't too far behind him. Pete Turner's callin ahead to Al Johnson, sayin, "You better spends your money fore I get in there, cause I'm goin to get every penny you got."

Al Johnson keeps comin up the path, but he's yellin back over his shoulder at Pete Turner, tellin him, "If I were you, I'd be worryin more about that money you goin to be losin. You damn sure ain't gettin a penny out of my pocket, you ugly motherfucker."

Pete Turner laughs, then yells, "You better spends what you got whiles you have it."

Ain't nothin left of that far glow in the sky. It's gone, been gone. Just them alley cats' eyes are glowin out in that alley. Them cats are doin them quick meows, runnin back up into the dark every time folks comin get near them. Dicky Bird's done had his chicken dinner and got him another one, too. Ain't nothin left of it either, cept a few bones. But he's still sittin on that back porch. He's got him a little drink he's sippin on and watchin folks comin up that dark path. Sometimes he tries to see if he can tell who's comin. But it don't make no difference when they get up on that porch. He still gives them a respectful greetin. Folks give him one back, then hurry themselves on through that door. That loud jukebox music comin out that door already got their hips swayin and is tellin them they goin to have a good time.

Pete Turner and Al Johnson got their card game goin. Richard Norris, Gary Morgan, and Carl Hughes is playin, too. That Friday night money is that quick kind of money. It's jumpin back and forth from one hand to another. But it ain't jumpin nowhere near Al Johnson's hands. The skin on Al Johnson's face is tight. It ain't stretchin nowhere close to a smile. He's starin at them cards he's holdin in his hands. The longer he's starin the more his eyes are glowin that red, mad. Pete Turner ain't gettin a hold of that Friday night money he wants to get, but he ain't losin what he had. He can hardly keep that cigar he got stuck in his mouth in there. All that laughin and talkin he's doin got that cigar danglin and lookin like it's about to fall. It's Al Johnson's play, but Pete Turner ain't lookin at Al Johnson. He's lookin at Gary Morgan and sayin, "See now, a smart man can look at somethin and see it ain't nothin." Now he's lookin at Al Johnson and askin, "Al, did you get to six grade? Did they give you some arithmatic?"

Al Johnson ain't takin his eyes away from them cards he's holdin and ain't sayin nothin back. Pete Turner's lookin back at Gary Morgan and sayin, "See now, he don't even know what grade he went to. Now you know he don't know nothin else, cept Um goin to get his money. He know that now, that's one thing he know."

Al Johnson looks up and over them cards he's holdin. He looks at Pete Turner and says, "Nigger, you gots a better chance of gettin some pretty white Mississippi pussy with your ugly ass than you do gettin my money."

Pete Turner laughs, then says, "I already had me some of that."

Al Johnson says, "The last time you had some pussy was when you first come slidin out of one. Now shut up, you ugly motherfucker, or I ain't goin to let you leave here with your pants."

Al Johnson still ain't made his play yet. But that nice, long, slow song comin out of Gus Goins's new jukebox got Bobby Rose thinkin he can make his play. He's already had enough of that gin he's been drinkin to have his head swayin without that music playin. He's dancin with Olinda Harris. Got her all close and his mouth down on her neck. She ain't carin either and the way she's slow-thrustin herself up against him is tellin him things he ain't hearin. Folks that ain't doin that dancin is sittin back in their chairs listenin to that music and seein what they can see. Sam Barnett got his old self sittin back there. All day he had told himself he wasn't goin down to Gus's, didn't need them policemens comin back with that trouble. But he ain't thinkin about what he told himself now. He's sippin on that drink he has and watchin Olinda Harris's ass roll around with that music.

.   .   .

The sound of music is down on that Elmira Avenue, too. Folks don't have to be inside them clubs to hear that music. It's comin out the doors and windows and fillin that night air with its beats. The front of them nightclubs are all lit up with them pretty colored lights. Some of them lights are real bright and flash them pretty colors out into the street. They make some of them sidewalks look red, blue, and them other pretty colors. That music comin out of the Satin Club is bringin folks in. Nicole Lynch is goin in there wearin a light purple dress. The look she got in her eyes says she knows she's wearin that dress well. When she walks, she can make it flow the way she feels. She can balance on them high heels she's got on like a good ballerina balances on her toes. She looks like one, too; tall and slender with big dark eyes. Kenny Douglas is makin that horn sound like it's callin her, beggin her to come to it. But she ain't lookin at that stage where that horn is blowin from. She's lookin at Mack Jack.

Kenny Douglas is takin that trumpet out his mouth and

wipin at his forehead. But Vann Irvis ain't gettin off them drums, he's gettin down on them. He's got them drumsticks swishin through the air, goin back and forth from them drums to them cymbals. But his foot ain't swishin, it's poundin down on that bass drum pedal. It's makin that bass drum pound out that loud, deep thump. That bass drum beat got folks shakin their hips and poppin their fingers.

Nicole Lynch is sittin herself up on one of them bar stools. She's gettin herself comfortable, gettin a cigarette out and lit. Vann Irvis is still poundin on them drums. But she's quietly lookin in that mirror behind the bar. She's lookin at herself, then she's lookin to see if she can see Mack Jack.

Kenny Douglas got that horn back up to his mouth. He's blowin one of them long, high, squealin notes. Some of them folks sittin down done slid up on the edge of their seats. They got their heads noddin and don't want that long high sound to come down. That high note's all up in Mack Jack's head. It's swirlin around in it. It got in but it can't get out. Mack Jack ain't lettin it get out. He still got that drum beatin up there, too. He's standin back by that back wall. But he ain't shakin or swayin nothin. He's standin still like he ain't never moved, never goin to move. It's dark back there where he's standin at. But some of them stage lights are flashin on his face. Them lights are flashin in his mind, too. Nicole Lynch can't see him in that mirror. She's takin them quick peeks over her shoulder at him, tryin to catch his eyes. But Mack Jack ain't lookin back.

Kenny Douglas done took that horn out his mouth, had to give it some rest. But Sweet Man Sam got that guitar makin them real low, long sounds. It sounds like it's talkin, tellin that horn, "Go on and takes your rest." It's tellin them folks sittin on the edge of their seats to "Go on and set back. Take it while you can get it. Make it last for you. Let it feel good to you." It's tellin Nicole Lynch, "Go on and look back there at that man with them pretty eyes."

Sweet Man Sam's playin that guitar nice and slow. It's slowin down them lights flashin up in Mack Jack's mind. They ain't flashin fast no more, they're just flickerin. They're lookin like little faraway candles. But they're gettin hot, makin Mack Jack hot. Sweat's rollin down his face, but it's rollin real slow. He can feel it movin down his face. He ain't feelin nothin else cept that sweat movin on his face. Ain't nobody turned around to look at that sweat rollin down his face. But somethin is in his mind, lookin at him. It ain't got no face, just eyes. Mack Jack's movin, runnin, but he ain't went nowhere. He's still standin against that wall. Them lights are flashin in his eyes again. He's lookin away from them, lookin everywhere. He's lookin up at the ceilin, back down to the floor. He ain't hot no more, he's cool. Sweet Man Sam's guitar is tellin him, "Looks back up here at me, Um nice."

Nicole Lynch is watchin Mack Jack, seein him look back at that stage, seein him slowly turnin his head and lookin at her. She's turnin around real slow, lettin her look linger in his eyes. Charley Lennwood's fingers are dancin on them piano keys. They're dancin real slow, takin their time gettin up and down them keys. Nicole Lynch is strikin a match, lighting her cigarette, then lookin back into that mirror behind the bar. She's starin in it, tryin to see if she can see Mack Jack lookin back at her. But it's dark way back in that mirror and she can't find what she's lookin for.

That music ain't playin no more. But folks's still sittin around in that Satin Club doin their talkin and sippin on them drinks. Wee little Charley Lennwood is down from behind his piano and up sittin at that bar. He's got up there on that stool next to Nicole Lynch. He's tryin to drink his drink, get some good word from Nicole Lynch, but Ray Nelson is leanin over his shoulder and won't stop talkin in his ear. Ray Nelson's sayin, "You all had it tonight. Yeal, you all had it tonight."

"Thanks man, thanks man," Charley Lennwood's sayin back, then turnin to Nicole Lynch. With that little voice of his. "How did you like the set, baby?"

Nicole Lynch is lookin over and down at Charley Lennwood lookin up at her. She's givin him a little smile and sayin, "I enjoyed it."

Charley Lennwood's smilin and askin, "What's your name, baby?"

Nicole Lynch ain't lookin at Charley Lennwood no more. She's lookin back over her shoulder. Mack Jack's still standin by that wall. Kenny Douglas and Sweet Man Sam's back there with him. Kenny Douglas is talkin to Mack Jack, sayin, "Yeal, man, we got us a nice thing goin. We could use us a good sax."

Sweet Man Sam says, "Yeal, man, it would be nice if you set in with us. Man, we could really get down then."

Mack Jack's lookin at Sweet Man Sam, then lookin down at the floor. Sweet Man Sam says, "Yeal, we could use us a good sax man."

Mack Jack's lookin back up past Sweet Man Sam. He's lookin at them eyes that are lookin back at him. Nicole Lynch is lettin Mack Jack see her lookin at him fore she slowly turns her head. Charley Lennwood's lookin at her and askin, "Let me get you a drink. What you drinkin, baby?"

Nicole Lynch looks at Charley Lennwood and says, "I like vodka and orange juice."

Charley Lennwood's callin up over the bar, tryin to get a bartender to know he's sittin there and needs some service. Nicole Lynch is lookin in that mirror. She can see Mack Jack now. He's behind that trumpet player, they're nearin the bar. Charley Lennwood's tellin the bartender what he wants for the lady sittin next to him. He's gettin a drink for himself, too. Nicole Lynch is still lookin in that mirror.

Kenny Douglas and Sweet Man Sam are passin behind them folks sittin at the bar. Mack Jack's followin them. Sweet Man Sam's stoppin behind Charley Lennwood and sayin, "Hey, Charley, man."

Charley Lennwood's turnin around on his stool. Sweet Man Sam starts tellin him about Mack Jack. Nicole Lynch is takin a quick look over her shoulder. She's lookin right up into Mack Jack's eyes. He's lookin back at her. Charley Lennwood's stickin out his hand and tellin Mack Jack, "Hey, it's nice to meet you, I heard about you."

Mack Jack's turnin and lookin at the little man sittin on the bar stool. Slowly he reaches out and shakes Charley Lennwood's hand. Sweet Man Sam's lookin at Nicole Lynch and askin Charley Lennwood, "Who's this beautiful lady here?"

Slowly, Nicole Lynch turns to Sweet Man Sam and says, "My name is Nicole."

Charley Lennwood's smilin and sayin, "Yeal, this is Nicole."

Sweet Man Sam likes what he sees. He's thinkin fast and talkin faster. He's tellin Nicole Lynch they're on the way to Judy's Place, he's tellin her to come on with them. He's sayin, "We goin to have us a nice time."

Nicole Lynch is givin Sweet Man Sam a little smile, but

she ain't tellin him she's goin to Judy's Place. He's sayin, "Come on with us, it's right around the corner."

"I know where Judy's is. I might stop by a little later," Nicole Lynch is sayin to Sweet Man Sam. Then slowly she's turnin back around to the bar and pickin up her drink. But she's sure Mack Jack was lookin at her, saw her give him the look she wanted him to have.

The night at home on Elmira Avenue seems like it never wants to leave. Them folks out on the avenue can look like they were born for the dark, come alive at night. Them street corner women got them short tight skirts on. They got them night men lookin even if they don't do that stoppin for them. Them corner-standin men always got somethin to sell and will take anything they can get for it. Everybody knows where Judy's Place is, but Judy don't let everybody come in her place. She don't let them empty-pocket, low-down folks in her place and she tells them that, too. Judy ain't real big. She's a short, skinny woman. But folks know she's quick with that razor if somebody gets wrong with her. She got her a little restaurant that stays open all night. But folks know that little restaurant ain't nothin but a front for that big room she got in the back. Night folks know they can get anything, anytime in Judy's back room.

Sweet Man Sam ain't sayin anything now. He ain't doin nothin but noddin, noddin and listenin to that soft jukebox music in Judy's back room. Kenny Douglas is talkin, but he ain't talkin much. He's takin them hard drags on that marijuana he's smokin. Then he's passin it to Mack Jack and sayin, "Yeal, man, you know, man, we could do New York. Maybe we could do them Paris gigs. We could play your stuff. You good on that sax, too. You real good."

Mack Jack ain't hearin nothin but sounds of things. Them words he's hearin ain't nothin but faraway sounds. That soft jukebox music ain't in his mind, his mind's in it. It's in that jukebox lookin out through all them pretty colors painted over it. Every long, slow beat is keepin him in it til the next one comes along, takes him and keeps him for a while. He got that joint up to his mouth, suckin on it hard. He's keepin that smoke sucked in til it's time to let it out. Then he lets it come slow, like one of them long, slow beats comin out of that jukebox his mind is in. Kenny Douglas is leanin back in his chair, got his head lowered but his eyes up. He's lookin around that room, but them other night folks in there ain't lookin back. They're deep into their own little corners, cept for them soft-colored lights. It's dark in that room.

Mack Jack's passin that joint to Sweet Man Sam, then leanin back in his chair. Sweet Man Sam's suckin on that joint, makin its little end tip glow real red. Kenny Douglas is doin that slow talkin, but Mack Jack ain't listenin. He's lookin over at them pretty lights comin from the jukebox. He's turnin his head and watchin Nicole Lynch. She's comin in that room, gettin up in his mind. She's floatin in it like some spirit of the night. She's nearin, Sweet Man Sam's sayin something to her. She's smiling, sittin down, and lookin at Mack Jack. He's lookin back at her, lookin at her eyes. He's talkin softly to her, hearin his words way after he's said them. Nicole Lynch is smilin, sayin things back. Her voice is low, soft, and gettin up into Mack Jack's head with that slow beat of the music up in his mind. Sweet Man Sam's lookin at Nicole Lynch, noddin his head and sayin, "You want some of this? It's nice."

Mack Jack's watchin the little end tip of that joint glow red.

He's lookin at them red lips suckin on it and makin it glow. Some woman's voice is comin out that jukebox, soft and sweet. She's singin, tellin some man somewhere to bring his lovin on back home. Nicole Lynch is leanin back in her chair. Mack Jack's leanin to her, he's whisperin to her. She's smilin and sayin, "My name's Nicole, what's yours?"

Them little dark moments in Judy's back room are passin real slow. They go on and go somewhere, then come back with the same time they left with. Sweet Man Sam ain't thinkin about that time, don't care whether it's comin or goin. His eyes ain't open anyway, but his head still doin that slow noddin. He ain't lookin up, ain't sayin nothin. Kenny Douglas is lookin up, watchin Mack Jack followin that pretty woman out the door. He's sayin, "Yeal, man, I'll see you tomorrow. Bring that horn."

Them nighttime lights out on Elmira Avenue ain't out. Some of them sidewalks still got them pretty colors flashin on them. The sounds of Nicole Lynch's heels clickin across them pretty colors sound like faraway echoes in Mack Jack's mind. She's walkin close to him, talkin that soft talk up in his ear. Mack Jack's smilin, then widening that smile, then them soft words get up in his head and stay there. She's turnin off Elmira Avenue. It's dark on that street she's takin Mack Jack down. Them Elmira Avenue lights ain't followin her. She's turnin off that dark street and goin up into one of them roomin houses. Mack Jack's followin her up some dark steps. Them steps he's goin up keep goin, don't end. But he ain't tryin to see them steps. He's lookin at the skirt of that light purple dress. He can see it in the dark, watch it swirl and flow. It's dancin in his mind, leadin him up through that dark. Some key is makin a noise goin in and wigglin in a lock. It's dark in that room Mack

Jack's goin in. He's standin, starin into the dark. A soft low light is comin on. Nicole Lynch is standin in that soft light. She's lookin at Mack Jack, starin in his eyes. Mack Jack's lookin back, ain't seein nothin but them dark eyes lookin at him.

That soft light is off. That soft talk that came, lingered, is gone. That room Mack Jack's in ain't still, it's movin. He's still. That purple dress is slowly movin, slidin, fallin to the floor. That pretty woman is movin through the dark. Her breath is warm on his lips, her tongue is hot in his mouth. Her soft bare breasts are rubbin over the hair on his chest. He's movin over her, lookin down into her eyes. Her tongue is makin little chills come to his neck. His eyes are closin, his face is slidin down, his tongue is lickin at her breast. She's moanin, suckin breaths, tiltin her head back. Them moanin sounds are far away, but they're comin, gettin closer. They're down in Mack Jack's mind now. He's hearin them, feelin them. It's hot and wet between her legs. Slowly, she's spreadin them. Her scent is seepin up into Mack Jack's nose, sneakin up in his mind. Slowly Mack Jack's pushin himself into her. She's suckin at the air, reachin and scratchin at Mack Jack's back. He's hearin them loud gruntin sounds he's makin comin from far away. But that warm, juicy feelin wrapped around his penis is close. That warm feelin is gettin up in his mind, makin them faraway sounds seem farther away.

Elmira Avenue is quiet now, almost empty. That early light is comin, makin it look all gray. Somebody is lyin in one of them storefront doorways. He's got some small stack of old papers under his head and a piece of cardboard box lyin over him. He ain't payin no mind to Mack Jack walkin by. Some of them nighttime alley cats are still out in that early light lookin for somethin to eat. The ones that are seein Mack Jack comin through that narrow walkway are doin them quick meows, then scootin away. That big black cat of Bella's is sittin on her windowsill. It's listenin to them squeaky sounds them steps are makin. Mack Jack's comin up them squeaky steps.

Bella's sleepin in that back room of hers. The sound of that soft tappin on her door is slowly creepin into her sleep. She's openin her eyes, seein that night is gone, that early light has come. It's silent for a moment fore she hears them tappin sounds again.

Mack Jack's standin at Bella's door when she opens it. He has his head lowered and his eyes lookin down, too. Bella's lookin up in his face, but she ain't sayin nothin. She's openin up that door wider. Mack Jack's comin in the door, but he's keepin his eyes lowered. Bella's closin the door and askin, "Where have you been all night?"

Mack Jack shrugs his shoulders. Bella's starin at him, tryin to see his eyes. Slowly, softly she's askin, "Where have you been?"

Mack Jack ain't answerin her, he's sittin down in one of them chairs, then he's starin down at the floor. Bella's comin to him, slowly reachin out and touchin his cheek. She's gently rubbin it, then slidin her hand around to the back of his neck. Softly she's rubbin his neck and sayin, "Where were you? You can't stay away. They will hurt you again."

Mack Jack's keepin his head down. Bella's askin, "You're tired, arn't you? You want to sleep, don't you?"

That early-mornin light is comin through Bella's windows. But it ain't gettin no brighter. Them dark curtains ain't lettin it.

Mack Jack's lyin on Bella's couch, his eyes are closed. Bella's coverin him up with a light bedspread and whisperin, "I'll take care of you now."

. . .

That early Saturday mornin sunlight comin through them windows and fallin on his face ain't puttin no life on it. Tommy Moses's mother ain't watchin that sun come up, but she knows it's comin. She's up, been up, couldn't sleep. She's sittin near that coffin just starin at it. Sometimes she gets up, goes to it, and looks down at Tommy Moses. Sometimes she whispers, "Oh, Tommy. Oh, Tommy." But she doesn't look out that window to see how light that day is gettin. She doesn't want that sun to get any higher. She doesn't want that undertaker man comin and takin her boy and puttin him in that ground.

Mister Hopewell's up and sippin on his coffee. He knows he got him a busy day, got him three funerals he got to do and another body that needs pickin up. He's lookin at his watch now and wonderin if he should go down to the morgue and get Clifford Dawkins on out of there or wait til after he finishes his funerals. Mister Hopewell's sighin now, lookin out his window and wonderin how long it's goin to be fore them bodies start comin back from Korea. Now he's wishin he had enough money to retire. Let somebody else do all this buryin.

. . .

Snake Town never takes long to wake up. Folks up way fore that sun sends its first light to get them up. Folks that ain't goin to the field get up and help do that mornin feedin. Them women that do the house cleanin and cookin in Stoney Town, they got to get up fore that sun come, too. They got to get themselves cleaned and fed fore they do that feedin and cookin for them white folks.

The field folks had gone on down that Snake Town road and on past Gertrude Mercer's house. She had heard them passin, didn't have to look out her window to know it was them early-mornin hours. Those early-mornin hours are gone and Gertrude Mercer has done them mornin chores. She got them chickens and mules fed, got her some eggs for her and Mason's breakfast. She's done her prayin, too. She did it, wanted to get it done fore Mason got up and started to ask questions again. She did that knee-prayin, got down beside her bed with her Bible in her hands. She asked her God to show her the ways she can't see, can't find for herself.

Mason's up now, eatin his breakfast and ain't sayin much. Gertrude Mercer's sittin across the table from him, sippin on her coffee. When she knows Mason has his eyes lowered to his plate, she looks at him, then tries to sigh quietly. She doesn't quiver or shake when she hears someone callin for her. Mason looks up and says, "Mama Gert, that's Aunt Lulu comin."

Lulu's comin up that yard path, she's walkin slow, knowin she can't carry that child in her much farther. She's nearin them porch steps and callin out, "Mama . . . Mama . . . It's Lulu . . . It's just me, Mama."

Willet's out sittin on Lulu's porch steps. She ain't took her eyes from off that Snake Town road. She watched as Lulu went down it and she's waitin for her to come back up it. Jeremiah's out on that porch, too. He's standin and leanin against that porch post. He ain't lookin down the road, he's lookin up. That road's quiet. Them children ain't doin all that runnin and playin yet. That Snake Town heat ain't come yet either. But them porch-sittin women are already out on their porches, doin that sittin and watchin.

Jeremiah's takin a long deep breath, then saying, "We can't stay here too much longer."

Willet's silent and ain't takin her eyes off that road. Jeremiah sighs, then says, "I just got a feelin. We got to get out of here."

Willet turns her head, looks up at Jeremiah. She stares at him for a moment, then turns and looks back at the road. Jeremiah sighs, then looks down the road. Standin, he can see farther. He can see Lulu comin and bringin some child by the hand. Softly Jeremiah says, "She's comin. I think she has him."

Quickly Willet gets up on her feet, steps back up on the porch, and looks down the road. She can see Lulu comin, see Mason with her. She keeps lookin. Jeremiah's sayin something, but she ain't listenin, ain't takin her mind off of what she's seein. She's gatherin her skirt and hurryin down them steps, then lettin go of her skirt and runnin down that yard path. She's runnin past Tommy Moses's car and out onto the road. Them porch-sittin women are gettin up off their chairs and goin to the edge of their porches. They're doin that quick lookin and ain't carin if somebody sees them doin it. Some of them children out on that road see that woman comin and runnin. They're gettin out her way. Yard dogs are hearin that runnin noise, lookin and startin that barkin. But Willet ain't payin them dogs no mind. She ain't seein them either. Ain't nothin in her eyes cept the blurs of things she's runnin by.

Lulu's holdin Mason's hand, got her head down lookin at him while she talkin to him. Mason's all dressed up, got his

Sunday clothes on. He ain't lookin up at Lulu, he's lookin down at that road. He's lookin at anything he can see to look at. Lulu's tellin him things he didn't know, can't understand.

Willet's runnin and ain't carin about them tears she feels comin out of her eyes and runnin down her cheeks.

Lulu's lettin them last words she was sayin drift, then fade into silence. She's heard them sounds of runnin footsteps comin down the road. She's lookin up, but she ain't sayin anything, just lookin. Mason's lookin up, too. He ain't sayin anything either, but Lulu feels him squeezin her hand.

Willet's slowin down, she's walkin now. She's got her hands up to her face, tryin to wipe them tears from her face and get her hair out of her eyes. But she ain't takin her eyes off Mason. She's close enough to see his face, see him starin at her.

Slowly Mason's lookin up at Lulu and askin, "That be my mama?"

Softly Lulu says, "Yes, that's your mama, Mason."

Mason looks back up the road. Lulu's stoppin and standin still. Mason stops, too, but he keeps lookin up the road. Willet's close to him now, close enough to feel herself shakin as she nears. She's sayin, "Mason . . . Mason . . ."

Mason's silent, but he's still lookin at Willet comin to him. She's close enough to look down in his eyes, touch him. Mason's lookin up into her eyes. She's bendin down, reachin out and puttin her hands on his arms and softly sayin, "Mason."

Lulu's lettin Mason's hand go. Willet's bringin him into her arms, huggin him. Her eyes are closed, she feels the softness of his cheek touchin hers. She can hear him askin, "You my mama?"

Gently Willet's movin her face away from Mason's so she can see his eyes. She's lookin in them and sayin, "I'm your mother, Mason. Yes, I'm your mother."

Mason's silent.

Willet pulls him back into her arms.

Lulu's lookin down at Willet and whisperin, "Mama say he can stay til suppertime. Then she say Ah have to brings him on back then."

Willet's eyes are closed again, she ain't openin them up, ain't lookin up at Lulu. But Lulu's still lookin down at her, seein them tears runnin down her cheeks, seein her pullin Mason closer to her.

Mason's little arms are hangin loosely at his sides. His chin is down, restin on Willet's shoulder. But his eyes are open, he's starin up the road. Willet's slowly loosing him from her arms, puttin her hands on his face and lookin into his eyes. Mason looks back, then down. Willet says, "I'm your mother, I've come back just for you, just to see you."

Mason looks up, then looks back down.

Them yard dogs ain't doin that barkin no more. That Snake Town road is quiet. Them children out on it ain't doin nothin but that quiet lookin. Della Stucky was standin on her porch, watchin Willet runnin down the road. She ain't standin no more, she's sittin, but she's still lookin down the road. Willet got Mason by the hand and she's bringin him on up the road. She's walkin real slow and lookin down at Mason. He's lookin down, too, but he ain't lookin at nothin but them little stones lyin on the ground. Lulu's walkin beside her sister. Sometimes she has a little smile on her face.

Jeremiah's still leanin against that porch post. He's lit up a cigarette and is blowin the smoke out his mouth. But he's still lookin down the road, lookin at Willet comin with Mason. Dorothy Webb and Pauline Russell are on their porches doin that lookin, that lookin down the road and then that lookin back and forth at one another. Mason's nearin that big dark car and lookin up at it. Willet sees him lookin at the car and asks, "Do you want to go for a ride in the car?"

Mason looks slowly up at Willet and asks, "That be your car? Can ya drive one?"

Tommy Moses hurries up and gets in Willet's mind and won't leave. But she's smilin anyway and sayin, "That's the car I came down here to see you in. I can't drive, but if you want to, you can go for a ride in it. Me and Jeremiah will take you for a ride. Do you want to go for a ride after a while?"

Mason's smilin.

"We'll go for a ride after a while." Willet says, then leans over and kisses Mason's cheek.

Softly Lulu's sayin, "Wil, Mama might not want Mason bein in no car. Ya know how Mama is, she might not want Mason goin nowhere cept here."

Willet's rollin her eyes at Lulu, then starin at her. Lulu's sayin, "Wil, Mama ain't had to let Mason come up here. She's tryin to do right, now. Ya gots to do right, too."

"This is my child," Willet says, then looks back to Mason.

.   .   .

It don't take long for that Snake Town sun to get high, get everything under it to glarin. But that high sun ain't stoppin folks from doin that lunchtime eatin. Lulu's feedin them children of hers and fixin Jeremiah something to eat, too. But whenever she gets a chance, she peeks out that door and looks out to the road. Sometimes Jeremiah looks out to that road, too, wonderin when Willet's comin back from where she took Mason to.

That noon hour's gone, them children are back out on the road playin. Lulu's cleanin up that cookin room, but she's still takin them peeks out the window. Jeremiah went back out on that porch, stayed out there for a while. He did that lookin up the road and that hopin he could drive up it soon. But he's sittin back in that cookin room now, doin that waitin. Lulu's takin one of them peeks out the window and sayin, "She ought to be back here soon. Mason ain't had his lunch. Poor child gots ta be hungry."

Jeremiah sighs and says, "She'll be back soon. She knows we got to go."

Lulu says, "Ah hates ta see her go again. Seems like she always gots to do that runnin. That got her in that trouble, that runnin she got to do."

Jeremiah's silent.

Lulu says, "Ah guess ya knows about Wilmington. Wil had to always do that runnin, went up there and did that runnin. That's what broke Mama's heart. She knew Wil was up there doin no good. She knew. Wil said she wasn't doin nothin but workin at that place . . ."

Jeremiah ain't sayin anything, but Lulu ain't waitin on him to say anything. She's still talkin. "When Wil came back here carryin Mason, Mama lets her stay. But soon she have Mason, she went and did that runnin. Left Mason there with Mama. She could have sends a letter, send some kind of word. Ah hates ta sees her goes again. Seems like she gots ta do that runnin. She should have just left Mason be. Ah hopes she brings him on back here soon. Ah knows that boy's hungry."

Willet didn't have to take Mason far to get where she wanted to go. That big tree down by the creek was still there, that little grassy spot under it was as quiet as she wanted it to be. Mason done run up and down alongside that creek, poked a long stick in it to see if he could make fishes come up. Willet had run with him, stuck that stick in the water, too. But she's sittin under that tree now, got Mason sittin right beside her. Mason's askin, "Is it big up there in the north? Trains go up there, too?"

Willet smiles, says, "There's lots of trains. The north is real big."

Mason looks up to her, askin, "It be big like Wilingtons, it be that big?"

"It's bigger that Wilmington."

"It's bigger than Wilingtons? It be that big? Its trains be bigger, too?"

Willet's silent for a moment, then she softly says, "It's bigger. Do you want to come with me? We can ride on a train up there. And we can go see picture shows. And we can go see the animals in the zoo. Do you want to come with me? Do you want to be with your mother?"

"Mama Gert say Ah come back fore dinner, she say that."

Willet looks in Mason's eyes and whispers, "I'm your mother, you belong with me."

Jeremiah's back out on the porch and leanin up against that post. He's doin that lookin and waitin, but he don't have to look too far and wait too long. He sees Willet comin down the road, she's got Mason by the hand and she's walkin fast. He goes over to the screen door and tells Lulu Willet's comin. Mason's smilin and almost skippin to keep up with Willet. He's nearin that big car and askin, "We go in the car now?"

Willet slows, quickly bends over, kisses Mason on his cheek and whispers, "Yes, we're going now."

Lulu's standin on the porch watchin Willet and Mason comin up the steps. She smiles at Mason and says, "Boy, Ah knows ya must be hungry."

Willet lets Mason's hand go and tells him, "Go on in the house and let Aunt Lulu fix you something to eat."

Mason's goin on into the house, Lulu's followin him in. Willet's stayin on the porch, watchin them go in. When she can see Mason sittin down at that table and Lulu goin to that icebox, she looks at Jeremiah and whispers, "We goin to go soon?"

It ain't takin long for Mason to eat that sandwich and drink the glass of milk Lulu gave to him. Willet's in the cookin room waitin on him to finish. Lulu's talkin to her, sayin, "Ah knows he be hungry. Where did ya all go?"

Willet smiles, says, "We went down by the creek. You know, where that big tree is, the one Papa went fishin by."

Lulu gets a big smile on her face and says, "Lord, Ah ain't been down there since Papa takes us down there when we littles."

Willet sighs, slowly lowers her eyes, then looks up and says, "Lulu, we goin to go now. Jeremiah wants to go, his brother is expectin us. I promised Mason we ride him in the car. We goin to ride him down to Mama's. Maybe she come out and say something to me. Maybe she won't be so mad when I come back again."

Mason's runnin to that car, them other children see him tryin to get that door open, stop that playin and come over to that car, too. Jeremiah didn't take no extra time to tell Lulu good-bye. He's openin that car door for Mason. Lulu's standin on the porch with tears comin down her cheeks. Willet got them tears comin down her cheeks, too. She's huggin her sister and sayin, "Lulu, don't be mad at me. I got to go now. Just remember, I love you. I'll write this time, let you know where I'm at. I hope you have the baby soon. Don't be mad at me. I'm goin now."

Jeremiah's startin that car up. Mason's sittin between him and Willet, lookin at all them knobs on the dashboard. Them other children are standin around the car, watchin it start to move. Them porch-sittin women are up on their feet, watchin that car move, too. Lulu's on her porch with them tears still rollin down her cheeks. She's wavin til she sees that car turn up the road instead of down. She's startin down them steps quickly and yellin, "WIL . . . WIL . . . WHERE YA GOIN? . . . WIL!"

Gertrude Mercer's out on her porch, but she ain't sittin. She's standin, watchin Lulu comin down the road. She's lookin for Mason, but she don't see him. She's hurryin down them steps and down that yard path. She's hurryin up to that road, lookin past Lulu, but she still don't see Mason. She's yellin, "WHERE'S MASON, LULU? WHERE'S MASON? WHERE IS HE?"

· THIRTEEN ·

Folks livin in them houses around Gus Goins's don't need nobody to tell them it's Saturday night. All that noise comin from out of Gus Goins's is tellin them it's Saturday night and must have been payday at the mill. Folks livin out on Fiance Street and sittin out on their porches can't even hear themselves talk. To hear them tell it, they can't even hear them loud old night trains goin by. Bill Lovit ain't hearin nothin, he's down in that front room of Gus Goins's where all that noise is comin from. He's sittin up in one of them corners, sleepin and snorin. Them folks in there dancin and doin all that loud talkin ain't payin him no mind. That card game is goin on in the back room, but Al Johnson had to come on out of there. He's standin out on that back porch, gettin him some air, havin him a cigarette, and tryin to save him that money he got left. Gary Morgan's comin up through that dark yard path, seein Al Johnson standin out on the porch and askin, "What you doin out here? Pete got your money already?"

Al Johnson laughs some, then says, "No, I been waitin on your black ass to get in here. I know you got that big money today."

Luther Duffs comin up through that dark path. Folks don't

see much of him during weekdays. He got one of them steady nighttime jobs at the post office. But come them weekend nights folks see Luther Duffs all over the place, spendin and showin that good money he makes. He's short, got that dark reddish-colored skin. He keeps his black hair slicked back and shiny all the time. Al Johnson sees him comin up them porch steps and calls out, "Hey, Luther, let me hold one of them hundreds you got."

Luther Duffs laughs and says, "Man, the last hundred Ah done see was fore they put George Washington's pitchure on it."

"You a lyin motherfucker," Al Johnson says, then laughs. "Where you been spendin all that money?"

Luther Duffs says, "Oh, man, just around, you know. I was over on Elmira, you know, had to take care of a little business."

Gary Morgan's still out on that porch with Al Johnson. He gives Luther Duffs a little laugh and says, "Yeal, you over there takin care of that midnight business."

Luther Duffs gets one of them big smiles on his face, then says, "Man, guess who I saw over there? Man, I'm comin out the Flamingo and I looks and I looks and here comes Mack Jack. He ain't had his shirt on. It's hot but it ain't that hot. I looks at him, you know, goin to say something anyway. Shit, I get a good look at him. Shit if I was a fuckin elephant he wouldn't have known I was standing there. I don't know what he got a hold of, but it damn sure had a hold of him."

Gus Goins ain't happy doin all that runnin around in that business he's doin. But he knows he's goin to be happy when he gets done countin that money he's makin. That new jukebox he got ain't new no more. Folks in that front room are wearin it out, ain't givin that little arm a break at all. That music it's makin is gettin out them windows, gettin way up in that dark Saturday night sky.

Ain't no more noise left in the night cept for them sudden meows of alley cats dartin through the dark. And Bill Lovit tryin to find his way back home, singin, "WAIT TIL THE SUN SHINES NELLY . . . AND THE CLOUDS GO DRIFTIN BY . . . WAIT TIL THE SUN SHINES NELLY."

That Sunday mornin sun seems to have its own way of comin to light up Homewood. It got that way of sorta waitin for Saturday night to go on, be gone, fore it sends its first light. Bill Lovit's asleep now, ain't seein that sun comin up at all. But them church-goin folks, if they ain't up, they're gettin up.

Mister Allen's up, he likes them Sunday mornins, he likes that quiet it brings. He's sittin at his kitchen table, drinkin his coffee. He got that radio on, that Sunday mornin news is on. But Mister Allen knows that news he's hearin about Korea ain't no good news. He's shakin his head and mutterin, "Don't need it . . . No, sir, don't need it."

Mister Allen's gettin up and turnin that radio dial. He's lookin for some nice Sunday mornin music. He don't want to think about that Korea anymore, don't want that kind of news messin up his Sunday like that Pearl Harbor news did. He's found him some music, but he ain't sittin back down. He's lookin toward that kitchen window, seein it gettin brighter outside. He's figurin he better go on and get his breakfast fixed fore it's time to get ready for church. Mister Allen doesn't like to be late for church.

Miss Alberta's up and hurryin around that roomin house of hers. Sunday mornin ain't no rest time for her. She's done got Edmund Yates cleaned up, hand-fed, and out on her porch already. She knows she got to get some of that Sunday supper ready, get them greens clean and them potatoes cut up. She keeps lookin up at that clock on the wall, lookin to see how much time she got fore she got to get ready for church. Sometimes she wonders where that Mack Jack is and that money he owes her. But as soon as she does, she hurries and tries to think of somethin else. She don't want her God knowin she's doin that kind of thinkin on Sunday.

Edmund Yates don't even know it's Sunday. He's sittin in that chair of his, got his head down. Miss Alberta put his shawl up over his shoulders, but he don't know it's there. Only thing he's feelin is that little bit of sunlight startin to get on his face. He likes that feelin when he can remember he's feelin it.

Miss Alberta done got herself out of the bathroom and out from in front of her mirror. She got her hair lookin the way she wants it and that light blue dress lookin the way she wants it to look on her. She's got her big black purse and is hurryin out her front door. She's on her porch now, gettin ready to tell Edmund Yates she's goin to church, til she sees Mack Jack comin up them porch steps. Her eyes are gettin big and her mouth is hangin open. Before she knows it, she's sayin, "Man, where is your shirt? It is Sunday mornin and I am not goin to have you comin in here likes you are. Don't you have no respect for yourself?"

Mack Jack got some little smile on his face. But he ain't smilin at Miss Alberta, he ain't payin her no mind. She sees him sorta stumble, steppin up from that last step and weavin some like he's drunk. She don't like that at all. She's sayin, "I am not havin this here. This is my house and I'm goin to have my respect here. It is Sunday mornin and I am not goin to put up with this, I'll tell you that right now."

Mack Jack still got that little smile on his face. Now he's close enough to Miss Alberta for her to see that walkin sweat on his face and chest. She don't like what she's seein and she don't like what she's smellin. That stinky sweat smell comin from under Mack Jack's arms is gettin up in her nose. She's sayin, "You gots to find yourself someplace else to live. You gets my money and you gets yourself out of my house today. And I want that money slid under my door and you out of here fore I get back here."

Miss Alberta's hurryin on down the steps and she ain't lookin back. Mack Jack's standin on the porch, still got that little smile on his face. He looks over at Edmund Yates sittin on the porch with his head sunk down, then looks at that front door and stares at it. It ain't swayin back and forth like he thinks it is, it's him doin that swayin. He's in the hallway now and that early-mornin shade in there is floatin around like some dark gray mist. Mack Jack likes that mist in his mind, stands there and lets it float around in his mind fore he starts up them dark, shady steps.

· · ·

Sunday came slow to Snake Town, brought that day some folks were waitin on. It brought them that time to rest their backs, stay out them pickin fields. But that Sunday mornin didn't bring that Sunday peace Gertrude Mercer was waitin for. It didn't bring back what that Saturday took away from her. The sunlight comin through them windows and gettin on that table she's sittin at ain't lightin up her eyes. Them dried tearstains on her face don't stay dry too long. She's done some of the things she had to do. Fed them mules and chickens. But she didn't pluck them eggs. She passed that little wooden wagon, had to look in it. She tried to let that turtle in it go, but it ain't gone. She picked it up out of there, but put it back. She's up from the table now, standin and lookin out the door. She's starin out at the road again. She knows it's church time, she knows Mason's goin to miss his Sunday schoolin. But she knows her God got to come down the road and get her this mornin, cause she can't go up by herself without Mason.

Folks that done come into that A.M.E. church don't like to bring no bad talk in there with them. They got to hushin them whispers about that Willet takin that boy way fore they got there. Folks like to come in that church nice and quiet, show their respect for that cross way up on top that steeple. Mamas hush them children quick.

It's quiet in that church now. Folks in there can't hear nothin but their own breathin sounds. Elsie Stokely was playin that piano, playin it nice and slow while folks came in, took them seats. But she ain't playin no more, she knows when to stop. Reverend Bell likes to let that quietness settle into silence fore he gets up behind his pulpit.

Lulu's sittin in that church, sittin in that same seat she always does. She got her children on one side of her and her husband on the other. They're lookin up, watchin Reverend Bell gettin up behind his pulpit. But Lulu's lookin down into some shadow beneath the seat in front of hers.

Reverend Bell is one of them big dark-faced men. He's got one of them deep voices that can make words roll like thunder. He's got his Bible open to the page he wants to tell about. But folks know he doesn't have to open up his Bible at all. He can tell anybody about any page in his Bible and have his eyes closed while he's tellin them. They know as soon as he gets to preachin he ain't goin to be lookin down at his Bible anyway. They know he's goin to start with that slow talkin. But it ain't goin to be long fore he gets to shoutin about what he's tellin about. He can get to pointin to what he's tryin to tell them and show them about. He can get silent, wait in that silence til somebody sees what he's pointin at, hears what he's tellin and shouts back, "Hallelujah! Hallelujah!"

Lulu's lookin up.

Reverend Bell's doin that shoutin, tellin folks, "YA GOTS TA LOOKS UP . . . LOOKS UP TO THE HILLS FROM WHENCE THAT HELP BE COMIN DOWN FROM. YA GOTS TO BELIEVES IT'S COMIN . . . BELIEVES IT'S . . . GOD CAN SENDS HIS HELP DOWN TO ANY VALLEY . . . ANY VALLEY OF DESPAIR . . ."

Them preachin words are still rollin around that church. Them echoes ain't even went away. Elsie Stokely's playin that piano again, gots folks singin and clappin with that music.

Jeremiah's tired, tryin to keep himself awake. He's passed them road signs again, them ones that told him how to get back to Snake Town. He's turned that car off that big highway and is drivin it real slow through Stoney Town. Mason's asleep. He's got his head restin against Willet's bosom, she has her arm around him. She ain't sayin anything, ain't lookin back at them Stoney Town folks lookin at that big car with them Coloreds in it going by. Jeremiah's takin a deep breath and holdin it. But he ain't lookin back at the cowboy-lookin sheriff that's lookin at him, watchin him pass.

Jeremiah's drivin that car slowly over that old creek bridge. It's shakin and rattlin. But Jeremiah ain't thinkin about that noise he's hearin. He's lookin in that rearview mirror and thinkin about gettin that gun from up under the seat. Willet ain't lookin back, ain't thinkin about that Sheriff Elmer Jeremiah saw. But Sheriff Elmer's still lookin, seein them Pennsylvania license plates on that car.

That Snake Town road is empty, quiet cept for them dogs runnin and barkin at that passin car. Jeremiah's slowin the car down by Lulu's house. Softly Willet's tellin him, "Keep goin, I'm goin to take him on down to Mama."

Jeremiah's nearin that white-painted church sittin off the road. That music is comin from it through them open car windows. But he ain't payin that music no mind, he keeps lookin in that rearview mirror. Willet hears that music, but she doesn't want to look and see where it's comin from. She lowers her eyes from it and looks down at Mason, gently rubs her hand over his face.

Gertrude Mercer's sittin at that table of hers. That silence she's sittin in she doesn't want to get out of. But that truck-soundin noise is snappin at her silence and makin it go away. She's up, lookin out the window, seein that big car stoppin down at the end of her yard path. She's hurryin out onto the porch. But she ain't goin no farther, she's just standin there and starin at that big car.

Gently Willet's kissin Mason on his cheek and softly whisperin something in his ear. Mason's openin his eyes, then closin them again. Softly Willet whispers in his ear again, then feels them tears comin bubblin up in her eyes.

Gertrude Mercer sees that big car door openin and Willet slowly gettin out of that car. She can see Willet reachin back in that car and bringin Mason out. Gertrude Mercer starts going down her porch steps and starts walkin down that path.

Willet's got Mason by his hand and is leadin him up the path. His head is lowered and his eyes are barely open. But

Willet's lookin up, lookin at her mother comin and softly callin out, "I'm bringin him back, Mama. I'm bringin him back."

Gertrude Mercer's close enough to see the tears comin down Willet's cheeks, see her eyes starin into hers. She looks down at Mason, then looks back up and just stares silently at her daughter. Willet's sayin, "I'm bringin him back, Mama. I love him, but I want him to be here with you, Mama. He can't be with me. It wasn't like you thought it was. I wasn't doin what you thought I was doin. It wasn't what you thought, Mama. I didn't want to go away and leave Mason, but I couldn't tell you what happened. I couldn't tell nobody. Here, Mama, you take Mason. Take him, Mama."

Willet's leanin over, kissin Mason on his cheek, then givin his hand to her mother. Gertrude Mercer's sighin, her voice is quiverin as she asks, "Why did you leave, why did you leave him?"

"I had to, Mama," Willet's sayin. "I couldn't stay down here and I couldn't take him with me. But I ain't never forgot about him, Mama."

"You didn't have to leave. I loved you."

"I know, Mama. I know, Mama, but you didn't understand. You didn't . . . I wanted to go places, that's why I went up to Wilmington. But I wasn't what you thought I was, Mama. I just workin there, Mama. I wasn't what you thought I was. Two men came in that hotel, Mama. I was doin cleanin there, that's all, Mama. Tryin to get some money so I could have things, but them two men, Mama . . . That's what happened, Mama. That's what happened. That's why I couldn't tell you who Mason's daddy was. I didn't want anybody to ever know. But you keep Mason now, Mama . . . You keep him."

Willet's turnin, hurryin to the car. Gertrude Mercer's callin out, "Wil . . . Wil."

Willet ain't stoppin.

"Wil . . . Come back."

"No, Mama," Willet yells over her shoulder, then stops and turns around and says, "I can't stay, Mama. I got troubles, Mama. I don't want Mason around my troubles. You keep him, you keep him."

"Wil, stay."

"No, Mama, I can't."

"Wil . . . Wil, there ain't nothin God can't take care of . . ."

"I can't wait on God, Mama. I got to go." Willet turns and starts runnin back to the car. Then stops when she gets to that car door, looks back at Mason. He's leanin against her mother's waist, got his face restin against her side.

Gertrude Mercer yells, "Wil, please . . ."

Jeremiah's leanin across the front seat, whisperin out of the car, sayin, "Come on, we got to get out of here. Come on."

Willet looks away from Mason and her mother. She's gettin in that car and ain't thinkin about them tears gushin out of her eyes. Quickly Jeremiah's turnin that car around on that narrow Snake Town road, then steppin down on the gas pedal. Them wheels are spinnin, kickin up that loose road dirt and makin dust out of it. Willet's turnin around in her seat, lookin out of that back window.

Jeremiah's nearin that church, but he ain't slowin that car down. Them folks comin out of the church done stopped that hand-shakin and got to lookin at that car comin up the road. Lulu got one of her children by the hand. She lets the child's

hand go and hurries up to the road. Willet sees her hurryin up
to the road, but Jeremiah ain't slowin that car down. Willet
yells, "STOP . . . STOP."

Jeremiah slows down, but shouts, "We got to go fore that
sheriff comes down here, damn it."

That car's slidin to a stop. Willet's gettin out, runnin over
to Lulu, puttin her arms around her sister and sayin, "I brought
him back. Mama got him. But I got to go now."

Lulu's tryin to hug her sister back, say things to her. But
Willet's pushin away, runnin back to that car. Them folks
watchin ain't sayin nothin to each other, just doin that watchin.
Willet's back in that car. Jeremiah's speedin up that Snake
Town road, he ain't slowin down. Them dogs comin at that car,
doin that barkin, ain't gettin too close. He's lookin up that
road, tryin to see that old creek bridge. But Willet ain't lookin
up and out that window. She's got her eyes lowered and ain't
lookin at nothin cept the things she sees in her mind. That air
rushin through the window is blowin them tears all over her
face.

·   ·   ·

That Tioga Street church was fillin up. Them folks that weren't
already in there was on their way. Mamas walkin their children, not lettin them run, fall down, and get dirty fore they goes
in the church. Them clean and pretty-colored clothes folks had
on were makin things they were passin pretty, too. That old
dark beaten-down wooden fence was lookin lighter with them
bright pinks, reds, and blues them mamas had dressed their
little girls in. Some folks that had had their heads hangin low
all week was tryin to look up, see that better time comin. They

could see the cross up above them church doors, hear that soft piano music seepin out onto the street. That cross and piano music was tellin them they didn't have to drag their burdens much farther.

Mack Jack's up in that dark room of his, but he's down on his hands and knees, lookin into that dark under his bed. He's stickin his hand into it, feelin around in it. He's touchin what he wants to feel. He's pullin that horn case out of the dark. He's openin it up, starin down into it. He's rubbin his fingers over that saxophone in the case. He's gently takin that horn out of its case. He's standin up with that horn in his hands, but leanin over and puttin his lips down on the top of the horn. He's puffin up his cheeks, blowin down into that horn. His breath is curlin down through it, swirlin around in it. His fingers are pushin down on them horn keys, keepin them down, quiverin down on them fore he lets them back up and pushes them back down again. A long, low, pretty sound is comin out of the mouth of that horn. It keeps comin, makin that air swell. Mack Jack's closin his eyes, leanin back and blowin harder into that horn. He's makin some high pretty tone come out that horn. It's whirlin around that room, goin out that window, gettin high up in the sky.

Some of them folks still on the way to that Tioga Street church can hear that horn music in the air. It got them smilin and lookin up for it. That horn music keeps comin out of Mack Jack's window and goin out into that Sunday mornin air. Some folks that ain't headin to the Tioga Street church are standin on their porches or got their heads stuck out of their windows, listenin to that music. If they ain't smilin, they're noddin their heads and tellin that music it's soundin good to them. Edmund Yates still got his head down. But his old, wrinkled, bony fingers are startin to quiver. Some long, low, pretty sound is gettin up in his mind. It's gettin past all that almost-dead time that just been lyin around up there. Some of that time ain't moved in years, but it's movin now, movin out the way and lettin that long, low, pretty sound get up in there. Slowly Edmund Yates is tryin to get his head up, get his eyes open. He's wonderin where that music's comin from, if it's comin at all.

Sweat's rollin down Mack Jack's face now. He's got his eyes closed real tight. He's leanin back, raisin that horn up to that window. But he ain't blowin into it no more. He's inside it, crawlin down through its dark curvy tube, blowin that music up out of the dark.